THE TWELVE THIEVES OF CHRISTMAS

THE FIFTH CHRONICLE OF A LADY DETECTIVE

K.B. OWEN

MISTERIO PRESS

The Twelve Thieves of Christmas
The Fifth Chronicle of a Lady Detective
Copyright © 2021 Kathleen Belin Owen

Published in the United States of America

～

Cover design by Melinda VanLone, BookCoverCorner(dot)com

ISBN: 978-1-947287-28-0

CHAPTER 1

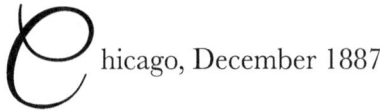 hicago, December 1887

The Christmas gift-shopping season was full upon us at Marshall Field's department store. It was evident in the décor, of course—the evergreen swags tied with bright-red bows and affixed along the glass display cases, the gleaming tin stars dangling from the ceiling, and the gaily painted plywood sleigh filled with colorfully wrapped empty boxes, perched on a dais beside the main lobby entrance.

But for a private detective tasked with catching any light-fingered customers among the crowd, the season was most noticeable upon the expressions of the shoppers, where anticipation and annoyance fought for dominion. I'm attentive to faces. Where the eyes go, the hands are bound to follow.

I smothered a yawn behind my glove as I strolled along the aisles of the main floor. Even though much of the daily routine was humdrum—it's a perverse streak in my nature to find disappointment in people behaving themselves—I was nonetheless happy for the work. My last case with the Pinkerton Agency had been several months ago.

I browsed the merchandise at the counters—notions, laces, gloves, jewelry—and nodded to the shopgirls occupied with customers. They knew who I was and what I was about. To the patrons, however, I appeared to be one of their own—a female shopper looking to spend money and the store's most sought-after demographic.

Mr. Field—the "great merchant prince," as the newspapers referred to him—had built a successful retail empire on the maxim "give the lady what she wants." Needless to say, the ladies had responded with a loyal patronage beyond what even he might have first imagined.

But courteous, deferential service didn't extend to allowing thievery, which was why I was here. Christmas-time in a department store as large as Field's produces a chaos all its own, an environment rife with opportunities for professional shoplifters, or *hoisters*, as they call themselves, to ply their trade.

"Can I help you, miss?" Lizzie asked solicitously as I approached the silk scarves. She kept her deep-brown-eyed expression neutral, bless her. Some of the other shopgirls couldn't resist a wink or a knowing look, which didn't help my undercover efforts in the least.

I nodded toward the stack of scarves at her elbow. "I'd like a closer look at the peacock blue, if you please."

"Excellent choice." She gently slipped it from the pile. "As you can see, it's one-hundred percent silk, not a snag or trailing thread anywhere."

"Indeed." Grasping it with both hands, I turned my back to the counter and held the silk up to the light, angling it for a better view. Now I could unobtrusively keep my eye on the pair of ladies who hunched over the Versailles laces nearby. One of the women, a sturdy-framed, dark brunette with a long, narrow face, cradled a chunky babe. He was well wrapped in a gray woolen shawl against the mid-December chill. Of course, the store's gas heating kept it a comfortable temperature indoors, so much so that the child was starting to fuss at his confinement. The woman grimaced but didn't unwrap him, instead shifting him to bounce on her hip.

The woman beside her seemed a bit younger—in her middle twenties, by my estimate—slightly built, thin-shouldered, with soft, fluffy brown hair peeking out from beneath her dark hat. It was her nervous behavior that had first drawn my notice. She frequently glanced around, jaw stiff and hands clenched, while her companion pawed the merchandise.

They must have come in while I'd been upstairs in the manager's office, finishing up a report from an incident yesterday—a woman who'd tried to make off with five spools of grosgrain ribbon in her muff. That one had been an amateur, the kind who steal for the thrill of it rather than as a livelihood. Though she'd been caught by the man in charge of first floor operations, Mr. Flynder, I was tasked with escorting the pleading, hand-wringing woman to the ladies' lounge, conducting a search of her person, and turning her over to the manager on duty. I was glad to be spared the rest of it. As I've been reminded time and again, you can't have a heart in this business. Writing up the report helped clear my mind—to leave behind the theatricals and reduce the incident to its solid, unassailable facts.

The ladies currently in my sights were now moving on to the jewelry counter. I handed back the scarf, sidled over to the laces, and made a quick survey. Everything seemed to be there. I glanced over my shoulder to find Flynder watching me from across the store. A frown tugged at his heavy salt-and-pepper brows.

I turned away with a sigh. I'd seen nothing but that disapproving look these past few days since I'd started this job. First floor operations were his domain, but he'd had no choice in my hiring when Mr. Selfridge, general manager of Marshall Field's, had decided that too much merchandise was walking away and had turned to the Pinkerton Agency. William Pinkerton, my employer, had recommended a lady's touch since, whether professional or amateur, shoplifters were overwhelmingly female. "Who better to catch a woman than one of her own kind," he'd pointed out.

So here I was.

The thin, nervous lady hovered over a tray of brooches, picking up one after another to show her friend. The shopgirl in charge of the jewelry section stood close by, watching.

I'd just approached for a closer look myself when I was jostled by a slim-built gentleman in a tan mohair coat. He passed me without a glance, walked straight up to the watches case on the far side of the jewelry counter, and rapped his knuckles impatiently. "Miss...*miss*! Young lady...I could use some help over here."

The girl turned toward him, and that's when it happened. The woman with the baby swept a brooch into the cuff of her glove, draped the child's wrap back over her arm, and turned aside while her companion dropped another pin—secreted in her sleeve—into the gap on the tray.

"We-we'll have to think about it," the thin woman called out to the shopgirl, still occupied with the gentleman. "Thank you for your help."

The two headed briskly towards the exit. I tried to catch Flynder's eye as I moved to follow, but he was occupied with taking the cash girl to task, judging by her flushed face and the way she clutched the money tray.

So be it—I'd do it alone. The thieves couldn't make a quick getaway with an infant in tow.

I didn't plan to confront them before they were out upon the sidewalk—it wasn't thievery until the unpaid merchandise left the store—but the nervous woman had noticed my advance. She nudged her companion. They bolted for the door, the baby gurgling in delight over the vigorous, bouncing ride upon her shoulder.

Flynder had noticed, finally. Out of the corner of my eye, I saw him crossing the floor toward them as hastily as his profound sense of dignity allowed.

Thankfully, I wasn't hampered by such considerations. I picked up my skirts and ran like a hoyden.

They were just ahead of me, pushing through the doors.

I glimpsed a flash of trousered leg before a man's foot sent me sprawling into the wooden sleigh of wrapped boxes, tipping the flimsy construction atop myself in a cascade of spurious presents from Saint Nick.

Flynder helped me to my feet. "What were you thinking, young lady, alerting them like that?" he thundered. "You're not supposed to chase them out of the store."

"They've stolen—an-an expensive brooch," I gasped. "We have to stop them."

His face reddened. "Wh-what? How valuable?"

We were wasting time. "Either help me or get out of my way."

His jaw went slack.

I impatiently clambered over the debris, pushed through the doors, and scanned the sidewalk. No sign of them, of course.

I gestured to the liveried doorman who was tipping his hat and holding the door for an elderly lady. "James, the two women with a baby who hurried out just now—which way did they go?"

He jerked a thumb to his left. "Headed down State, miss—toward the post office. A gentleman followed them right out."

I was willing to bet every brass button on James's jacket that it was the fellow who'd distracted the shopgirl and then tripped me. "Slim, wearing a tan mohair coat?"

"Yep, that's him."

"Thanks." I hurried in that direction.

I finally caught sight of them several blocks later, in front of McCabe's, a discount dry goods store. The women lingered outside, but there was no sign of their male companion. I loitered across the street, beside a newspaper stand in front of

5

the post office, where I could keep an eye on them without attracting notice. They'd gotten a good look at me back at Field's, and I'd learned from sad experience that a woman of my height can be conspicuous. I picked up a newspaper from the stack and pretended to eye it.

Christmas shoppers hurried to and fro, only a few stopping at the open-air stands. It was nearly noon, but the leaden gray sky and nip in the air portended freezing precipitation. Vendors called out cheery greetings and lit their lamps to dispel the gloom.

"Are ya gonna read, or buy?" the news seller growled, looking me up and down.

I set down the paper and drifted over to a nearby candy-and-cigar cart.

Within minutes, the man with the mohair coat came out of the store to confer with the ladies. They went inside but he didn't follow, instead lighting a cigarette and leaning against the wall to wait. Likely keeping a lookout, I reasoned. I would have done the same. I had a better look at him now. He wore his reddish hair long beneath his bowler, and the red-gold whiskers didn't entirely conceal pockmarked cheeks. His resting expression was hardened, watchful.

I bit my lip. How was I to get in without him seeing me and alerting his companions?

As I was debating my options, the skies opened up in a sleety downpour. Up and down the sidewalk, umbrellas unfurled. The man in the mohair coat stepped to a nearby overhang, flicked away his cigarette, and turned up his collar. I envied him that bit of shelter as I pulled my jacket lapels closer against my shivering frame and leaned under the cart's striped awning, pretending to dither over the peppermint sticks.

"Buy an umbrella, miss?" The plump lady running the stand, well wrapped in a bright-green shawl, smiled at me as she handed back change to another patron. "I sell those, too."

I shook my head. "Some other time."

A carriage was pulling up in front of McCabe's. I might be wet, cold, and uncomfortable, but I had an idea.

I reached the other side of the street as two matrons were handed out of the conveyance. As expected, McCabe's doorman gallantly stepped forward with his large umbrella, and I slipped in to join them. Their surprise at my sudden familiarity was confined to a few odd looks, since no one cared to debate my breach of manners out upon the frozen sidewalk. Between the umbrella and the other women, I was effectively blocked from the lookout's view.

I tidied myself in the vestibule, stamping my shoes, brushing my jacket, and smoothing my hair. If I was to enlist the store manager's help, he'd have difficulty believing a damp, wild-haired woman with a tale of chasing thieves from another store, and my identification was sitting in a staff locker back at Field's.

Briefly, I wondered what Mr. Flynder was doing. He'd obviously declined to aid me in the chase. Perhaps he considered the loss of an expensive brooch a fair trade for getting rid of me for good. I was sure my failure to recover it would mean the end of my employment. He was likely spinning a tale of me abandoning my post.

I spied the hoisters at the glove counter. The thin one with the ever-present nervous expression was now holding the baby, while the long-faced brunette smoothed a pair of burgundy suede gloves and matching pocketbook. The shopgirl was showing them all the little cavities in the purse and the quality of the lining. That should keep them occupied for a minute or so.

Careful to avoid their field of view, I headed for the cash window in search of the floorwalker. In contrast with Marshall Field's, McCabe's aisles were narrower and the lighting rather sparse, creating a cramped feeling.

"Oh, you want Mr. Andrews," one of the girls said, pointing to a tall, barrel-chested gentleman in a brown pinstripe suit. He was occupied with tidying the greeting card rack beside a case of men's handkerchiefs.

Mr. Andrews looked up at my approach. "Something I can do for you, Miss—?"

"Hamilton." I drew him a bit farther out of sight of the glove counter. "I'm a detective, currently employed at Marshall Field's."

His eyes widened. "*You* are a detective?"

"A bit more quietly, if you please," I hissed. Quickly, I explained the reason for my presence.

"Do you have any identification?"

I grimaced. "It's back at the store. You can certainly call Mr. Selfridge to confirm I am who I say, but we really don't have time for that."

He cast a frowning glance at the ladies in question before ducking back out of their sight. "One of them has an infant. Hardly likely to be stealing. Perhaps you're mistaken."

I shook my head. "I saw them take the brooch. There's also a male confederate who helped them. He's waiting outside. Thin, medium height, red whiskers, wearing a tan mohair coat. Perhaps your doorman can be of assistance in that regard?"

He gave me a long, measuring look before blowing out a breath. "Very well. I'll have the man escorted somewhere private to be questioned." He gestured toward the women. "Do you need help getting those two to come along?"

"They may bolt again," I conceded. "It would be best if we approached them together."

He nodded. "Let me speak to the doorman first."

I kept my eye on the women as I awaited his return. They drifted over to the laces, and from this distance it looked as if the burgundy gloves had drifted with them. The shopgirl was busy with other customers and hadn't noticed. The pocketbook, too large to be concealed effectively, was still on the counter.

Mr. Andrews returned from the vestibule and made a line for the laces counter. I hurried to join him.

The women turned to face us, the babe now sleeping across the thin woman's shoulder.

"Good day, ladies," he began, "I'm Mr. Andrews, in charge of day-to-day operations here at McCabe's. This lady, Miss Hamilton"—he inclined his head in my direction—"has brought a serious matter to my attention. Would you step upstairs with us to the office, please?"

The long-faced woman sucked in a breath with a sharp hiss. "We'll do no such thing! How dare you accuse us of—of—" She broke off, as Andrews hadn't accused them of anything as yet.

The child woke and began to wail. Nearby, several female patrons swiveled their heads and moved protectively closer.

Mercy, the last thing we needed was a scene.

Andrews attempted to guide the sturdy brunette by the elbow, but she shook him off and pushed him full in the chest.

"My dear woman!" he exclaimed. "You conduct is…most unseemly."

The thin woman, trying to soothe the baby, shot me a quick, pleading glance. She seemed the more docile of the two, so I focused my attention on her. "Let's take the little fellow upstairs where it's quieter. We can sit down and talk this over."

She shrugged and kept her eyes on the child, fussing with its shawl.

Andrews indicated a small service elevator towards the back of the store. The brunette—now compliant but no less wary— walked between us, darting a glance from side to side. I could only hope the doorman had been able to take charge of the man outside. I hadn't seen any sign of him.

Andrews directed a female supervisor to lead us into the privacy of a staff cloakroom. She held the child while I carefully searched the women. Nothing was on them.

"See?" the brunette said triumphantly, as the employee handed back the infant and led us down the hall to the manager's office. "This is an outrage. My husband will be contacting the owner about this, let me assure you."

9

The thin, nervous woman flashed me another pleading look.

I wondered about this one. She seemed a reluctant partici-pant. "What's your name?"

She hesitated. "Mrs. Mathilda Sohren. People call me Tilly. And this is my sister, Olivia—"

"*Mrs.* Clement Moser," the woman finished, through gritted teeth.

"And who's the little fellow?" I asked.

Tilly clutched the infant protectively. "My son, Henry."

Andrews pulled out chairs for us, then flicked a troubled glance my way. "Nothing?"

"Not on their persons." I watched Tilly fuss again with the shawl wrapped around the baby, "but Master Henry may be obliged to give an accounting of himself." I whipped back the shawl and reached beneath the little boy's shirt. Sure enough, there were the burgundy gloves.

Mrs. Moser gritted her teeth.

"He feels rather warm," I continued. "Let us make him more comfortable."

Further inspection of the baby's clothing—and bonnet—revealed a silk scarf, two millinery feathers, and a card of lace trimming. None of the items were from Marshall Field's depart-ment store, however. And no brooch. My heart sank.

Mrs. Moser tossed her head in defiance as the pile of goods grew before her eyes. "You know babies are always grabbing at things. And with the shawl catching on the tables we passed, these must have been accidentally scooped up. It doesn't prove a thing."

Andrews and I exchanged a look. She was a cool one.

But she wasn't done yet. "Besides, we have yet to leave the premises. Which means we haven't *stolen* anything." She folded her arms and sat back with a triumphant glare.

Andrews gestured for me to follow him out of the room. "She's right, you know," he murmured, once we were out of earshot. "The only reason I took them in hand on the spot was because you said they'd already stolen something from Field's."

"Where's their gentleman accomplice?" I asked.

"We have him in the stock room. The doorman's with him."

"He's been searched?"

Andrews nodded. "I did that myself, while you were with the ladies. He has nothing he shouldn't have. I was going to return to question him after we spoke with the women, but now—" He blew out a breath. "It looks like I'm going to have to let them all go."

"Just like that?" I asked incredulously. "Even without the brooch, you saw what they would have gotten away with. This is a professional thieving ring."

"It's store policy. The ladies aren't on our list of chronic, repeat offenders, and the gentleman didn't steal anything at all. Frankly, prosecuting them is more trouble than it's worth. Families are embarrassed—or worse, offended. Word gets around. It hurts our patronage. We'll ban them from the store, of course."

I looked back through the partly open door at Mrs. Moser. She was calmly re-tying the baby's bonnet, her lips curled in a smug smile.

Where had the brooch gone? I'd been thorough, also checking their shoes, under their hats, even in their hair. Had she hidden it downstairs among the merchandise on the counter? No—she'd had no advance warning to get rid of it before we were upon her. And she hadn't dropped it—the clatter on the wood floor would have been unmistakable. In fact, she hadn't seemed alarmed at all. When confronted, she'd been angry, and even so bold as to push her accuser...

A laugh bubbled out of me in spite of myself. *Oh, she was good. Very, very good.*

Andrews looked at me as if I were demented. I didn't keep him in suspense.

"Check your handkerchief pocket, sir."

CHAPTER 2

*I*t was long past the dinner hour when I finally let myself into our lodging house and wearily hung up my coat and hat.

Sadie, our maid, came bustling down the hall. "I kept a plate warm for you, miss."

"Thanks. Where is everyone? It's so quiet." I'd grown accustomed to the comings and goings involved in running a boarding house. Though we had only a few lodgers at the moment, the first floor had an unoccupied feel tonight.

"Mr. Grissom retired after dinner, and Miss Leigh recruited Mrs. Hodges and Miss Walterson to help with the stage set for the Sunday school's Christmas play."

Cassie Leigh, my best friend and confidante, helped me run the boarding house we lived in. Since detective cases requiring "a woman's touch" didn't come my way as often as I'd like, taking in lodgers was our primary means of keeping body and soul together. During lean times, we also gave lessons in china-painting and the pianoforte.

After finishing my vegetable soup and buttered roll, I tucked up in an afghan by the parlor fire to read. A short time later

Cassie came in, her usual pale-complexioned cheeks flushed from the cold, her dark eyes sparkling with animation.

"Hello, dear," I said. "Have you had a good evening?"

"Oh, Pen! The play is coming along wonderfully. And I've convinced Reverend Fargo to make an appearance as Santa Claus when it's time to give out presents." She smirked. "He'd been holding out for the longest time."

"Reverend Fargo?" I asked skeptically. "The man's barely a hundred pounds soaking wet."

I heard a snort on the other side of the parlor door, followed by light footsteps hurrying away.

Cassie rolled her eyes. "Sadie's listening at doors again."

I chuckled, having listened at my share of closed doors. "Leave her be. We'd have to pay a *proper* maid more than she earns."

"It's your fault, you know. She thinks you lead an adventurous life. She wants to be a detective now."

Adventurous? Well, sometimes. "I just thought she enjoys being a snoop."

"What's the difference?" Cassie's eyes gleamed in mischief.

I half-heartedly threw a pillow at her. "It could work to our advantage, you know. I could train her to protect the valuable silver from thieves."

"We sold the silver long ago," she pointed out.

I gave a tired smile and closed my eyes. "That should make the job easier, then."

She sat beside me. "Hard day at Field's?"

I opened my eyes and shrugged. "You could say that."

"How many shoplifters did you catch today?"

"A group of three. And I had to work plenty hard to do it." I recounted the particulars.

She let out a low whistle. "You destroyed the entire Christmas display in the front lobby of Marshall Field's department store?"

"*That's* what you're focusing on?" I asked testily. "Three

thieves were stopped, the stolen goods were returned—including an expensive ruby-and-diamond brooch—and, most importantly, I still have my job." Much to Flynder's consternation, I reflected gleefully. Seeing his expression when I came back with the brooch was worth the aggravation.

"And it's only your third day," she said. "What's the total up to now?"

It was a little game Cassie liked to play, as if I were collecting thieves like picture postcards.

"Six." I couldn't help a small smile.

"What about Flynder?" she asked. "How many has he caught?"

"Four. But it hardly matters. He'd resent my presence even if I rounded up every hoister in Chicago."

"I'm curious—why did the thieves leave a brooch in place of the one they took? It seems simpler to just grab what they want and get out of there."

"It buys them time. When the store gets busy, the shopgirl in charge of that counter has only a moment to glance at the tray she's putting away before turning her attention to another customer. When she sees that every slot has a brooch, nothing looks amiss."

"The thieves left behind something cheap, I assume?"

I nodded. "I checked afterward. The shape, size, and coloring of the glass stones were similar to the expensive one. Someone must have gotten a good look at it ahead of time."

"How much is the real one worth?"

"I didn't ask, but it has to be substantial, given how thankful the manager was to have it back."

We were quiet for a while, staring at the fire.

"What's going to happen to the baby?" she asked suddenly. "He won't be taken away from his mother, I hope?"

"I doubt Fields will prosecute, for that very reason." A clever strategy on the part of the hoisters, to bring along a baby. "Can you imagine the negative publicity of wrenching a child from its mother? The store would want to avoid that. The only exception would be if one of them has a long record of thieving." I thought back to the nervous woman with the pleading eyes. "I have a feeling this is the first time the young mother has broken the law. I doubt she'll be in any trouble."

I didn't know it at the time, but I was quite mistaken about Tilly Sohren, and it was going to complicate our lives very soon.

Flynder checked his watch as I walked in the next day, ten minutes early.

"I'm on time," I said pointedly. I nodded towards the now-restored sleigh display. "You've added some garland. Very nice."

His lip curled. "That was necessary, young lady, in order to conceal a broken runner we haven't had time to repair. We were here until late last night, thanks to your little escapade."

I straightened my shoulders. "I'd say it's an improvement. Excuse me, I have to get ready. I wouldn't want to be late."

After stowing my purse in an employee locker and signing in, I hurried downstairs to mingle with the incoming customers. A man in a gray-checked suit and brown felt hat walked through the doors, his tall, lanky frame, firm chin, and sharp hazel eyes all too familiar. My stomach clenched. Frank Wynch.

Whatever my estranged husband wanted of me, I doubted it was anything to my benefit.

If Frank was bound and determined to have a conversation, I certainly didn't want to be overheard by the floorwalker—who remained standing beside the front doors to greet the customers at the start of the day. I sidled over to the perfumes counter on the far side of the store to put some distance between myself and Flynder. I picked up an atomizer, sniffed, and waited.

"Hello, Pen."

Frank smiled down at me—few men are taller than I—as if we'd only just chatted last week instead of five months ago, at the successful conclusion of our last case. I'd assumed he'd been busy with work when he'd returned to Chicago. It had been a relief not having to fend off his persistent attempts at reconciliation.

But if I were honest with myself, I missed his company. Our case in Newport had gone a long way toward clearing the air between us after living apart for four years.

Ah, well, a woman's nature is ever perverse, as Reverend Fargo is always telling us.

"You're limping." I drew Frank away from the girl staffing the perfume counter, who watched Frank with a gleam in her eye. I must admit, my husband *is* a handsome fellow—charming, even. When sober. "Your injury hasn't fully healed?" He'd broken his leg badly during our Newport adventure.

He grimaced and leaned against the counter. "I tripped and re-injured it recently. But don't worry about that. I need to discuss something urgent with you."

I stifled a sigh. "I assume Mr. Pinkerton told you where to find me?"

He shook his head. "Mrs. Hodges."

Our gossipy lodger. And how she'd found out…Sadie, most likely. I'd have to have a talk with them both.

"I didn't want to ask Pinkerton," he went on. "He mustn't see me like this." He gestured toward his leg. "He'd transfer my assignment to someone else."

"Maybe he should, don't you think? And you ought to see a doctor." I glanced over Frank's shoulder. Flynder was striding purposefully toward us, a scowl creasing the cavernous folds of his face. "I can't talk now. Come to the house after dinner tonight."

His eyes lit up and he clasped my hand, which I quickly drew away.

"You'd better go," I urged.

Frank limped past Flynder, tipping his hat.

The floorwalker barely gave Frank a nod as he bore down upon me. "*Miss Hamilton.* We expect more decorous behavior from our female employees. If you had paid attention to our employees' handbook for ladies, you would have known that personal conversations with gentlemen during working hours is not allowed." He pulled out his pad. "I shall have to put a notation in your file."

The rest of the day was less remarkable—reuniting a lost child with its mother, helping set to rights a collapsed pedestal display of wrapped confectioneries, listening to stories of love and heartache from the shopgirls during the lunch break. Not a thief in sight.

I was just thinking I'd have nothing new to report to Cassie in that regard when, a half an hour before closing, I observed a pair of gentlemen engage a stout, matronly lady in conversation in the toy section. One of the men—sporting a befuddled expression—gestured toward the case of baby dolls. The matron obligingly leaned closer, squinting through her pince-nez, to deliver her opinion on which he should choose.

That's when the other man slipped his hand into her reticule. In a flash, he'd retrieved something and stuck his hand back in his overcoat pocket. He touched his companion on the sleeve. I was close enough now to hear them.

"It's getting late," the pickpocket said. "We shouldn't impose upon this gracious woman any longer."

"By Jove, you're right," the other fellow exclaimed. He bowed to the woman. "My apologies, ma'am. I shall have to give the purchase further consideration. Thank you for your time."

They turned to leave, and I stepped in their path. "I don't think so, gentlemen." I nodded toward the lady shopper. "I believe you're missing something, ma'am. Would you check your reticule, please?"

The pickpocket shifted his weight and flashed an uneasy glance at his friend. I half-expected them to bolt for the door, but perhaps a woman challenging them had thrown them off their game.

"Who are *you*?" the pickpocket demanded. The man who'd acted as decoy was edging away.

"Someone who saw you put your hand where it does not belong," I retorted. I raised my voice to the girl working the nearby small-clothes counter. "Annie, fetch Mr. Flynder. Then see if James can leave his post and help us." I didn't know what to expect from these two.

Annie craned her neck, took in the spectacle of the matron frantically pawing through her purse and a man trying to sidle away, and hurried to get the floorwalker.

The matron emptied the purse's contents on the counter. "My money's *gone!*" She turned her soft gray eyes, wide with disbelief, first at the pickpocket, then at me. "He took it?"

I gave a brief nod before addressing the pickpocket. "Hand it over."

She applied a scented handkerchief to her nose. I hoped she wasn't going to faint.

But she was made of sterner stuff than I credited her for, and now curiosity overruled panic. She leaned toward me. "But how did he do it? I didn't feel a thing."

The pickpocket rolled his eyes. "That was the point," he snarled.

His friend groaned in disgust. "Why would ya say *that*? Dumber than a stump you are, Charlie."

"I said, *hand it over*," I repeated, watching Flynder and James approach from opposite ends of the store.

"You're sure the money's all there, ma'am?" the assistant manager asked, for about the fifth time. He set down a tea tray in front of us.

The woman—Mrs. Lockwood—nodded. "And thank heaven, too. I don't know what my husband would say if I'd lost it." Her smile deepened her already apple-plump cheeks as she turned to me. "Thank you, dear, for stopping those odious men!"

The matron had required a restorative cup of tea in the quiet of the office while Flynder summoned the police and dealt with the pickpockets. She'd insisted upon my company. That was fine—I could do with a cup of tea.

He flashed me a grateful glance. "Miss Hamilton's perspicacity in such matters is quite commendable. But ma'am—it would be safer in the future if you simply charged the items and left the cash at home. The Lockwood name is always good here."

"I know I should have done, but I didn't want my husband to see the charges. The gifts are to be a surprise, you see."

He shrugged and bent over her hand. "If you'll excuse me, I have several matters to attend to. Stay as long as you like."

After he left, the woman shifted in her chair to look me full in the face. "He called you Miss Hamilton—any relation to Curtis and Honoria Hamilton, of Boston?"

My stomach clenched, as it often did, when my blueblood lineage is at risk of discovery.

I suspected there was no use bluffing it out this time. "Yes. They are my parents."

She settled back with a sigh. "I do see a bit of your mother in you, now that I look for it. The blue eyes, the pale blonde hair, and perhaps a hint of the same determined jaw... Oh, don't take offense, dear," she added with a laugh at my expression. "A stubborn streak will serve you well. Especially if you're a—what is it you do, exactly?"

"I'm a detective." There was no denying it, of course, but she looked to be the gossipy sort, and Mother would not be happy if word of her daughter's sordid profession circulated among her set. I'd only just managed to squash such rumors in Newport this past summer.

"Indeed? Lordy. But do call me Aunt Lou—that's what you called me as a child, don't you remember?"

I sat back. Stray remembrances of my early years—pigtails and pinafores and spinning tops and jacks—and yes, she was there, a comfortably plump young woman, the nice sort of visitor who doesn't snitch on a girl she caught jumping on the divan. "*You're* Aunt Lou? I do remember. I didn't recognize you at first. It's been a long time."

She nodded vigorously. "Decades. You were only five years old when I married my first husband and moved away. It's little wonder you didn't recognize me." She grimaced ruefully at her capacious lap. "People change a great deal in that time."

I smiled. "As do we all."

"It broke my heart to leave Boston," she said, her deep-set eyes growing misty. "Honoria was a dear friend, almost like a mother to me after the loss of my own. We've kept up a correspondence, but it isn't the same, is it?" She pursed her lips in a puzzled expression. "She never mentioned that you'd moved to Chicago."

I winced as I considered what such a missive would look like.

Dear Mrs. Lockwood,

My daughter, Penelope, has moved to Chicago, having married beneath her station. She currently runs a boarding establishment and engages in detective work in her spare time. Be a dear and invite her to your next illustrious affair. She has not had occasion to wear her diamonds of late.

"That surprises you?" I answered with a sharp laugh. "If you two are the close friends you say, you must realize she would not want my profession to become common knowledge." A bitter taste flooded my mouth. Perhaps it was the tea. I reached for the sugar tongs.

"Honoria is rather on the stuffy side," Aunt Lou conceded. She bit her lip. "It's actually propitious that you're a detective. I have a little problem—" She broke off as the assistant manager came back in.

"Excuse me—forgot my key." He fetched it and scurried out at the woman's glare.

"Perhaps this isn't the best place to discuss it," I said.

She stood. "Good point. Are you heading home? I have a carriage waiting—we can talk on the way."

Aunt Lou's carriage was a well-appointed affair, the interior inlaid with polished mahogany paneling, the cushioned seats upholstered in crushed maroon velvet. It even smelled pleasant, of citrus and sandalwood.

She raised an eyebrow briefly when I recited the address to the driver—ours is a quiet neighborhood of shopkeepers, plumbers, and underpaid clerks, conveniently situated near one of the main streetcar lines.

Once we were comfortably tucked in and on our way, I looked at the woman expectantly. "What's the nature of the problem?" I asked, as we turned the corner and left State Street behind.

She hesitated. "I must have your promise of confidentiality first. It's a most delicate matter."

"Naturally. Though my employer, Mr. Pinkerton, will need to be informed of the particulars."

Her eyes widened in alarm. "Mr. Pinkerton? Why?"

"Any case I take on—I assume you wish to engage my services—must go through him. He's the soul of discretion, I assure you. He could not have achieved success without such."

She was quiet for a few moments. I waited.

"I suppose that is acceptable," she said grudgingly. "However, I cannot be seen traipsing into his office—it could excite notice."

"That shouldn't be a problem. I'll lay out the case for him, get his approval, and we'll proceed from there. So—tell me about it."

"I lost a piece of jewelry over a year ago," she began.

"Valuable?"

"Valuable enough—it was part of the Countess Margharita's famed ruby collection."

"I'm not familiar with that."

"Oh, it goes back eighty years. The necklace was made especially for her on the occasion of her marriage, with earrings and a bracelet to match. But her husband proved unfaithful and later abandoned her with a great deal of debt to settle. Everything was sold off. I believe she entered a convent afterward."

"Do you have the remainder of the collection—the earrings and bracelet?"

"I never had those. Only the necklace. My first husband gave it to me. After he died and I remarried, I kept it locked away in the safe. Edgar—my current husband—doesn't like me wearing anything that isn't from him. He's rather sentimental that way," she added with an indulgent smile. "And I thought only women paid attention to such things. But he's generous in his own right," she added hastily. "I have a number of lovely pieces to wear."

I touched the outline in my pocket of the engraved silver pocket-knife Frank had given me on our first wedding anniversary. He'd never showered me in jewels save for my wedding band, which was currently tucked in a drawer of woolen stockings. He'd preferred more practical gifts—the pocket-knife, a set of lockpicks, my double-barrel derringer. "So how did you come to misplace the necklace? You conducted a search, I assume?"

"No, no," she said quickly, "that's not what I meant. It wasn't exactly *lost*. It was stolen after I'd lent it to a friend. Mrs. Crofton."

"She told you it was stolen?"

Aunt Lou looked down at her gloved hands. "She couldn't tell me anything. She was dead."

A chill pricked at my spine. "Illness, or accident?" I had a feeling it was neither.

"Murder." She swallowed. "The way I understand it, a burglar broke in, killed her, and fled with her jewels and other valuables. Her maid found her dead the next morning." Her voice thickened with emotion. "Smothered."

"I'm sorry. Was the killer caught?"

"No."

"Did she live alone?"

"No—she was married, but her husband, John, was out of town."

"I see. Did you tell the police of the necklace?"

She looked up, surprised. "No."

"Why not?"

"I didn't want my husband to know I'd been so foolish as to lend such an expensive piece of jewelry. Besides, Eileen's death had upset me greatly. I had no wish to be subjected to a police inquiry on top of that."

"But if the item is as valuable as you say…" I began, but the expression on her face told me the argument was pointless. I dropped it. "You want me to find the necklace after all this time? I don't think that's possible, frankly." And not quite in my line.

"Actually, I know exactly where it is. I saw it two nights ago, around Allison Rowe's neck."

I gnashed my teeth in exasperation. Aunt Lou had trouble getting to the point. "And who is *she*, pray?"

"The daughter of Judge Lucius Rowe and his wife Clara. We know them through our charity work with the Widows' Benevolent Association, mostly, though we attend many of the same fetes and musicales as well."

"What did you do when you saw it?"

"Once I recovered from the shock, I inquired of Clara where her daughter had come by such a lovely necklace. I didn't say anything of it being mine, of course."

"How did she answer?"

"The judge had given it to their daughter on the occasion of her birthday the day before. The Shermans' winter cotillion seemed the perfect time for her to wear it, Clara said, as it set off Allison's crimson gown."

"You're sure it's yours? Did you get a close look at it?"

She frowned. "Not close enough to be sure. Perhaps it's a copy. It's a well-known piece—there are bound to be imitations. But you can see the awkwardness either way."

I nodded. "One cannot ask if it's counterfeit and risk implying that the Rowes are in financial difficulties. And if it is indeed yours, Judge Rowe must have purchased it from someone who deals in stolen goods." I gave her a long look. "There's more to this, isn't there?"

"Yes." She bit her lip. "I've had my suspicions for quite some time as to who murdered Eileen, and I want you to look into it."

"Whom do you suspect?"

She swallowed. "Judge Rowe."

CHAPTER 3

*A*t last we were getting somewhere, though I couldn't make sense of it all yet. "What makes you think he's responsible for your friend's death?"

She blew out a breath. "They'd had an affair years ago, before her marriage. I'm not sure whether it was still going on after that, but..." She cleared her throat. "It's a sensitive subject."

"So you believe he killed her—in the heat of an argument, perhaps—then took her valuables to make it look like a robbery gone wrong?"

She nodded.

"That's a bit of a stretch, don't you think? Why would he be so foolish as to give his daughter a piece of jewelry from the woman he'd murdered?"

"Maybe his wife found it tucked away and he came up with that as a last-minute excuse? Besides, it's been a year. And it wasn't on the list of stolen items—he would have known that."

"Oh? The list was published in the paper?"

"I couldn't say, but as a retired judge, he regularly entertains the district attorney and chief of police."

I suppressed a groan. "He's *that* Judge Rowe?" Marvelous. Mr. Pinkerton wasn't going to like this one bit.

She blinked. "I thought you knew."

"I don't exactly move in such circles nowadays," I said dryly. "You're certain they were having an affair? Why would you associate with such a woman, let alone call her your friend?"

"I didn't condone it, if that's what you mean," she snapped. "Despite such a… weakness, Eileen was an intelligent, kind person. She deserved better than that sort of death. The Croftons had been our neighbors for five years—her husband still lives there. She and I had grown close. We're the same age, though she married late and never had children. We collaborated on several volunteer projects." She smiled in memory.

"You admired her greatly," I noted.

"I'd never met anyone like her. She became the only female member of the board of the Widows' Benevolent Society and eventually was elected Treasurer. She wasn't always the easiest person to get along with, though. Single-minded in purpose and rather opinionated, but those tend to go hand in hand, don't you think?"

"Did Mrs. Crofton have other affairs?"

"There were rumors," she said grudgingly. "The ladies of our set had begun leaving her off their guest lists. And she resigned as the board's treasurer last year so as not to impugn its reputation." She shrugged. "That's all she would tell me about it."

"What about your husband? How did he feel about your friendship? Ah," I added, watching her brow furrow, "that's why you didn't report the loss of your necklace. You didn't want him to know you were still close friends."

"He didn't *forbid* me to socialize with her," Aunt Lou said defensively, "but he seemed rather awkward in her company."

What a tangle. "If I can determine whether or not Judge Rowe is to blame for your friend's death, would this be for your personal knowledge or for public consumption? And what do you want to do about your necklace?"

Her gray eyes hardened in a defiant glint. "If the judge is responsible, I want him to pay for his actions. As far as the necklace—it's a loss. I'm certainly not going to cause embarrassment by laying claim to it. Can you imagine the gossip? They'd say I was practically ripping it off a young girl's neck. I'd never live it down."

"So instead of depriving a young girl of her necklace, you want me to deprive her of her peace of mind and prove her father a murderer," I said dryly.

Aunt Lou flinched. "It's not what I want, but we must get at the truth. Don't I owe Eileen that?"

"I'm as opposed as you are to allowing a man to get away with murder. However, a year has passed. I'm not sure my inquiry could prove anything definitively."

She patted my hand. "You'll figure out a way. You always were a clever girl, Penelope. But remember, no one else besides your Mr. Pinkerton must know I've hired you to look into this."

We'd pulled up to my house several minutes ago. The coachman stood outside, respectfully waiting.

I blew out a breath. "All right." I fished out a pad and pencil from my reticule. "Write down the names and addresses of the people involved and the date of Mrs. Crofton's death."

As she squinted over her writing in the dim light, I added, "Our first step will be to establish definitively whether the necklace is yours. Is there anything that would distinguish it from a copy, short of having a jeweler examine the stones?"

"Let me think… Well, there's a small scuff in the metal filigree, along the left side. I never got around to having it repaired. It's barely noticeable."

"Write that down, along with a general description of the piece itself—size, shape, number of gemstones—that sort of thing. When might she wear it again?"

"The Rowes are hosting a Christmas ball on Saturday. A girl

Allison's age wouldn't have many pieces to circulate through, so chances are good she'll wear it again then. You can accompany me and see for yourself." She passed back both pad and pencil.

"Mrs. Rowe won't consider it an inconvenience to receive an extra guest?" I asked, mentally reflecting upon my slim collection of gowns. Fortunately, I had one of myrtle green that should do the trick. A dressmaker had given it to me last year, when I'd solved a little problem for her.

"I'll worry about that," Aunt Lou said. "You concern yourself with getting a good look at the necklace."

I was just catching Cassie up on the events of the day—except for Aunt Lou's problem, of course—when we heard the doorbell and Sadie's footsteps hurrying down the hall to answer.

I glanced over at Cassie, feet comfortably propped on the ottoman, darning a sock by the light of the gas lamps. "I forgot to tell you—Frank's coming over. That's probably him now."

Her thin hands stilled as she scowled. "You invited him here? Why?"

"He stopped at Field's today to talk to me. He said it was urgent. I certainly couldn't discuss it then, so I told him to come tonight."

She shook her head. "When are you going to get him out of your life for good, Pen?"

"That is hardly your concern, Miss Leigh." Frank stood in the parlor doorway. He crossed to the hearth in careful strides, with only a hint of the limp I'd noticed earlier. "The matter is between my wife and me."

"Have a seat, Frank." I gestured to a rocker well away from my friend and her tightly gripped darning needle. "Cassie, would you mind—?"

Frank remained standing, waiting.

Cassie gave a mighty sigh and got up. On her way out of the

room, however, she walked straight over to Frank and stood on tiptoe to meet his eye, her diminutive frame looking almost childlike against his height.

But size never intimidated Cassie. She shook a finger in his face—thankfully she'd set down the needle—and said, "Pen may still be your wife, but she is my friend. *Tread carefully*."

He blinked at the ferocity in her tone.

I blew out a breath. "*Cassie*. Close the door on your way out. And take Sadie with you," I added in a raised voice. The hallway floorboards squeaked under retreating footsteps.

Once we were alone, Frank lowered himself into the chair. "Interesting household you run here. A snooping maid and a she-tiger for a housemate." He rested his derby upon his knee and fiddled with the brim.

I shrugged. "It suits us. If you think that's noteworthy, you should spend time with our lodgers." I ticked off the list on my fingers. "We have a gossipy, middle-aged widow, an elderly gentleman who spends most of his time trying to avoid the aforementioned widow's attentions, and an annoyingly cheerful young schoolteacher with a predilection for excessive holiday decorations." I gestured toward the paper snowflake cut-outs festooned upon the walls.

He chuckled and extended his leg stiffly toward the hearth fender. "I've met the widow."

"That you have," I said curtly, still annoyed at him for simply showing up at my door in my absence.

The mantel clock ticked in the silence.

"Well?" I asked finally. "What's so urgent that you had to get me in trouble at work today?"

He grimaced. "It's this case I'm on. I could use some advice."

My favorite kind of problem. I settled back in my chair. "Tell me about it."

"Two years ago, a shipment of bonds and cash—close to two million dollars' worth—went missing on its way from the train depot to the First National Bank of Chicago. The shipment was inspected when it arrived at the depot from Minneapolis. The lock was recorded as intact and the trunk released to the driver to deliver to the bank. But he never made it. The abandoned vehicle was found later, with the trunk inside, smashed and empty."

"What happened to the driver?" I asked.

"Disappeared. Samuel Brinkerhoff. He'd been with the company for years. There'd never been any doubt about his honesty before that."

"Looks bad for him, though. If someone had waylaid the vehicle and attacked him, he would have been found, either injured or dead."

"We'd also considered the possibility that someone killed him before he got to the depot, stole his credentials, and passed himself off as Brinkerhoff. But however it happened, he's disappeared completely. Not even a body has turned up in all this time."

I frowned in Frank's direction. "What have you to do with a two-year-old case?"

"Ever hear of a fellow named Dutch Dan?"

I shook my head.

"He has a long history of sneak thieving. Runs the occasional boodle swindle for variety. Several of the missing bonds were found in his possession."

"How did Dutch come to be searched to begin with?"

"Officials were keeping a watch on known dealers in stolen bonds around the area. Dutch was caught when he went to pay one of them a visit in Edgewater." Frank clucked his tongue. "Dutch isn't the smartest of fellows. He should have waited a while."

"He didn't tell them where the rest of the stolen goods were?"

"Denied all knowledge of the robbery. Said an anonymous person left them under his door. Written on the envelope was 'In payment of an old debt.'"

I snorted. "A rather thin story. But if we're assuming Dutch was working with Brinkerhoff, have they questioned Brinkerhoff's close relations?"

He nodded. "There's a wife. She was questioned extensively, though it was difficult for them to get anything coherent out of her. His disappearance had her in near hysterics."

"Naturally. She still doesn't know whether or not she's a widow," I mused.

"Or whether she's married to a thief who abandoned her," Frank said. "The remaining bonds and cash never turned up. Brinkerhoff must be in hiding with the rest of the stash."

"What happened to Dutch?"

"He served twenty months in prison for possession of stolen goods and just got out a few weeks ago. He works at Temple's Grocery, off Madison. Lives in a flat over the store."

"You're monitoring Dutch, I take it?"

"Right. The express company still hopes to recover the missing bonds. They believe he'll lead us either to Brinkerhoff or—if Dutch killed him—wherever the cache is hidden."

"What have you learned from your surveillance so far?"

"Not much. It may take a while for him to let down his guard, after his big mistake the first time. He works at the grocery during the day and stays in his flat at night. No after-hours visitors so far. He has a woman come in a few times a week to fetch his laundry, clean, and cook for him."

"You've searched his quarters over the shop?"

He flashed me a look of barely suppressed impatience. "Of course. Nothing."

"What do you need from me, then?"

"There are three of us watching the building right now, working in shifts. I'm concerned about one of the other operatives. Bert O'Neill."

"Concerned? How so?"

His hazel eyes clouded as he stared at the hearth. "Two days ago I saw him—he was off-duty—chatting with the woman who cleans for Dutch. Her name's Abby. They were at a magazine stall about a block away. He doesn't know I saw them together."

"He could be pursuing a lead. Maybe he's befriending her in hopes of getting information about Dutch."

"I thought of that, too. But why wouldn't he have told me?"

"You don't want to ask O'Neill directly, I assume, because if he's up to something it will tip him off?"

"Exactly."

"It seems your best option is to have someone follow the cleaning woman when she leaves for the day—" I broke off at his grin. "Oh, *no*—you can't mean *I* should follow her?"

"Why not? I'm sure you can avoid being spotted."

"That isn't the issue. I have two jobs already. I haven't time to take on anything more."

"It should only be for short time," Frank wheedled, "just to see where she goes and who she associates with." He paused. "What do you mean—two jobs? You work at the department store. What else are you doing?"

He didn't need to know about Louisa's problem. "I run this." I gestured to the walls. "A boarding house is a job in itself." Make that *three* jobs.

He grunted. "I suppose. Still, you're the only one I can ask who'd be able to pull it off. I don't want to cause trouble for the fellow if I'm wrong. He's new to the agency."

I suppressed a sigh. "Very well—but just a night or two. Give me a description and everything you already know about her, particularly what days she's there and what time she leaves."

He grinned as he reached for the pad and pencil he habitually kept tucked in his jacket pocket. "I knew I could count on you, Pen."

I visited William Pinkerton's office early the next day to ensure I'd be on time for my afternoon shift at Field's. With Flynder already breathing down my neck, I didn't want any more demerits in my file.

I knocked on his door, and Pinkerton looked up in surprise. "Mrs. Wynch? How propitious." He tapped the sheet he'd been reading. "I was about to send for you."

My curiosity overrode my annoyance at his continued insistence on calling me by my married name. He never gave up hope that Frank and I would reconcile our differences.

I took a seat. "Send for me—why?"

"Marshall Field's is terminating your employment. Quite generously, however." He passed over a slip of paper.

I gaped at the check made out to me. It was as much as I would have made at the department store between now and Christmas, and then some.

Pinkerton waved another check. "They've also included a bonus to the agency for your successful recovery of the diamond-and-ruby brooch."

"It's the nicest way I've ever been fired from a position, but why are they letting me go? Did they say?"

He leaned back and hooked his thumbs in the armholes of his waistcoat. "There's mention of 'retaining a long-valued employee,' but no wrongdoing on your part is put forward."

"I see." So Flynder had gotten his way, after all. Their Christmas decorations may be safe from hoydenish lady detectives from now on, but good luck keeping valuable merchandise from walking out of the store.

Pinkerton was closely watching my face. "I take it someone has expressed his objections to working alongside a woman detective?"

"When is that *not* the case?" I said mildly. "It's surprising, though, that the store would prioritize the delicate sensibilities of a tyrannical floorwalker over their bottom line."

"Well, it's their problem now." Pinkerton closed the folder and placed it in a tray for filing. "What is it you came to see me about?"

"We may have a new case." I outlined what Louisa Lockwood had told me. His brows lowered when I got to the part about her suspicion of Judge Rowe having killed her friend, but I pressed on. "Can your staff gather the known details of Mrs. Crofton's death and what the police were able to determine? I'll need to catch up."

"It will have to be carefully done." He grimaced. "If the judge gets word of our agency delving into his personal affairs…"

I saw his point. Maintaining a good working relationship with the local authorities was crucial to the agency's success. "I'm not suggesting we investigate the judge—yet. Just that we familiarize ourselves with Mrs. Crofton and the circumstances of her death."

He scowled. "We don't even know if the necklace Mrs. Lockwood saw is hers. We should establish that first."

"She's arranging an invitation to Saturday's affair at the Rowes'. I may get a look at it then."

He shifted restlessly. "What if Mrs. Lockwood never had such a necklace and has fabricated the story? She could have a personal grudge against the man and is trying to use you to smear his reputation."

"That's a possibility," I conceded. "We'll want to learn more about the provenance of the Margharita necklace. There must be a record of Louisa's first husband having purchased it. That at least would confirm part of her story."

He pursed his lips. "We need an expert in legacy jewels. There's a man I got a letter from recently—just a moment."

I waited as he rummaged in a stack of files.

"Ah, here we go." He adjusted his glasses, skimmed the page, then looked over at me. "Do you remember Phillip Kendall?"

"The jewel thief? Of course."

"I wouldn't characterize him as such anymore," Pinkerton said.

"Maybe so. Still, I'm surprised you've been in contact with him."

"I reached out to him after your report on the Cullom case. I told him to contact me if he was ever in need of employment." He re-folded the letter and tucked it away. "He's in town and available."

Kendall's aid had been indispensable in Washington and at Schroon Lake before that, when we'd set a trap for a killer. And yet— "You really believe him to be reformed? Otherwise, it's a complication we can do without."

I didn't tell Pinkerton that Kendall's particular brand of charm was also a complication *I* could do without. Working with him was rife with distractions of a more personal nature.

"I've had him checked out," Pinkerton said, "and I'm confident he's left that life behind. I'll set him to work on investigating the most recent owner of the Margharita necklace. He'll report his findings directly to you to save time. The event is Saturday, you say?" He frowned. "Three days isn't much time, but we'll see what he can accomplish. You'll write up all the reports, since he's not familiar with our procedures."

There didn't seem to be any more to discuss. I stood, as did Pinkerton. "I'll inform Mrs. Lockwood."

"At least you'll have more time to pursue the matter now," he said.

I smiled to myself as I tucked the department store check in my pocketbook. And perhaps take care of some Christmas shopping.

CHAPTER 4

*S*ince ladies' footwear is not conducive to prolonged shopping excursions, it was a relief to finally slip off my boots in my bedroom, toss the packages on the bed, and turn to my wardrobe to consider what options would suit my upcoming assignments.

My needs were a study in contrasts. Saturday's ball would require an evening gown with more layers than I cared to contemplate, heeled pumps that were the devil to walk in, and a collection of female frippery to complete the look.

I pulled out my myrtle satin brocade for close inspection. It had cap sleeves of gold *mousseline de soie*, the color picked up in the embroidery of the gored skirt. The simplicity of the close-fitting corsage bodice was brightened by a wide panel of inset antique lace, but I grimaced over the squared neckline. It showed a rather broad expanse of neck and bosom. Though I'm not amply endowed with the latter, the snug fit was designed to bring a lady's natural charms to the forefront. One could only hope I wouldn't be called upon to do anything more active than standing around fanning myself and engaging in vacuous conversation before I got a look at Miss Rowe's necklace. With a sigh, I hung it up on the dressing screen and considered my next set of choices.

Covertly following Dutch's maid home in the dark required something else entirely. I pushed aside my dark, serviceable dresses, sturdy walking skirts, and crisp shirt waists, reaching deep along the left side of the wardrobe for the one item I'd never worn in the years I've had it—a man's suit jacket and trousers in charcoal gray. They were Frank's, left behind when he'd moved out. I'd never returned them to him, sensing they might come in handy one day. The jacket pockets were deep enough to hold my double-barrel derringer and lockpicks. I gave the items a good going-over. The trouser hems would need taking up a bit, but the waist should stay in place with suspenders.

I was reaching for my sewing basket when there was a tap on the door frame.

Cassie leaned in, shifting a stack of sheets in her arms. "I'm surprised to find you here. Shouldn't you be at Field's?"

I rearranged the gown on the bed to hide my packages. "I've been dismissed."

"Dismissed! Why?"

"Apparently I ruffled Flynder's feathers enough that he threatened to quit. That's what Mr. Pinkerton and I surmise, anyway. But I received a generous severance check." I picked up my sewing basket and sat down beside the brightest window to work on the trousers.

"Still, it's awfully unfair," she protested. "You were doing a much better job than he was!"

I shrugged. "I have another case, anyway. And I'll have more time here at home to help with chores."

Cassie brightened. "What's the case?"

"I can't get into the particulars, unfortunately. Only Mr. Pinkerton knows. It took a bit of coaxing to get the client to agree even to that." I stifled a sigh. Kendall being pulled into the investigation meant yet another person who knew.

But for all the jewel thief's faults, Kendall wasn't a gossip.

I caught myself. Why did I continue to refer to him as a thief? Maybe I was as stubborn as my employer, who insisted on calling me *Mrs. Wynch*. Why was I trying so hard to keep Kendall relegated to the category of criminal when he was turning his talents to helping people?

The ready answer—I still didn't trust him.

Cassie watched me as I bit off the thread from one cuff and started on the other. "Why are you sewing for Frank?"

"I'm not." I squinted as I re-threaded my needle. "These are for me."

"You're wearing *trousers* for your new case?" she asked incredulously.

I chuckled. "It's a different case, one I'm helping Frank with. But it's night work, outdoors. Safest to be taken for a man under such circumstances, rather than invite unwanted attention as an unaccompanied woman."

She frowned. "Are you sure that's a good idea? Helping Frank, I mean. His assignments tend to be more dangerous than yours."

I snorted. "That hasn't been my experience. Besides, this is simple surveillance. I plan to keep my distance from the criminal element—don't worry."

I should have known that such plans can quickly unravel.

Dutch's maid, Abby, left her employer's flat at eight o'clock in the evening on the days she worked for him. I stationed myself in the shadows of a blocked alley across the street from the grocer's promptly at 7:45. As I waited, I stooped to re-tie a shoe. Bert O'Neill was currently the one on watch tonight. I straightened, then tugged at the brim of the brown felt hat I'd found in the depths of the coat closet. Lodgers leave all sorts of things behind when they move out.

From my vantage point, I could observe the side door that

led from the upper flat—the front doors leading into the shop itself were locked for the night—without being seen by anyone watching from either inside or outside the house. The sun had set hours ago, which had the benefit of concealment and the disadvantage of chilling me through my jacket. I stamped my feet and huddled into my collar. At least it wasn't snowing, though it felt cold enough to be.

O'Neill lit a cigarette as he loitered beside a wagon parked in the drive next to a bookseller's. Every once in a while, I caught a glint of his light brown mustache in the glow of the cigarette ember. The moon was mostly obscured by clouds, so all I could make of him was his wide-shouldered bulk. I couldn't tell his age or much else, and Frank hadn't seen fit to contribute that information. My quarry was Abby the maid, and my mission tonight was to establish where she lived and observe whether O'Neill would attempt to interact with her when she left.

The door opened, and a woman stepped out. The street-lamp lit up her form—thin-shouldered and slightly built, with fluffy, light-brown hair straggling beneath her bonnet.

I froze. Even from this distance—the nervous movement, the clenching of her hands, her figure—I knew her. It was Tilly Sohren, one of the women who'd made off with the brooch from Field's. Either Abby was an alias, or the name she'd given at the department store had been. Probably the former. Far easier to get away with lying to a grocer's boy.

She gathered her coat collar at her neck, shivered, and walked briskly up Madison toward Rockwell. I watched O'Neill. He stubbed out his cigarette and retreated farther into the shadow of the wagon. She glanced furtively in his direction, then looked away and kept going. Had she seen him? I couldn't tell.

I blew out a quiet breath. That was a terrible lapse on his part. A cigarette ember on a dark night was sure to attract attention, especially if one is waving it around. Was that the point? Did he want her to know he was there?

He made no move to follow her. I hardly expected him to, since his job was keeping watch on the building and reporting any comings and goings of people who might collude with Dutch Dan. At least he was keeping to his post.

O'Neill had turned away from me sufficiently that I could slip out of the alley and trail Tilly. I kept a half block of distance between us. Not many were out walking on such a night—most were climbing in or out of conveyances that pulled up to the houses.

I followed her for three blocks. She didn't glance over her shoulder or give any indication of being aware of my presence. I drew a little closer, weighing my options for something to retreat behind should she look around.

My precautions were justified a block after she passed West Jackson Street—and several large mansions—and crossed over to a narrower side street. She stopped suddenly and started to turn. I ducked behind an overgrown shrub, and only came out of hiding when I heard her footsteps ringing upon the pavement once more.

She stopped again in front of an Italianate-style, three-story house, part of a row of four well-kept residences. She fumbled in her purse, then rang the bell. I slipped closer, hiding behind the stone balustrade of the adjacent house, where I could hear but not see.

I heard the door open.

"Oh, ma'am!" a young, female voice said. "Forgot your key again?"

"I'm afraid so, Lucy." It was unquestionably Tilly's voice. "I'll be sure to remember next time."

"No trouble, ma'am."

The door closed upon the voices, and I slipped out of my hiding place. I wanted a look at the house number.

I should have allowed a few more minutes, however. Just as I noted the number, the curtain in the front window twitched. Heart thumping in my throat, I turned my face aside and hurried away, hoping the gloom—and my male attire—had obscured me sufficiently to prevent her from recognizing me.

But I had a feeling she had.

Frank had the day watch at Dutch's flat, so I didn't expect him to show up for my report until the evening. I had plenty to keep me busy in the meantime. Even though Cassie and Sadie manage the bulk of the housework, there's a lot to be done when running a boarding house.

As I sat at the kitchen table, sorting through stacks of linens to determine which needed mending, my mind kept going over the puzzle of Tilly Sohren. The house she was living in—an obvious conclusion, as she had a key and was known by the staff—was situated in one of the more prosperous sections of the city. So why was she working as a maid for the likes of Dutch Dan? And why steal from department stores? Though it was not unheard of for some wealthy women to steal from compulsion rather than need, Tilly had been working with two others the day I caught her. Only a professional operated in such a fashion. Frank would look into who owned the property, of course, but now I was curious as to whether the department store had reported Tilly to the police or let her go. Did she have a record? What was her background?

"Miss Hamilton?" a tentative lady's voice inquired.

I looked up to see one of our lodgers, Miss Walterson, in the doorway. Though in her mid-twenties, the diminutive woman looked quite a bit younger, with freckles across a snub nose and an animated expression only wide-eyed youth can achieve. I wondered how she managed unruly pupils at the day school.

"Yes?"

"There's a gentleman to see you. Sadie's getting coal out of the cellar so I answered the door. Was it all right to put him in the parlor to wait?"

Mercy, I'd been so lost in thought I hadn't heard the bell at all. I glanced at the mantel clock. Frank shouldn't be here so early. Was something wrong?

"I'll be right there."

She smiled. "He's quite a handsome gentleman. I hope he's come to inquire about lodging."

"Hardly," I retorted. The last thing I needed was my estranged husband living under our roof again.

But it wasn't Frank waiting in the parlor. My breath caught in my throat at the sight of the tall, wiry, dark-haired man who turned from examining the mantel at the sound of my approach. Phillip Kendall.

"Pen. It's good to see you after so long," he said warmly, reaching out and clasping my hands. "You're looking well."

The gesture was not unwelcome—I had to admit, the familiar pressure of his warm grasp was a pleasant sensation— but I pulled away for the sake of propriety. "This is a surprise, Mr. Kendall. Please, have a seat."

As we settled ourselves, I got a good look at him, noting the well-defined jaw, the dark, neatly trimmed pencil mustache, and the quirk of the mouth, ready to laugh at the unexpected or the absurd. Not much about him had changed since I'd seen him last, though perhaps there were a few threads of silver in the sweep of dark hair at his temple. I'd never known his age. I assumed he was only a bit older than my thirty-three years.

He smoothed a crease on his impeccable trousers as he sat. "I do wish you'd call me by my Christian name. We're friends, are we not? After all, I've seen you in your stockinged feet. That should allow us some degree of familiarity."

I flushed. "*That* was an extraordinary circumstance. As you may recall, someone was trying to kill me at the time. I most certainly do not run around unshod on a regular basis."

He grinned but said nothing.

45

"We *are* friends," I added grudgingly, "but one must be careful when addressing a handsome gentleman so familiarly in the company of others. It could be misconstrued."

His eyes twinkled mischievously. "We aren't in the company of others at the moment."

Had the room grown warm? Where was our busybody Widow Hodges when I needed her?

A change of topic was in order. "I hadn't heard much of you since February."

"I meant to keep up a correspondence after we parted, but —" He waved a hand. "Things got busy in a hurry. I wasn't at any fixed address for long."

I resisted giving in to curiosity about the nature of his occupation. Best to keep things impersonal. "It's no matter. I was busy as well. I understand you're between jobs at the moment and ready to take on the task for Mr. Pinkerton?"

"Better than that. I have the answer already. But before I get to that"—he pulled out an envelope from his pocket and passed it over—"he wanted me to give you this."

A quick glance revealed it to be a copy of the police report on Eileen Crofton's death. Good. I set it aside to read later.

"I found out what you wanted to know about the neck—" He broke off as I stood, checked the hallway, and closed the door. He raised an eyebrow.

"We have a snooping maid," I explained. "Continue. So, is Mrs. Lockwood the current owner of Countess Margharita's ruby necklace?"

He shrugged. "You tell me. A man named Colin Adair purchased the necklace at an estate auction fifteen years ago."

"He was Louisa Lockwood's first husband, now deceased. She's remarried."

"That confirms it, then. Of course, it's possible the piece was later sold, discreetly—if the family found itself in financial difficulties, for instance. But I looked into that possibility—the piece is distinctive—and I'm confident it hasn't been sold since."

He narrowed his eyes when I didn't answer. "Isn't this the information you were looking for?"

"Oh—sorry. I was thinking ahead." I made a face. "I'm unsure how I'll go about ascertaining whether Allison Rowe's necklace is the genuine article and not a copy. After all, I can't exactly breathe down her neck while I take my time examining it."

A gleam came to his eye. "That, dear lady, is my area of expertise. Mr. Pinkerton said I might be of assistance in that regard."

"Breathing down ladies' necks is a specialty of yours?" I quipped. I didn't doubt it—particularly when the neck in question was young, comely, and draped with an expensive piece of jewelry. I recalled the last time I'd seen him in such a setting. He'd proved himself adept at liberating a strand of costly pearls straight from the lady's neck without her noticing. "Keep in mind, Mr. Kendall, we're not *stealing* the necklace—we simply need to examine it."

He winked. "Understood. When and where is the affair?"

I told him.

"The Rowes? I'm on good terms with the judge—haven't met his wife yet. I should be able to cadge an invitation, even with only two days' notice."

I gave a snort. "You're on good terms with a *judge*?"

He blinked in a mock-wounded expression. "My acquaintance with any judge is purely social, I assure you. You act as if I've spent half my life in criminal court. While I may have been a jewel thief, I was never *caught*. Well...except by you," he amended at the sight of my raised eyebrow.

"Looks like you ended your career just in time," I retorted. Why was I needling him this way? I wished I knew.

He narrowed his dark eyes. "Do you want my help or not?"

CHAPTER 5

$\mathcal{W}$ith only Sadie and myself in the house that evening—Cassie and the others were helping Reverend Fargo with the children's rehearsal, and Mr. Grissom was dining with a friend—I finally had a few quiet minutes to review the report Pinkerton had sent.

Mrs. Crofton's maid had found her mistress dead in her bed when she'd gone in at six o'clock that morning to start the fire. At first, it appeared the lady had had some sort of fit during the night—the covers were mightily disturbed as if she had thrashed in her sleep, with one of the pillows on the floor and the contents of the night-table knocked over. But after the rest of the household had been roused and the police summoned, it became evident that a burglar had gotten in. Mrs. Crofton's jewel case had been cleaned out and cash taken from a dresser drawer.

There were no signs of the killer having forced his way in, but a side door leading to the porch was found unlocked. The butler, in charge of locking up each night, swore that every door and window on the first floor had been secured before he retired. The report made clear that the butler's assertion was not to be taken at face value, and he could very well be covering up his own oversight.

The victim's husband, John Crofton, was visiting his ailing mother in Cleveland at the time. A telegram was sent at once, and he returned to learn that his wife had been smothered with a pillow as she slept—as confirmed by the coroner, who also concluded she'd been dead at least three hours before she was found.

The police questioned Crofton, but he could provide them with nothing useful, save for details of his whereabouts that night—subsequently verified by Crofton's mother and her household servants. The police extensively questioned Crofton's staff and the surrounding neighbors on Prairie Avenue as well. The Lockwoods were included in the round of questioning, of course, as their rear garden adjoined the Croftons'. Louisa had asserted that she, her daughter Susannah, and Susannah's friend Allison had returned quite late from a concert, and they'd retired right away. None of them had heard anything of an unusual nature. Edgar Lockwood stated that he'd been poring over papers in his study until two in the morning but had heard nothing but the family dog whining on one occasion to be let out.

I grimaced. What good was a dog that didn't bark when an intruder is prowling through an adjacent backyard?

The Lockwoods' servants were no help, either. Edgar Lockwood had dismissed the footman for the night after he'd brought him brandy at eleven o'clock. All of the Lockwoods' servants had retired soon after.

The accounts from the other neighbors were much the same. No suspicious persons had been seen lurking in the neighborhood that night or in the days beforehand. No one had heard anything untoward in the middle of the night, such as the clatter of a conveyance.

I turned back to the account given by Eileen's maid. She said her mistress seemed perfectly fine and in a cheerful mood when she'd brought her the usual warm milk and sleeping tonic around ten o'clock. That was the last time she saw her alive.

By midnight, the maid and everyone in the Crofton household had retired, the house had settled down for the night, and that was all anyone was aware of until the morning.

I blew out a breath of disappointment. It looked to be the work of someone who knew Mrs. Crofton's husband would be away. Perhaps the burglar was in collusion with one of the servants? If the butler had indeed locked the door, any of the other servants could have gone back after he'd gone to bed and let in a confederate.

I scanned the list of staff that lived in. The officer in charge of the case had been thorough, listing the names, references, and length of service. None had been in service for the Croftons fewer than four years, and none had any known criminal associates. No surprise there—they wouldn't have been hired otherwise.

I turned to the list of stolen items. The Margharita necklace was not among them, just as Aunt Lou had said.

The windows were dark when I finally tucked away the report and Sadie ushered in Frank. He didn't even bother to take off his hat, simply collapsing upon the settee and propping his stiff leg on the coffee table. Sadie flashed me a frown, pulled down the window shades, and left us.

I wasn't about to chide him for his poor manners. Pain and fatigue were plainly visible on his face. I sat down across from him. "Long day?"

"And boring, watching Dutch do nothing but sweep the sidewalk and unload expressmen's wagons all day." He gave me a hopeful glance. "I hope you had better luck with Dutch's maid. Learn anything about her?"

"More than I expected." I handed him the report I'd

compiled. "It's all in there. She's one of the hoisters I caught at Marshall Field's a few days ago."

His hazel eyes brightened with interest as I related the details of my earlier adventure. "That's a fine piece of work, Pen. I'll ask Pinkerton to find out whether Tilly and her companion have criminal records—that must be how she knows Dutch—and if they ended up being charged."

"There's something that doesn't make sense, though. The address I followed her to last night is in an affluent neighborhood."

He arched an eyebrow. "Really? Odd. She went in by the front door?"

"Yes, and she usually carries a key, based on what I overheard between her and the servant who let her in. The servant addressed her respectfully, as one would an employer."

"I'll have to get a look at the house. Abby—I mean, Tilly—didn't know she was being followed, did she?"

"I'm not sure. I was able to avoid being spotted on the two occasions she stopped to check behind her, but after she went inside and I went up to check the house number, the curtain in the front window twitched. I'm hoping it wasn't her—or if it was, that she didn't recognize me in the dark. I was disguised."

"Disguised? How?"

I waved a hand. "Never mind that now." I didn't care to explain that I'd made liberal use of his trousers. "What if she recognized me?"

He gave a grunt. "Well, nothing we can do about it now. What about Bert O'Neill? Anything suspicious there?"

I explained what I observed—the glowing cigarette ember and Tilly's reaction. "It's hard to know if that was a lapse on his part or a signal."

"But if a signal," Frank mused, "a signal of what? He didn't leave his post and try to communicate with her?"

I shook my head.

"So perhaps a lapse, then. As I mentioned, he's new. There's one last favor I want to ask."

"Another?"

He smiled at my teasing tone. "O'Neill's off tomorrow night. Can you keep watch at Tilly's house and see if he shows up there? Just so we're sure."

"All right—but only if you agree to see a doctor about that leg," I said, watching him wince as he stood to go.

He rolled his eyes. "*Women.* Okay—when I have the time."

Sadie saw him out and returned to the parlor where I stood, staring into the fire. "Um, miss—I..." She bit her lip.

"What?"

"When I let Mr. Wynch out, I could'a sworn I saw movement in the shrubbery. Too large for an animal. I think it was a man."

My heart clenched as I hurried down the hall for my cloak. "Exactly where?" I asked over my shoulder.

"The right side, on the corner between the houses. Oh miss," she wailed, "you shouldn't go out there."

"*Shh.*" I fastened the cloak at my neck, switched off the hall lamp, and tentatively cracked the door open. Sadie crept up from behind.

A thick mist had drifted in, and I strained to see the clump of holly bushes along the right side of the house where we bordered the alley. The shrubbery was in definite need of a trim, but I hadn't considered it a security threat because it's so prickly.

"There's no one there now." I opened the door wider. "Which way did Frank leave?"

"By the alleyway."

Bless the sharp-eyed girl.

"Lock the door behind me. I'll be back." I snatched up the umbrella with the heavy wood handle—there was no time to run back for my derringer—and hurried out.

The clamminess of the night air was palpable as I peeked

around the corner of the short alleyway. Empty. I hugged the shadowed side and quickly headed for the next street. Given Frank's fatigue, it was a safe bet that he would head straight home and not make any detours. My plan was to follow the most direct route he would take to his lodging on South Water Street. I shouldn't be too far behind them—Frank wasn't walking all that briskly these days.

Who was following him, and why? I bit my lip as I considered. Had Dutch spotted Frank during his surveillance and set someone on his trail?

A block farther along, I caught sight of my husband. He'd stopped to buy an evening paper from the boy at the street corner.

But where was his shadow? I inched closer, crouching behind a stack of wooden crates left outside a bakery.

Then I saw the man. He was about twenty yards away, leaning against an unlit lamp post—one of many that hadn't worked along this street for weeks. In the gloom I could only tell that he was short and squat, wearing a dark raincoat and derby, with a dark-patterned scarf wound around the lower part of his face. His left hand was in his pocket, but he held his right arm stiffly downward, along the coat folds.

Just beyond, Frank nodded to the boy and stepped away. The man at the lamp post raised his arm. That's when I saw the pistol.

"Frank!" I yelled, running toward them.

Both men—and the newsboy—turned and gaped as I ran at the gunman, wielding my umbrella like a barbarian with a battle-axe storming the castle. He swiveled and aimed at me. Out of the corner of my eye, I saw Frank rushing towards him.

The sequence of what happened next was a blur. All in the space of a few seconds, I tripped, saw the wood from the umbrella handle splinter as it jerked out of my hand, heard the gun go off, and felt a biting pain in my shoulder. I struck my head on the cold pavement and was senseless for a time.

~

"Thank heaven you're all right," Cassie said, for the third time that night. She fussed with the pillows behind my back.

Cassie and our two female lodgers, on their way home from the rehearsal, had come upon the distressing scene out on the street just as the newsboy was rousing me and a patrolman had joined Frank to give chase. The ladies had brought me home while the rest of the affair was being sorted out.

"I'll be fine, though I wish I hadn't been so clumsy as to stumble over myself."

"That could be why he missed you and hit the umbrella handle instead."

I grimaced. "I'm afraid the umbrella's unsalvageable."

"I'll take that trade," she declared. "Sadie's fetching the doctor to look at your head." She peeked under the makeshift bandage on my right shoulder. "One of the larger wood fragments is still in there. I'd rather leave it for him to remove."

"At least it's not a bullet." One must be grateful for unexpected blessings.

It was close to midnight before the doctor, Cassie, and our hovering lodgers finally left me to rest. Neither Frank nor the police had come, surprisingly. Had they caught the gunman? No doubt I'd hear tomorrow. In the meantime, I lay propped up in my bed, puzzling over the man who'd tried to shoot Frank. Did he work for Dutch? Were the other detectives keeping watch on Dutch also in danger?

It made no sense. Frank and his team had been monitoring the ex-convict for more than a week. Dutch had to be aware. So why come after Frank now? Unless he was getting ready to retrieve the stolen goods he had secreted.

I wasn't satisfied with that, however. Even if Dutch wanted the detectives out of the way, this method was too confrontational. The Pinkerton Agency was not going to allow its detectives to be picked off one by one. Another possibility gripped my spine with cold fingers. Tilly Sohren. I'd discovered both her identity and where she lived. Perhaps that was a threat to her or someone else.

If so, was Frank the only target, or were we all in danger? The question sent me scrambling out of bed. If the gunman had a confederate, we might be under observation even now.

I groped for slippers and, with difficulty, put one arm through the sleeve of my dressing gown and shrugged the other side over my sore shoulder. Everyone had retired for the night. The house was quiet. I slipped downstairs to look through the window on the landing. No one loitering in the street or the front yard. I waited a while, just to be sure, as the air of the cold, drafty stairwell crept up my bare ankles.

After checking that the front door was latched, I headed for the kitchen. There was no upper window that would afford me a view of the entire backyard except for Sadie's, and I was not about to visit her room at this hour and frighten the girl to death.

I stood on the back stoop, listening and waiting for my eyes to adjust. Our small garden was brown and bare this time of year, the breeze rattling the few clinging leaves. No one there.

Still feeling unsettled, I latched the back door, returned to bed, and lay awake, staring at the ceiling for a good long time.

My shoulder was throbbing so badly the next morning that Cassie had to help me dress. She also insisted upon putting my arm in the sling the doctor had left.

"I can't walk around like this," I grumbled. "Especially not at the dance tomorrow."

I'd given Cassie the barest of explanations when the invitation had arrived. After all, she would have caught on when she saw me leaving the house in my ball gown.

"If you wear the sling today and early tomorrow," she

THE TWELVE THIEVES OF CHRISTMAS

chided, "your shoulder should improve enough to go without it that night. How's your head?"

"Better." I gently touched the receding lump. Fortunately, my hair hid it on that side.

We heard the bell.

"That will be the police," I said. "We should hurry and finish."

Cassie clucked her tongue. "Sadie will put him in the parlor. He can wait."

Mercy, our parlor was becoming a veritable hub for detective investigations these days.

Frank was waiting along with a uniformed policeman, a sharp-eyed, stiff-necked fellow of indeterminate age. Both rose politely.

Frank paled when he caught sight of me. "Pen!" He crossed the room as quickly as his limping strides would allow and gently helped me into a chair. "You're hurt worse than I feared."

I shook my head, which I immediately regretted. "The sling's just to help the shoulder heal. I'll be fine." I squinted at him as seated himself. "Your leg is worse. Did you reinjure it last night?"

He waved a hand. "Not worth talking about."

The policeman, whom we'd ignored up until now, cleared his throat. "A bullet struck you, miss?"

"No—shards of wood from the umbrella I was holding. Officer—?"

"Morgan, miss. Lieutenant Morgan."

"I see. Do you need a statement from me, lieutenant?"

"Nothing so official. I simply want to get your side of the story and try to make sense of things." He pulled out a pad and pencil from his tunic, the brass buttons so shiny I could practically see myself in them. "First of all, how did you come to be out on the street at that time of night?" His expression was skeptical and faintly disapproving. I wondered what Frank had told him.

I detailed what our maid had noticed when Frank was leaving the house and my subsequent actions in response.

His skeptical look shifted to one of grudging respect. "The gentleman here"—he gestured to Frank—"told me you were a lady detective working with him at the Pinkerton Agency. I thought he was pulling my leg. I can see I was wrong."

That's more deference than I usually get. "Who was the gunman, lieutenant? Is he in jail?"

Morgan grimaced. "He got away."

I lifted an eyebrow in Frank's direction. "Indeed? Wasn't a patrolman giving chase as well?"

"The gunman had a confederate waiting around the corner in a cart," Frank said.

"We'll be keeping a lookout, of course," the lieutenant said, "but we don't have much to go by. Can you give me a description?"

"It was too dark and foggy to see much. I could tell he was a short, stocky fellow, wearing a dark raincoat and hat. The brim was pulled down too low for me to get a look at his eyes. However, I think he was clean-shaven. He wore a scarf, but it slipped when he pointed his gun. No sideburns."

"A youth, perhaps." Morgan made a note.

I glanced over at Frank. "Do you think Dutch is trying to have you killed?"

"Maybe." He waved an impatient hand toward the lieutenant. "*He* certainly can't go up to Dutch and ask. It would only tip him off to our surveillance."

"I'm sure he's well aware you're monitoring him," I said dryly. "Have there been attempts on the other two detectives keeping watch?"

Frank shook his head.

"So why you and not the others?" I asked.

Morgan leaned forward in interest. "Good question. Care to speculate, Mr. Wynch?"

Frank shot me a look I knew all too well. We were straying

into a topic not meant for the policeman's ears. "On second thought, it probably isn't Dutch Dan," Frank amended. "I'm sure you can understand, lieutenant—my line of work involves making enemies as a matter of course."

"I see." The policeman stood. "Well, then, I'll be going. Thank you for your time, miss." He turned to Frank. "Somewhere I can drop you?"

"No, thanks." Frank glanced at me. "I'll be staying a bit longer, to discuss a few matters with Pe—Miss Hamilton."

Morgan flashed us one last look of curiosity before letting himself out.

Once we heard the front door close, Frank slumped in his chair. "Thanks for not saying anything about O'Neill and Tilly."

"I'm not sure I did you a favor. You should tell the police—and Mr. Pinkerton—the whole story. Let them sort out whether O'Neill's involved with the maid and Dutch's scheme, whatever that is."

Frank's jaw clenched. "I was caught off-guard last night, that's all. But I'm sorry you're mixed up in it."

"There's no help for that now. We must face the conclusion that the attempt on your life is connected to the woman I followed. It's the only new development to come up since you started watching Dutch. Which could mean O'Neill is involved."

"Perhaps. If she recognized you from the department store —" He paused. "Would she have known your name?"

I nodded. "The floorwalker referred to me by name when taking them in charge."

"So she must have gotten word to Dutch yesterday—she doesn't work for him on Thursdays—and warned him you were on her trail."

I nodded. "And it wouldn't be hard to find out where I live."

Frank stood. "My next step will be finding out more about this woman and that house she's living in."

K.B. OWEN

"It's a pity the gunman escaped." I frowned. "Do you think he was planning to come back for me after dispatching you?"

He walked over to my chair and put a hand on my uninjured shoulder. "Don't worry, Pen. I'll always protect you."

As I watched him leave, I realized his words weren't as reassuring as they might have been before.

CHAPTER 6

*C*assie wove the finishing touch of a gold-edged green ribbon in my hair and stood back to admire her handiwork. "You look lovely."

I shook out the folds of my myrtle-green brocade in front of the mirror. Though the bodice and sleeves were not trimmed as ornately as current fashion prescribed, the embroidery along the skirt panels was all the more eye-catching. I deemed it sufficiently presentable.

"Thank heavens that part of your shoulder's covered by the cap sleeve," she said.

My reflection frowned back at me. "I can glimpse the bulk of the bandage beneath, though."

She gently draped a cream cashmere shawl around me. "Keep this on, and you'll be fine."

Aunt Lou's carriage arrived soon after, and we were on our way.

As it was only the two of us in the conveyance, I felt it was appropriate to catch her up on what I'd learned thus far.

"I read the police report on Eileen's death. There isn't anything yet to indicate Judge Rowe was involved. More likely, someone in the household helped a burglar get in. And no one heard a carriage come down the street in the middle of the night. The Rowes live at the North end, correct? You told the driver Astor Street. Too far to walk."

Aunt Lou frowned. "I'm not saying he did it himself. He could have hired someone."

"Perhaps. I admit—one thing that doesn't make sense about the incident being a burglary is why the intruder killed her. The maid said Eileen took a sleeping draught every night. I doubt she was at risk of waking and surprising a thief."

We were quiet for a while before I asked my next question. "You say there were rumors of Eileen having another lover besides the judge. Do you think that was true?"

She winced. "I'm not sure. But she was acting rather secretive and standoffish the last few weeks before her death. I had a feeling she was keeping something from me."

"Is that why you were so eager to lend her your necklace? Were you trying to get back in her good graces?"

She plucked at her apricot satin. "I missed our friendship, it's true. I couldn't understand why she'd become so distant. We used to share all sorts of confidences with one another."

"You said earlier that Eileen knew she was being snubbed by your common group of acquaintances, correct?"

"It was hard not to see it."

"Then she could have been trying to protect your reputation by putting distance between you. A close association with her could have damaged your own standing."

"That may be so." She bit her lip. "Edgar wasn't happy about it, as I told you."

"Will your husband be attending tonight?"

"He's already there. He headed over early to speak with the judge about a business matter. Edgar's an attorney," she clarified.

"And your daughter—Susannah is her name? She isn't coming?"

Aunt Lou pressed her lips together and shook her head.

"She's too young for such a function?"

"No, she's fifteen. If anything, she puts on airs as if she's older."

"I suppose that isn't uncommon."

"Complicating the matter is that her only friend of consequence is Allison Rowe."

"You object to their friendship?"

"Only because Allison is two years older and her mother gives her a great deal more freedom than we permit. Consequently, Susannah resents our restrictions." She sighed. "She and Edgar argue quite often."

"I suppose it isn't so surprising, since he's her stepfather."

She nodded. "For all that, he's very involved in her upbringing and concerned for her welfare. Perhaps he's a bit too strict as a result. Last week she disobeyed him in some trifling matter—I forget the infraction—so she's not permitted to attend any entertainments this weekend. It happens often, I'm sorry to say. That's how we were able to secure you an invitation."

Serving as a replacement for a sulky girl was hardly a ringing endorsement of my desirability as a companion. Fortunately, I don't possess an inflated sense of my own importance.

The traffic approaching the Rowe home on Astor Street had slowed to a crawl, which indicated we'd arrived at the most fashionable time—along with everyone else.

"I fear it will be a dreadful crush," Aunt Lou warned, as a footman helped us alight and find our footing on the frosty pavement.

"No matter." I looked up at the four-story, Romanesque-revival-style mansion. It was hard not to stare at the formidable structure, with its deeply recessed arched entryway, crenellated turret, and wrought-iron terraces. Every light was blazing, and I could hear strains of a lively two-step through the open windows.

I suppressed a wince at the tug to my injured shoulder when a harried maid clumsily relieved us of our outer wraps. I kept the shawl firmly in place, though I was sure to regret it later. Such crowded occasions inevitably grow stifling.

The ballroom was on the second level. As we and the other guests waited upon the broad, hand-carved oak staircase for our turn to be announced, Aunt Lou introduced me to a light-haired, bony woman who stood upon the step above us, tapping her fan impatiently beneath an unfortunate beaky nose.

"Ah, Gladys, may I present Miss Penelope Hamilton? Penelope, this is Mrs. Cartwright. I'm sure you've heard of her husband, Richard Cartwright, the highly successful real-estate broker."

"Indeed I have," I lied, trying to look anywhere but at her nose. "A pleasure to meet you."

"I would imagine so." Mrs. Cartwright's glance swept over my gown, a sharp contrast to her own rose-tinted tulle-and-satin, with its up-to-the-minute bustle and cascade of flounces that did little to soften her angular frame. She arched a pale eyebrow. "Though I don't believe I've heard of *you*, my dear."

"Miss Hamilton is the daughter of my dear friend Honoria," Aunt Lou said. "She has recently returned from an extensive trip abroad and is visiting friends in town for the holidays."

Aunt Lou and I had decided upon the cover story to explain my presence. It wouldn't do to present me as the local landlady-turned-detective. The risk of discovery was minimal, of course. This social set had little occasion to ride a streetcar—where I'd caught a ring of fare-skimming conductors a few months ago— or rent a room in my lodging house.

I glanced around for her companion. "Is Mr. Cartwright joining the gathering?"

The woman's nostrils flared. "He's sequestered with Lucius, John, and your husband"—she waved a fan in Aunt Lou's direction—"at the moment. Widows' Benevolent Society business, I expect." She craned her neck. "Ah. There he is now." She gestured to a heavy-browed, portly gentleman at the top of the stairs. "If you'll excuse me."

Aunt Lou leaned close once she left. "Tiresome woman. Theirs is the mansion across the street from ours. Completed a few months ago. Resembles a medieval keep! She goes on about how much it cost to build, but I find it quite horrid-looking."

As we progressed up the stairs, Aunt Lou continued with the introductions. Each of the ladies of her acquaintance conducted a sweeping survey of my gown and, seeing that I was of little interest, inclined her head politely before turning back to her gentleman companion. The men in question—several of whom I towered over—muttered some inanity before the conversation waned.

The chandeliers were heating things up already. I slipped the shawl down my arms.

At last we reached the landing and handed our invitation to the house steward, who announced us. Louisa sailed right in and I followed behind, ignoring the curious glances cast my way. I doubted Phillip Kendall was here yet—the man embodied the term *fashionably late*—but I surveyed the room nonetheless. I'd come to count on his presence tonight. Odd, since the day before I was perfectly content to handle the matter on my own.

Aunt Lou wasted no time in bringing me forward to our hostess, who stood greeting the arrivals.

"Louisa! How delightful you've come," a delicate-browed matron with suspiciously dark hair exclaimed, leaning forward to lightly brush her cheek. Even from where I was standing I could pick up the heavy scent of her heliotrope perfume.

"It was so kind of you to invite us," Aunt Lou said promptly. She gestured in my direction. "May I present Miss Penelope Hamilton? She is my friend's daughter, of whom I spoke. She's visiting friends here for the holiday. Miss Hamilton, Mrs. Rowe."

"I'm grateful for your hospitality, Mrs. Rowe," I said.

Clara Rowe turned her china-blue eyes to me and smiled. "Why of course, dear, a pleasure. Hamilton...I've been puzzling to recall...there was talk of an extensive trip abroad some years ago, is that right?"

I'd wondered if my mother's fabrication—to conceal my elopement with Frank nine years ago—would catch up to me. I gave a serene smile. "I was feeling quite restive at the time and decided to explore the temple ruins in Siam." I hoped I was remembering Mother's falsehood correctly. "I've traveled widely since."

"Oh? Well, you must tell my Allison all about your adventures," Mrs. Rowe said smoothly, touching the elbow of a plump, blonde young lady in close conversation with a gentleman of middling age. "Miss Hamilton, may I present my daughter Allison? Allison, dear, this is Miss Penelope Hamilton, of Boston."

"Pleased to meet your acquaintance," Allison Rowe said in a well-modulated, ladylike voice. She gave a pretty little bob.

The girl was attired in a splendid emerald gown, ornately embroidered and trimmed with rows of antique white rosettes entwined with gold braid. The colors flattered her lily-white skin —and a liberal amount of it there was, as the snug neckline dipped rather low. She wore an emerald choker and diamond-and-emerald earrings to match.

My heart sank. There would be no rubies tonight. I gave Aunt Lou a sideways glance. She'd noticed, too.

After an exchange of platitudes, Aunt Lou gracefully disengaged us from our hostess and found an out-of-the-way corner beyond the orchestra room. "Now what?"

Good question. "Apparently Miss Rowe has more pieces than you'd anticipated. If you can find the opportunity tonight to converse about her jewels, perhaps you can learn when she might plan to wear the necklace again. Discreetly, of course." At seeing her crestfallen look, I added, "It's the only option I can think of at the mo—" I broke off at the brisk approach of a heavy-set gentleman of average height.

"My dear," he murmured, "I was wondering where you'd gotten to." He raised an inquiring eyebrow in my direction.

"Edgar," she said, "may I present Miss Hamilton? She's the daughter of a dear friend of mine."

He bowed with alacrity over my gloved hand. "A pleasure, Miss Hamilton."

I inclined my head. "Mr. Lockwood." He was a bulky-torsoed man—his collar looked uncomfortably tight—and I didn't realize it until now, but he must have been nearly ten years younger than Louisa, evident by his vigorous step and full head of thick, brown hair. Still, when his brow rested in the serious, no-nonsense expression currently on display, he appeared older.

"There are people I wish you to meet," he said to his wife, before giving a little bow in my direction. "If you'll excuse us?"

"Of course."

Aunt Lou cast an uncertain look over her shoulder as he led her away.

I was perfectly fine with being left to my own devices. My next task was to find Kendall in what had become a crowded room.

I finally spotted him near the head of the stairs, bowing gallantly over the hand of Miss Rowe, as the young lady flushed a becoming pink. Not that I could blame her—the man looked quite dashing tonight, in what was obviously a custom-tailored evening jacket, the fitted lines emphasizing his long-limbed frame and lean torso.

I didn't rush right over to him—that would have been undignified—but instead watched him circulate among the groupings of young ladies. He seemed to know a great many people for a man who didn't call Chicago his home.

He approached the punch table and was obviously looking around for me by this point, so I went over to greet him.

I have to admit to a certain degree of satisfaction—one might characterize it as uniquely female and undoubtedly vain

—when I noticed his glance sweep appreciatively over my gown and hover briefly at my décolletage. Or perhaps it was my shoulder. Drat it, I'd let the shawl slip.

"How delightful to see you again, Miss Hamilton. Care for some punch?" He gestured to the offering in the largest punch bowl, a mixture laden with cinnamon sticks and slices of clove-studded oranges. The scent evoked the Christmases of my childhood.

He handed me a cup of the spicy brew. I surreptitiously shifted my shawl back into place as I accepted it.

He leaned as close as propriety allowed. "You're injured. What happened?"

"A misadventure." I took a sip before continuing. "Someone tried to kill Frank."

He blinked. "Who?"

I'd forgotten Kendall didn't know much of my personal history.

As I was formulating a response, the strains of a waltz began. Kendall took the punch cup out of my hands. "We can talk more easily if we dance. Shall we?"

I could make no logical objection to this, so I allowed him to lead me onto the dance floor.

"Now," he said, putting his hand at my waist and clasping my gloved hand with the other, "tell me who Frank is, and what happened."

"His name is Frank Wynch," I began, waiting for him to put it together without my going into the sordid details.

His forehead cleared. "Ah. I remember…at Schroon Lake, the innkeeper referred to you as Mrs. Wynch. Your husband?" His grip shifted at my back.

"Yes. We live apart—it's been several years now—but we're on friendly enough terms to still confer with each other on cases. He's a Pinkerton, too." We were covering a good expanse of the floor as we danced, and I glimpsed the speculative looks cast our way. It was Kendall, of course, who excited such notice. I was merely the woman in the way of his next dance partner.

"I see." His expression was neutral and unreadable. "Why was someone trying to kill the man? How is it you got in the way?"

"That's a long story we don't have time for. I blame the umbrella," I quipped. "But never mind that. More urgent is the fact that Allison is not wearing the ruby necklace, as you no doubt noticed."

He grimaced. "An unfortunate setback."

"What do we do now?" I whispered, as the tune came to an end.

"Do?" he murmured. "Why, get a look at Allison's jewel case, of course."

I stepped out of his arms. "You cannot be serious."

We walked out to the terrace as the orchestra struck up the next arrangement.

"Of course I'm serious," he said. "Contrary to what you may believe, I'm not in the habit of casually breaking into a young lady's boudoir." His lips quirked in a wry smile.

No need to break in…has a lady ever refused you admittance to her boudoir?

I kept the thought to myself.

"I see no other option," he went on. "Besides, you likely won't have to deal with an outside lock, just an inner one. So it's not *actually* breaking in."

I leaned against the stone balustrade and looked out at the moon rising beyond the tops of the trees. "But what if there is a lock?" I swept a hand along my gown. "I couldn't secret any picks on my person tonight."

He grinned and tapped his pocket. "I brought a few, just in case."

The man's enthusiasm was infectious. "Well, then," I said briskly, "we'd better get started before supper-time. How are we to determine which room is Allison's?"

"I already know that. Her room is on the floor just above us, overlooking this very balcony."

The man was handy to have in an emergency, no doubt about that. Though one had to wonder about his methods. "And how did you discover such a personal item of information, pray?" I asked.

He shrugged. "Not important. How you'll get up there without being observed is the more pressing question."

"Me? Alone? Aren't you coming along?"

His eyes crinkled in amusement. "Two of us prowling along a bedroom hallway? A lone female guest is less likely to attract notice."

"But you're the one who needs to examine the necklace."

"Bring it to me, concealed in your shawl. Once I have a chance to look it over—won't take more than a minute—you can put it back." He turned to gaze out upon the carriage-lined avenue. A moment later, I felt the slim metal of a lockpick pressed into my hand. "If you need it, this one should do it."

I slipped it in my glove. "Wish me luck."

Luck was with me, at least in the beginning. I discovered the door to the servants' staircase, tucked along a hall beside the unoccupied library. I carried my shoes, took a breath, and crept up the bare wood stairs.

I was equally lucky when I turned down the bedroom hallway. It was empty of people and thickly carpeted. I put my pumps back on. Far better than being caught in stockinged feet.

If my orientation with the terrace below me was correct, Allison's room should be the left-hand door in the middle of the row. I turned the knob. As Kendall had guessed, it didn't lock from the outside. Nonetheless, my heart beat painfully in my chest as I hurried in and closed the door behind me.

The wall sconces had been dimmed, though I could still see the high poster bed heaped with thick quilts, the Persian rug that covered most of the floor, and the dressing table. The latter took pride of place in the room, ornately draped in a lacy table skirt with more swathes of lace gathered at the top of a large mirror and cascading gracefully to curtain the sides of the table.

I crossed the room for a closer look. The surface was littered with brushes, combs, and other female accoutrements, but I finally found an ornately worked silver box tucked into the center drawer. This must be it. Before I had a chance to lift the lid, however, I heard the approach of footsteps. I scurried behind the curtains and had just settled them when the door opened. Unconsciously, I held my breath. I didn't dare peek.

Someone was moving around, and then another set of rapid footsteps came from the hall beyond.

"Magda, what are you doing here?" an older woman's voice demanded from the hallway.

"Oh! You startled me. I was jes' fetching Miss Allison's fan."

"You're supposed to be helping replenish the hors d'oeuvres trays," the woman snapped.

"But Miss Allison sent me," the girl whined.

I rolled my eyes, wishing they'd take the fan and go.

What I heard next sounded like a cuff on the ear, followed by a muffled gasp.

"Don't talk back to me, girlie. Just give 'er the fan and get back to the kitchen. You hear?"

"Yes'm," came the subdued voice.

One set of footsteps faded down the hall. I waited.

After what seemed an eternity of sniffles—the girl was a dawdler, for sure—the maid finally left, too.

I grabbed the silver box and brought it over to the window to see better by moonlight. I didn't want to turn up a lamp and risk showing a light beneath the door.

After several minutes of lifting trays and carefully moving items aside, I had to acknowledge it wasn't there.

CHAPTER 7

I returned to the ballroom in search of Kendall. The dancers were in the middle of a mazurka, but since he was taller than most, it wasn't difficult to pick him out from among the couples. He was partnered with Allison, holding both her hands before spinning her in a graceful pirouette. The young lady's flawless porcelain complexion was touched with a glow of rose at her cheeks. They made quite the dashing couple, he dark-haired and lithe, she blonde-haired and curvaceous. Many an envious female glance was tossed their way, and I had no doubt both were well aware.

As Kendall turned slightly to execute a hop-glissade forward, he spotted me and his eyes crinkled in a smile. I pointedly headed in the direction of the terrace once again to wait.

I wasn't the only terrace visitor—the fresh air was a welcome relief to us all—and I questioned the wisdom of selecting it as a meeting place. I retreated to the part-shadow of a pillar at the far left end of the balcony, hoping that would be sufficient privacy.

About twenty yards away, a group of gentlemen congregated. They were too busy getting their cigars to light in the breeze to notice me. I recognized Edgar Lockwood and Richard Cartwright, but not the other two. One of the unknowns was a tall, broad-shouldered younger man—quite handsome, actually, with a pointed chin and a wide, intelligent forehead—and the other was much older, with sagging jowls and an air of ill-temper.

Since I wasn't doing anything at the moment, I shamelessly eavesdropped. Unfortunately, I could only pick up scraps during musical lulls.

"...meant to ask you," Lockwood said, "where the ledger has gotten to. Don't we keep it at...?"

The broad-shouldered gentleman waved a careless hand. "...my home. I'd fallen behind in...catching up."

Lockwood frowned. "...not supposed to leave the premises, Crofton."

Ah, so this was John Crofton, the widowed man.

Cartwright leaned forward. "As he's the treasurer, it's perfectly appropriate—" The rest was drowned out in the final strains of the mazurka and then applause.

A thin, wiry fellow wearing a gray business suit—not at all dressed for an evening affair—came through the terrace doors and hurried toward the men.

"Sir!" he gasped in a squeaky voice, addressing the man with the sagging jowls, "I've been looking for you everywhere. I've found the papers at last. I've laid them out on your desk, if you wish to sign them now."

Finally, I knew who the last man of the group was—one of our hosts and the subject of my inquiry, Judge Lucius Rowe.

Rowe scowled at the cringing little man. "Does it *look* like I'm available to do so now, Morris?" He waved his cigar in dismissal. "I'll attend to it later."

"Y-yes, sir." The man—likely his secretary—made a quick bow and left.

Lockwood chuckled. "Rather nervy, isn't he?"

Rowe grunted in disgust. "That one gets flustered all too easily. Mixes up files, misplaces things continually."

"Why do you keep him on, then?" Cartwright asked.

"He's my wife's cousin. I don't really have a choice. Speaking of wives..." He stubbed out his cigar in the ash stand positioned by the balustrade. "I should find mine. I promised her a dance before the midnight supper."

Cartwright nodded. "Quite right. Can't hide out here the entire evening."

Lockwood made to follow, then cast a look at Crofton, who had turned to stare gloomily out at the trees beyond. "Coming?"

Crofton shrugged. "I don't have a wife who's missing me at the moment."

Lockwood clapped him on the shoulder. "What you need, my good man, is a pretty young lady to dance with. Your mourning is nearly up, after all. And you're too young and too wealthy to be single for long—somebody's mama will be eyeing you as a marriage prospect soon enough."

A new melody drifted through as the band got started again.

"That's what I'm afraid of," Crofton said wryly.

Lockwood laughed and went in.

I glanced over my shoulder as Crofton stared moodily over the railing. Where was Kendall? I shivered as the chill started to seep through my shawl.

Then I saw him, making his way casually through the double doors of the terrace.

Crofton flicked away his cigar and headed inside, giving Kendall a nod as he passed.

"Miss Hamilton, how charming to see you again," Kendall said jovially. "It's rather cold out here, don't you think? I hear the arboretum is well-stocked with Mrs. Rowe's favorite orchids. Would you care to join me for a look around?"

I accepted his arm and accompanied him back through the ballroom and down the steps.

"Sorry it took me so long to extricate myself," he murmured, leaning in. "Did you get it?"

"It wasn't in her jewel box," I whispered, firmly schooling my senses to ignore the intimacy of his breath against my ear. "I haven't a clue where we can look next."

Other guests were enjoying the orchids prominently displayed in the middle of the arboretum, so Kendall steered us over to the more humble collection of African violets on the far side of the room and well out of earshot.

"It must be in a safe," he said. "My guess would be the judge's study."

I blinked. "Are you insane? You cannot mean to break into the man's safe."

He lifted an eyebrow. "We need to know if the necklace is the genuine article, do we not?"

"Louisa and I already came up with an alternate plan, before your first outrageous notion to break into Allison's bedroom." Which now, in retrospect, sounded quite tame compared to what he was currently proposing.

"And what plan is that?"

"Louisa will find out from Allison when she intends to wear the necklace again. Discreetly, of course," I added, at the sight of Kendall's skeptical eyebrow lift.

He folded his arms. "Oh, that won't excite notice in the least," he mocked.

I felt myself flush.

He clasped my hand. "Pen—trust me. I'll get into the safe, examine the necklace, restore it, and report back to you. Where should I look for you?"

The cheek of the man, expecting me to acquiesce. He was right, of course. That made it all the more maddening.

"You won't have to look for me at all. I'm coming with you," I said firmly.

. . .

In the end, we decided Kendall would wait out of sight just beyond the outer French doors of Rowe's study while I picked the lock of the inside door. Then I'd let him in to work on the safe.

Attuned to every creak and voice in my proximity, my hands were damp and my mouth dry by the time I got the door open. I shut it quietly behind me, crossed the room, and let him in.

He explored the walls, feeling behind the framed artwork by the judge's desk. I looked on with grudging respect as he removed a particularly grim-expressioned relation of the Rowe family and set it gently on the floor.

"Turn up that lamp, then keep an ear to the door," he whispered, leaning close to the dial.

Within a few minutes, he exhaled in satisfaction and swung the safe open. I joined him as he passed over packets and groped inside.

One of the packets caught my attention. Though wrapped in an ordinary banker's band, it smelled faintly of lavender and was addressed in a feminine hand.

Letters from a woman—Eileen Crofton, perhaps? I needed time to read them.

But I didn't have that luxury here.

"I am an idiot," came Kendall's frustrated voice.

I looked up to see him restoring the contents of the safe. "What's wrong?"

"I should have realized the safe in here would be exclusively for Rowe's business affairs, not his daughter's jewels. Meaning—"

"There must be another safe in the house," I finished with a sigh.

"My guess would be Mrs. Rowe's sitting room or bedroom. It's too risky to try to find that one tonight, much less search it." He reached for the packet in my hands. "Looks as if we'll have to revert to your plan after all, Pen."

I gripped the packet. "Not everything in there was business related. I'm taking this with us."

He frowned. "Risky, if he notices it's gone."

"Let's just worry about getting out of here," I said firmly.

He restored everything else and turned off the lamp.

We'd nearly reached the study door when the sound of a key turning in the lock made me jump. Drat—the judge must have decided to sign his papers, after all.

Heart in my mouth, I skittered to the French doors, Kendall right behind me. We'd barely eased the door closed behind us and stepped out of view as light spilled through a gap in the curtains.

Kendall led me down the flagstone path that led around to the kitchen. "You're trembling," he whispered.

"I'm cold," I said shortly. We tiptoed past the kitchen stoop. "Best to enter through the arboretum's outer door. That would excite the least notice."

The kitchen door swung open behind us. Kendall swiftly moved to block me from view as he gathered me in his arms and kissed me with the sort of ardor one would expect from an illicit tryst.

Over the pounding of my heart in my ears, I heard a young girl's giggle and the door being hastily shut.

It would have been tempting to lose myself in the careening sensations of the kiss—the warm lips pressing urgently upon mine, the fingers cradling my jaw, the other arm firmly encircling my waist.

This would not do. The embrace had only been for cover.

Kendall didn't seem inclined to be the one to end it. I drew a ragged breath and put my hands firmly upon his chest.

"Well, then," I said, ignoring the tingling of my lips, "we-we're past one hurdle. I'd best plead a headache and go home before we encounter any further mishap." I suppressed a wince. Kendall's swift embrace had aggravated my shoulder, though I hadn't noticed until now.

Kendall glanced down with a frown. "I forgot about your injury, sorry." He stooped to retrieve the pilfered bundle of letters I'd dropped in the commotion. "Let's fetch your coat and get you home."

"Would you mind explaining to Mrs. Lockwood and our hosts?" I didn't care to navigate that gauntlet, while my heart was still beating so wildly.

"Don't worry. I'll make your apologies to all involved."

"You're very kind." I looked up into his dark eyes, unreadable in the dim light. "I appreciate all you've done, even if it didn't turn out as expected."

He grinned. "On the contrary, I consider the evening quite a success."

My shoulder was much improved by the next morning, though I begged off accompanying Cassie to Sunday services.

"You don't want to miss the boys' choir, do you?" she asked. "They'll be doing a run-through of the Christmas songs they've been working on."

I suppressed a shudder at the memory of last year's thin-voiced rendition of "Good King Wenceslas." "I'd much rather wait until they've, um, practiced a bit more."

Once everyone had gone—including Sadie—I turned to the packet of letters from Judge Rowe's safe.

They were indeed from Eileen Crofton. I rifled through them first to check the dates. If she had been a regular correspondent, he had not kept them all, as there were only ten. The earliest was from four years ago, and the most recent was dated December 5th of 1886, several weeks before her death the following January. I read that one first.

Dear Lucius,

Thank you for granting my request to install E. on the board of the Widows' Benevolent Society. I hope you will ensure he eventually advances to the position of chairman. *Though you were averse to placing him so soon after he joined Riverside, you'll see it is for the best. I'm sorry I had to take the extreme step of threatening to reveal your secret in order to get my way. I renew my promise now to keep it safe.*

I only ask that I be allowed to live my life, free of further gossip and censure. After all, I am no longer a threat to you or Cartwright—the scandal got me removed from the board, and Cartwright won't have to worry about me questioning his decisions anymore. I would appreciate, however, if you used your influence to persuade him to stop maligning my name. My relationship with E. is my own business, and I don't wish to hurt John.

Your humble servant,
Eileen

A defiant woman, I reflected, as I skimmed through the rest. These were not the love letters I expected. They dealt with Benevolent Society business, particularly Eileen's concerns about Richard Cartwright's handling of the finances. I detected an early frustration with what she ascribed to be the judge's inaction in the matter, including an accusation that Rowe himself was collaborating in the scheme. I turned back to a letter from the year before, in July of 1885:

If you agree with my assessment, Lucius, then why not act? Is it because a mere female has raised the suspicion, or because you are complicit with Cartwright?

I slipped the band over the stack. Certainly, the motivation for Rowe to do away with Eileen Crofton was there. She'd alluded to a secret of his. Had he no longer trusted her to keep silent once she'd used it as leverage? But how would he have accomplished it? As I'd pointed out to Aunt Lou, he lived too far away to proceed by foot. No one had heard a carriage approach. He could have taken a conveyance up to a certain point and then walked the remaining blocks. It was even feasible that he would know John Crofton would be out of town. But how to get in? It was too risky to bribe a servant to leave the door unlocked.

Unless he still had a key.

Even as I considered the possibility, I knew I could make a better case for Cartwright's guilt. It would explain why Rowe kept her letters. One allusion to a secret wasn't necessarily damning for Rowe, especially now that she was dead. But—if the woman's words could be used against Cartwright later—that might make keeping them worthwhile. Had Eileen managed to come up with proof of Cartwright's malfeasance, but had been killed before she could reveal it?

Lockwood had asked Cartwright about a ledger last night—was it for the organization in question or something else? I'd have to learn more.

I was about to read through the police report again when I heard the bell.

It was Frank. "They're gone, Pen. Packed up and left." He pushed back his hat and mopped his forehead with a fraying kerchief.

I let him in. "Tilly's residence?"

He paced the hallway. "Right. My first opportunity to check it out was last night, after my surveillance shift at Dutch's. I was already worried, you see, because Tilly didn't show up for work yesterday like she was supposed to. So I went there after O'Neill took over. It's all shuttered up. The coach house is empty, too. Then I climbed through the kitchen window and poked around, just to be sure. Even in the dark it was easy to tell—their belongings are gone."

I grimaced. "If they're behind the attempt on your life, they must have taken off when they failed."

"I want to go there now and search in daylight," he said. "I've arranged with the landlord to see it." He held up a key. "We only have an hour. Will you come?"

Of course I would.

Soon we were rattling along the streets on our way to the west side. "What were you able to find out about the tenants when you spoke with the landlord?" I asked, clutching the hansom's door handle as we made a sharp left, which sent me nearly into Frank's lap.

"They were a small household—a married couple and the wife's sister, along with a maid. And a baby," he added.

"What name did they go by?"

"Moser. Mr. and Mrs. Clement Moser."

"That's the name of Tilly's sister. Was the wife's Christian name Olivia?" I asked.

He shrugged. "I don't know. The landlord met her, once, when they were moving in. He said she was brunette, sturdily built, a bit commanding in temperament."

"Sounds like her. How long did they live there? How did they pay?"

"They moved in a week before Thanksgiving. The husband brought the payment to the owner's place of business. In cash."

"This man…was he medium height, red hair and whiskers, tan mohair coat?"

"Exactly. Do you think he's the one who tried to take a shot at me?"

I shook my head. "I'm fairly confident I would have recognized his build, even in different attire. You said the Mosers moved in a few weeks ago—the middle of November, correct? When was Dutch Dan released?"

Frank's eyes gleamed in interest. "In time to have a turkey dinner at the Dearborn Mission—November twenty-third. Now I see what you're getting at. You believe they're working with Dutch?"

"I'd rather not speculate without more to go on. Let's see what we find at the house."

The interior had all the signs of a household packed in haste. There were dirty dishes standing in the sink, an overflowing rubbish bin, and a stack of newspapers in the corner by the stove.

While Frank sifted through the debris downstairs, I went up to check the bedrooms. Very little was left but furniture. The sitting room that connected to the larger bedroom seemed to have been put to use as a workroom. A long bench had been pushed under the double windows, with a scratched magnifying lens, metal filings, and bits of bronze wire the only things left behind.

Frank joined me. "Nothing of interest downstairs. Find anything here?"

"Apparently our ladies—or one of them—makes costume jewelry." I placed a few of the metal ends in his hand. "Cheap imitations to swap out for valuable pieces in jeweler shops. I saw them do it at Field's." I put my hands on my hips and looked around. "I have the sense, however, that they were simply passing time."

"What makes you say that?"

"The house is large and in a nice neighborhood. Trafficking in stolen brooches would barely pay the rent for this place."

"So why were they here?"

"The house is a few blocks from Dutch's flat over the grocery shop—close, but not too close. It makes a good temporary location for keeping an eye on him without being spotted. Probably the best they could do on short notice."

"So they've been watching him, too?"

"More than that. I suspect Tilly's cleaning duties involved searching Dutch's flat when he was downstairs working."

Frank grunted in satisfaction. "Searching—so they *don't* know where he hid the money and bonds."

"But they know *about* them," I said, "which tells me they were originally in on the plan."

"*Ah*—then he double-crossed them."

"Seems likely, doesn't it? Come on, I want to check the nursery."

"Why the nursery? I'd say that's the least likely place to find clues about what they're up to."

"I have a hunch Tilly wasn't part of the original robbery scheme. She may even be a reluctant participant in this whole affair. Perhaps she left us something to go by. If so, what better place than where she spent most of her time with the baby?"

"You consider her an unwilling party?" Frank frowned down at me. "I hope you're not going sentimental on me, Pen. Just because she's a mother doesn't mean she can't be a hardened criminal."

I rolled my eyes. "I don't harbor such notions, believe me. But if the Mosers wanted Dutch's flat searched under the guise of someone working as his maid, they'd need a person unknown to him."

"I suppose that's true," Frank mused. "They'd never get anywhere if Dutch recognized her."

"Exactly."

"Why is she helping them, then? Some sense of misguided loyalty, because Mrs. Moser is her sister?"

I thought back to when they were caught in the department store—Tilly's pleading eyes, the protective way she'd clutched the child, her nervous demeanor. But not mere nerves, I realized now. Fear.

"It's worse than that." I met his eye. "She has no choice but to comply."

He frowned. "No choice? Oh." His forehead cleared. "The baby."

"What better way to compel a mother to cooperate than to threaten harm to the child?"

His eyes hardened. "Well, then, we'd better find them."

As we pulled open drawers and shifted the crib, I asked, "What was the getaway driver's name...Brinkerhoff, yes? What does he look like?"

Frank pushed the dresser back into place before answering.

"I'd have to check. You think our man in the mohair coat could be him?"

"It's a wild conjecture, but best to be sure. Brinkerhoff's body was never found. He could still be alive."

"But you said this man was questioned in the department store theft," Frank pointed out, "along with the women. Seems foolish to risk contact with the authorities if you're trying to drop out of sight."

"True. But check with the police on all three of them, would you? We need to know more." I groped between the crib mattress and frame. "Ah, here's something." I pulled out an infant bonnet, along with a black-and-gray-houndstooth wool scarf with some sort of dust on it.

"Not very helpful," he said skeptically.

"On the contrary." I brought the items over to the window for a better look. "I recognize the scarf. The person who tried to kill you had it wrapped around the lower part of his face. Her face," I amended. "Perhaps Olivia. I wonder if she has a sharp-shooting background."

He frowned. "A *woman* is responsible?"

I chuckled. "Don't sound so astonished, Frank. It isn't the first time a female has tried to kill you. Fortunately, you're fairly indestructible." I ran a finger over the soiled segment of the material. "See? Face powder. I knew it wasn't my imagination that I didn't see sideburns on the gunman. She must have padded her middle to hide her figure. That's why she seemed stout."

"I have to admit, she wasn't a bad shot," he said grudgingly. "It's lucky you tripped."

I made a face. "Yes, isn't it, though?"

He picked up the baby bonnet. "What about this? The baby's name is stitched inside—Henry Sohren. We already know that."

I pointed to the bottom edge of the bonnet lining. "Here's a laundry mark."

He squinted for a better look. "Munger's. I'll inquire."

We heard the front door open.

"The owner's coming back for his key." Frank stuffed the scarf and bonnet in his coat pocket and clasped my hands warmly. "Thanks, Pen."

I blew out a breath. "Just find Tilly and her baby."

CHAPTER 8

$\mathcal{M}$onday morning came without any word from Frank. To take my mind off my worry—and because I owed Aunt Lou a report of some sort—I sent off a note asking if I could pay her a visit today.

Her response came in the form of her carriage arriving at four-thirty, for which I was grateful. A light snow had been falling for the past hour and I was happy to be spared a streetcar ride followed by a walk to her residence.

This was the first time I'd visited Aunt Lou at her home on Prairie Avenue. Nearly every building style was showcased along this stretch—French Revival, Romanesque, Queen Anne, Italianate—and each bespoke the sort of comfortable privilege my mother would appreciate.

Finally, we swung onto the Lockwoods' driveway and I got my first full look at the mansion. It was a stately structure, built in the Greek Revival style. Except for the black wrought iron fence around the property, everything about it was white—the façade, the wide stone steps, the columned porch extending two stories high. It conveyed a sense of tradition, simplicity, and purity in contrast to its ornately pilastered-and-turreted neighbors.

I was ushered into the parlor where Aunt Lou sat with what looked to be a shaggy white ball in her lap. Upon my approach, the creature jumped up and barked vehemently.

"Plato," Aunt Lou said reprovingly. "Settle down."

The little dog—a Maltese, I believe—gave one last yip and aimed a baleful look in my direction before curling up again.

A young lady close to debutante age sat across from Aunt Lou. She glanced up briefly, then resumed pouring the tea.

"You mustn't mind Plato," Aunt Lou said to me. "I'm so glad you could join us! Please, be comfortable."

I cautiously chose a plump, upholstered settee of rose silk, hoping I'd later be able to extricate myself from it gracefully.

She reached for the bell pull. "This is my daughter, Susannah. Susannah, dear, say hello to Miss Hamilton."

"Hullo, Miss Hamilton," Susannah echoed in a dutiful, but toneless, voice. Her sulky, downturned mouth would be appealing given a better temperament, but the rest of her appearance was quite lovely— rosy cheeks, a delicate pointed chin, a wide, clear forehead so like her mother's, and wavy, dark-brown hair pulled softly back and forming charming wisps at her temples.

The maid came in. "Ma'am, you rang for me?"

Aunt Lou picked up the drowsy dog and passed it over to the maid. "Plato needs a b-a-t-h, if you would take care of it."

The animal, perhaps knowing how to spell, jumped down with a whimper and bolted for the door, the maid giving chase.

Aunt Lou grimaced before turning back to me. "Would you care for a cup of tea?"

"Yes, thank you."

She gave her daughter a pointed look. Susannah poured out another cup and passed it over. I declined the sugar.

As I brought the cup to my lips, I gazed idly at the side window. To my astonishment, a young man's face appeared briefly. Before he ducked, I caught the tufted beginnings of a pale mustache, light eyes, and light-blond hair slicked down with pomade.

Aunt Lou hadn't noticed, but Susannah had. She shot me a swift glance, but I kept my face expressionless as I took a sip and smiled. "It's excellent, thank you."

Her shoulders relaxed. She poured another cup that she passed to her mother.

"Thank you, dear."

Susannah stood. "If you'll excuse me, Mama? I have to retrieve the pots from the kiln."

"Yes, of course. Do be careful. Wear your smock and work gloves."

With a final, curious glance in my direction, the girl left the room.

"Pots from the kiln?" I asked.

"Susannah has lately become interested in pottery-making. We've built a small studio for her use at the back of the property."

"Indeed." The wealthy found all sorts of interesting ways to spend their money. I wondered if the young man awaited her there.

Aunt Lou sighed as her gaze lingered at the door her daughter had just stepped through. "I apologize for Susannah. She isn't as interested in the social niceties as I would like."

"I expect it's the age," I answered, though I had no idea if that was true or not. It had been a long time since I was that young, and I had no children of my own to go by.

"I wish she and Edgar got along better. He's so strict, and she's rather...well, rebellious."

"I remember you mentioning that. A difficult combination, to be sure." I set my cup aside. "I'm glad we're alone. I need to talk with you about our next step in the investigation. I regret I had to leave the dance early on Saturday."

She shrugged. "There wasn't much else to be done, anyway, as Allison wasn't wearing the necklace."

"Were you able to learn when she plans to wear it again?"

"It will be a while, I fear. Clara's taking her to New York—they left yesterday—for a couple of days of Christmas shopping. She promises they'll return in time for the Cartwrights' charity auction Wednesday evening, but the girl certainly won't be wearing it there."

"True," I acknowledged. "Extravagant jewelry would be incongruous in such a setting. She'd wear something along the lines of a simple pearl strand or gold chain."

Aunt Lou gave me an approving glance. "Your mother has trained you well, my dear."

I shrugged. I didn't have occasion to make much use of such training. I considered the possibilities for examining the necklace. With Allison and her mother gone, perhaps it was feasible for Kendall to get into the bedroom safe. If there was one. But there had to be.

I shook my head. I couldn't believe I was condoning another break-in.

"Penelope?"

"Hmm? Oh. I beg your pardon. What were you saying?"

"I said, 'What's our next step?'"

"To what lengths are you willing to go?" I asked.

She blinked. "Lengths?"

"Allison likely left the necklace at home. What would you say if I found a way to discreetly get a look at it without the family's knowledge?"

Her eyes widened. "You mean, *steal* it?"

"No, no," I said quickly. "Merely examine it on the spot. No misadventure would come to it."

She was quiet for a while. I waited, watching sunbeams light up the dust motes that drifted into view.

She blew out a breath. "I suppose so, if you feel it's necessary."

"I do." I didn't mention the fact that attending several months' worth of whatever fetes and dances this social set had to offer—all for a close look at the necklace—held little appeal for me. "But there's something else I wanted to discuss with you. You mentioned the Widows' Benevolent Society earlier. What can you tell me about it?"

"It helps local widows—particularly those with children—who are in financial straits. We raise the money, and the board decides what agencies to disburse it to."

"So the money isn't given to the widows directly?"

"That was deemed in bad taste. The funds go to other agencies that serve the widows' various needs—food, clothing, appropriate employment, perhaps an apprenticeship for one of the older children. We're particularly active now." She smiled. "People are always more generous at Christmas-time. I mentioned the auction this week—that is to benefit the Society. Edgar and I are hosting another fundraising event next week—a musicale. You should come. We shall have Miss Stephens, the talented soprano from Minneapolis. Quite a treat to have her sing for us."

I waved off the distraction. "That sounds lovely, but to return to this Society...I found letters from Mrs. Crofton to Judge Rowe, in which she raises concerns about the organization."

Aunt Lou leaned forward in curiosity, at least as far as her stiff corset would allow. "What sort of concerns?"

"Financial malfeasance. She suspected Richard Cartwright but didn't offer any proof. Not in her letters, at least. Did she confide in you about it?"

She shook her head. "I haven't heard a whisper of scandal about Cartwright. He's president of the Riverside Club—the Benevolent Society operates under its auspices—and he's currently the chairman of the charity's funding board."

"I'll have to ask Mr. Pinkerton, then."

She narrowed her eyes at me. "You say Eileen wrote these letters to the judge? How did you get them?" As I started to speak, she held up a hand. "Never mind—I'd rather not know.

Just tell me what was in them, skimming over any sordid details."

"There really weren't any sordid details," I said. "They weren't love letters, though a level of familiarity was evident. In the early letters—written several years ago—she accused Rowe of resisting her efforts and allowing Cartwright free rein. Apparently Rowe was the board chairman back then. In her last letter, a few weeks before her death, she seemed to trust him to help her discover what Cartwright was up to, with the help of another man."

"That's all?" Aunt Lou's voice was tinged in disappointment.

"She did mention she knew a secret about Rowe and had used it to her advantage once."

Aunt Lou's eyes brightened. "So the judge did have a motive to kill her."

"Strictly speaking, yes, but it still doesn't make sense that he would give his own daughter a necklace taken from the woman he'd murdered. Cartwright appears a more promising suspect. I should like to look further into the possibility. You say the auction on Wednesday will be at the Cartwrights' mansion—can I get an invitation? And one for Mr. Kendall, too," I added. Perhaps a search through Cartwright's private correspondence would turn up something.

"That's easily done." Aunt Lou's gray eyes took on a merry glint. "Provided you're willing to pitch in. We ladies are running the auction, you see. I know Gladys Cartwright could use the help."

"The women are in charge?"

She laughed. "Indeed. I have a feeling it originally started out as a way to keep us from frivolously bidding on too many knick-knacks. But now everyone finds it exceptionally entertaining to watch the matrons of upper-crust society acting as runners and hawkers."

I could only imagine. "I'm happy to help."

"Excellent! I'll inform Gladys. She'll send an invitation

around to Mr. Kendall, as well. He's at Tremont House, isn't that right? I believe he mentioned that to Clara on Saturday."

I was about to answer that I hadn't a clue as to Kendall's accommodations when Edgar Lockwood filled the parlor doorway with his bulk.

"Edgar!" Aunt Lou exclaimed, as he crossed the room to clasp her hand. "You're home early. Would you care for some tea?"

He shook his head and turned to me with a questioning expression.

"You remember Miss Hamilton, from the Rowes' affair on Saturday?" she asked.

His forehead cleared, and he gave a little bow. "Yes, of course. Now I recall." He turned back to his wife. "I'm sorry, dear, I haven't time for tea. I came home early to resume work on my acceptance speech for the Society banquet." He must have noticed my start of surprise, as he smiled in my direction. "I'm not much of a speech-giver, you see. The proper words for such an occasion do not come easily."

"We were just speaking of the Benevolent Society." Aunt Lou turned back to me. "Edgar has been serving on the board this past year, and he's just been elected chairman, effective this January. A high honor, particularly to have advanced in so short a time." She beamed at her husband.

"My congratulations," I said faintly. My thoughts raced. Eileen had pressured Judge Rowe to nominate "E" for a place on the board, with an expectation of him later becoming chairman. It was too much of a coincidence.

But there was more to disturb me than that.

"Edgar, dear," Aunt Lou said, breaking into my thoughts, "perhaps you can clear something up. Are you aware of any financial difficulties with the charity? Money not going where it should—that sort of thing."

"No." His answer was curt. He moved toward the door. "I'd suggest, Louisa, that you ladies restrain your natural tendency to gossip and instead occupy yourselves with matters of hearth and home. Leave financial concerns to greater minds—those of us trained to deal with such concepts. If you'll excuse me."

In the silence that followed his departure, Aunt Lou cleared her throat. "I apologize for his sharp tone. Edgar abhors female gossip."

I nodded absently. Gossip… Mrs. Crofton had wanted Rowe to squelch the rumors about her and "E." *My relationship with E. is my own business, and I don't wish to hurt John.*

She hadn't bothered to deny it, but rather had worried what her own husband would believe. The conclusion was inescapable. Edgar Lockwood had had an affair with Eileen Crofton.

I stood. "I should be going, Aunt Lou."

If she was surprised by my abrupt departure, she didn't show it. "Yes, of course. I'm sure you have a great many things to take care of."

Indeed—one of them figuring out how to tell the woman who hired me, whom I cared about and respected, that her husband had cheated on her with her best friend.

"I'll see you on Wednesday," I managed to say.

I returned home to find two notes waiting for me. The first was a short one from Frank saying Pinkerton was conducting inquiries into the Mosers and Tilly Sohren but had nothing for me yet. The second one came from Phillip Kendall asking if he could call upon me at my earliest convenience.

Now was as good a time as any. I scribbled a note in reply, sealed it, and sent Sadie with it.

The maid, delighted to be spared cleaning up the tea dishes and starting on dinner, grabbed her cloak while I headed to the kitchen.

I had two capons in the oven and was just taking off my apron when I heard Sadie returning with Kendall. Mercy, that was fast. I smoothed my hair in the reflection of a soup ladle, shook out my skirt, and tugged at my cuffs before heading down the hall.

Kendall's wide smile at the sight of me felt positively restorative after the day I'd had. "Pen! Good to see you." He reached for my hand to bow gallantly over it. Just past his shoulder, Sadie made goggle-eyes at his back before leaving us alone. I stifled a laugh.

"You're looking well." He stepped back for a good look. "How's the shoulder?"

I led him into the parlor. "Much better, thanks."

"Tell me about the letters from the safe," he said. "I hadn't heard from you since Saturday night."

"I've been busy with another matter." After a peek through the gap in the partly open door—no sign of Sadie, thank goodness—I closed it.

Kendall stoked the fire for me, and we sat by its warmth. His expression grew grave as I recounted the gist of Eileen's letters to Judge Rowe.

"She was blackmailing him, then." Kendall sighed. "Plenty of reason for him to kill her."

"She certainly blackmailed him on one occasion. That's how she got a particular man installed on the board of the Benevolent Society." I wasn't ready to share my suspicions of "E" being Edgar, though it certainly looked that way.

"We can make a better case for Cartwright's guilt," I went on. "That would explain why Rowe kept these letters, even though she refers to a secret. They could be useful later when Rowe had evidence. I haven't had a chance to ask Mr. Pinkerton to look into Cartwright's finances yet."

I leaned past him to reach for the credenza drawer where I had the letters tucked away and noted the spicy scent of sandalwood in his aftershave. "I hope you're free Wednesday evening." I explained the auction at the Cartwrights'. "I want a look at Richard Cartwright's private correspondence while everyone's occupied. There may be something pertaining to Eileen."

"More lockpicking?" he said in mock despair.

"Just a quick look—I promise I won't take anything away with me this time." No sense in tempting fate.

He brightened. "Well, then, I'm your man."

I had to admit, he was turning out to be extraordinarily useful. I handed him the packet of letters. "In the meantime, you need to get these back into the judge's safe before he misses them."

He made a face. "He may have missed them already."

"I wouldn't worry. Rowe's secretary, Morris, strikes me as particularly scatter-brained. I suspect he'll be blamed if they aren't found right away."

He tucked the packet in his breast coat pocket. "All right, then. What about the necklace?"

"The mother and daughter are out of town until Wednesday. Louisa has given reluctant permission to use, *er*, unconventional methods to get a look at the necklace while they're gone." Of course, she wasn't aware we'd already employed such means.

"Perfect." He stood, as did I.

"To be clear," I said sternly, "I'm expecting you to return the letters to the judge's safe, find the other safe containing the necklace, examine it to determine if it's genuine, and put it *straight back* where you found it. Can you do all that in one…visit?"

"You don't trust me?"

"If I didn't trust you," I retorted, "I'd be accompanying you. You'll send word?"

"Naturally." His tone had a bit of a chill.

I reflexively moved closer to the fire. "When will you do it? Tonight?"

"Yes—sooner is best. The women may change their plans and return earlier than expected."

I nodded my thanks and let Sadie show him out.

That evening at dinner, I poked at my food in preoccupation.

"Something wrong?" Cassie asked.

I mustered a smile. "Merely tired."

She didn't inquire further but cast a number of glances my way.

We retired to the parlor afterward. Widow Hodges and Miss Walterson joined us, the two playing several lively rounds of checkers at the card table while Cassie and I worked on our Christmas gifts. Cassie was knitting a wool scarf for Sadie in a charming shade of kingfisher blue, and I'd decided to embroider a set of handkerchiefs for Frank. It would be the first time in years that I'd given him a Christmas present, but the sight of him wiping his forehead with a raggedy kerchief had apparently awakened some long-dormant, wifely protectiveness. A Christmas miracle of sorts, you could say.

The activity did help soothe me, though I glanced at the clock frequently as the hours went by. How would Kendall manage to break into the Rowe mansion? When would he make the attempt? As the evening progressed, my uneasiness grew. What if he was caught?

Finally, everyone except Cassie had retired. She kept me company until I noticed her smothering a yawn.

"It's nearly midnight," I said. "Why don't you go to bed?"

"Good idea." She wound her wool and speared it with her needles. "What about you? You said you were tired earlier."

"I'm feeling too restless now."

Her eyes narrowed. "Are you waiting up for anything in particular? Or any*one*? Frank, perhaps?"

Mercy, did she think I was planning an assignation? I snorted. "Not at all. I simply have a lot on my mind."

She gave me a long look, waiting for me to tell her what was preoccupying me so, then gave up. "Well, then—good night."

After she left, I set aside my work and paced the room.

CHAPTER 9

*I*t was about four o'clock in the morning when a sound awoke me. I was fully dressed and sitting in the wingback chair in the parlor. Heavens, I didn't even remember sitting down and nodding off.

The sound again—tapping, at the window. Cautiously, I twitched the curtain aside an inch. Kendall was outside, pointing frantically at the door. I ran to the hall, flung myself at the door, unlatched it, and yanked him in.

He put a finger to my lips as he eased the door shut and turned the latch. I switched off the light. We stood for I don't know how long, waiting. I strained to hear over the pulse pounding in my ears. Was that the sound of boot heels in the street? Yes—a light, careful tread. The steps paused, then continued up the street until they grew faint.

I leaned with my back to the door and took a deep, shuddering breath. "That was close. Do you think he saw which house you went into?"

"I don't know." In the dim hall, Phillip's dark eyes took on a liquid quality that I found unreadable. No doubt he was shaken, too.

I skipped the parlor and led him straight to the kitchen. If

K.B. OWEN

ever an occasion called for a hot, bracing drink, this was one of
them. He hovered at my elbow as I pulled out the saucepan.

"For heaven's sake, Phillip, don't stand on ceremony for me.
Go have a seat. This will take a few minutes."

As he complied, I got my first good look at his attire—black
wool trousers, a dark-colored fisherman's sweater, and a close-
fitting knit cap, which he now tugged off.

I refrained from questions until we were both seated in front
of steaming cups of milk laced with sherry.

Once I saw his shoulders loosen and his jaw unclench as he
sipped, I knew we could proceed.

"Who was following you?"

"I don't know. A man similarly attired for stealth." He waved
a hand at his clothing.

"Not quite—we heard heels on the pavement outside." I
nodded toward his rubber-soled footwear. "Your boating shoes
are better suited for the job."

"Yachting shoes, actually," he corrected with a grin.

I rolled my eyes. "As you say. All right, start from the beginning."

He drained his cup and set it aside. "I watched the Rowe
mansion, waiting until everyone had retired. I learned the judge
was taking advantage of the absence of the ladies to attend an
all-night smoker at his club tonight, so that was a break for me. I
got into the judge's study without a problem, opened the safe,
and put the letters back. I made it to the bedroom floor without
any issues and found the second safe."

"Where was it?"

"Behind a large mirror in Mrs. Rowe's dressing room. It's
mounted on hinges so she can make easier use of it."

"Clever. Go on."

"It took a while to get it open—it's a newer model with a
reinforced door." He patted the satchel he wore cross-ways over
his shoulder. "Fortunately, I have some tools to get around such
an obstacle, without leaving a mark."

As intrigued as I might have been under different circumstances to see the device in question, now was not the time to explore his criminal accoutrements. I blew out an impatient breath. "Fine. Then what?"

"The women have a number of jewel boxes between them, I can tell you. But I finally found it." He reached into his bag and laid out the necklace upon the table. The red gems gleamed in the light.

Oh, no.

"Phillip," I said faintly, "you weren't supposed to *take it away* with you. This complicates things terribly."

"I know, I know," he muttered, rubbing the back of his neck. "But I'd scarcely gotten my hands on it when I heard footsteps close by. There was no time to examine it then. I stuck it in my pocket, shut the safe, extinguished my lantern, and hid in the wardrobe just before a man came in."

"Mercy. This is the same man who later followed you?"

"I'd say so. Slightly built, medium height, walked around with his shoulders hunched. But he carried a lamp into the dressing room—either he belonged there or wasn't worried about being caught. I'd say he was also aware of the judge's plans to be out tonight. He went straight for the safe."

"Had you locked it?"

Phillip nodded. "But he had a slip of paper in his hand. Obviously, the combination."

"That's very interesting."

"Isn't it?" He held out his cup. "Another? Reliving the experience has made my mouth go dry."

I smirked. "Not used to coming so close to being caught?"

"Not often enough to grow inured to it," he retorted.

"Poor man," I tsked and went back to the stove. "Go on— don't keep me in suspense. What happened next?"

"He got it open in no time, of course, and rummaged around for several minutes. I have a feeling it was the

Margharita necklace he was looking for, because he left without taking away anything."

I set his cup in front of him and re-seated myself. "I assume he didn't really leave?"

Phillip made a face. "That was my mistake. I thought I was clear. However, once I left the house and was heading here, I realized I was being followed. I tried dodging between houses, but he must have picked up the trail again. Persistent fellow."

"But not an official one," I observed. "Otherwise, he would have raised the alarm. And you say you didn't recognize him?"

"It wasn't the judge, that I know. Whether it was an outside thief or a servant, we can only guess."

"True. So—someone else is after the necklace," I mused. "That's a bit of a wrinkle."

Phillip rummaged in his satchel. "Time to see if this is the real thing. Bring over the lamp, would you?"

As I did so, he pulled out a jeweler's lens.

I sat and watched as he deftly turned the necklace under the light.

At last, he set down the eyepiece and looked at me. "It's the Countess Margharita's necklace, without a doubt."

I'd already known it would be. With another man after it, the necklace had to be genuine. But who wanted it? And why now? And our next step—

"What's next?" he asked, echoing my own thoughts.

"First, we have to return it to the safe before it's missed," I said. "But there's a danger to you."

"I dare not go back there now," he said.

"I agree." I checked the clock above the stove. Four-thirty in the morning. "Rowe's servants will be getting up soon. Fortunately, we still have another two days until Mrs. Rowe and her daughter return."

He narrowed his eyes as I scooped up the necklace. "What are you doing?"

"I'll hold onto the necklace until you're ready to return it."

The last thing I wanted was to entrust such a valuable item to a jewel thief, reformed or not. Besides, I had an idea of how to turn this into an advantage.

Phillip raised an eyebrow. "But the man who followed me—he'll assume you have it. If he figures out which house I went into, he'll come for it."

I smiled. "That's what I'm counting on."

Whoever was after the necklace wouldn't make a try for it until late tonight.

In the meantime, there were preparations to be made.

It was going on midnight before the last lodger—the chatty Widow Hodges—finally retired. Cassie and Sadie waited for me in the kitchen while I double-checked the doors and windows on the first floor. Our burglar's best option for entry would be the kitchen window, as it was lower to the ground and faced the tiny backyard rather than the street. We'd wedged broom handles in the other windows just to be sure and, of course, moved Cassie's beloved "cuttings" from the window in the kitchen so they wouldn't be knocked over when he came through.

Back in the kitchen, we kept the lamps dimmed. Sadie crouched nervously behind the rubbish bin, Cassie at her elbow. I kept watch nearest the window, in the shadow of the open pantry door.

The minutes crawled by.

"I feel quite ridiculous," Cassie whispered, after a time. "Are you sure he's coming tonight?" She gave the dozing Sadie a nudge.

I made a shushing gesture as I heard something outside. I peeked through the slats of the pantry door. I couldn't see the window from my angle, but I could see the floor. The moonlight had been blocked briefly. Someone had looked in.

Silence followed. He was either working up his courage or fumbling with his tools.

We heard a faint rasp of metal on wood, followed by a sharp splintering noise.

We stayed still, waiting. I watched through the slat.

After a pause, we heard the scrape of the sash being pushed open and some shuffling noises. I glimpsed a trousered leg.

Now.

I came around the door and shoved him, hard, in the back. With a yelp, he stumbled to the floor.

"Sadie—lights!"

Sadie turned up the lamps as Cassie came over to help me pin the arms of the squirming man.

"Lordy, miss," Sadie breathed, coming over for a closer look.

"Let me go!" the man shrieked. Straight, greasy black hair had come down over his forehead during the scuffle, hiding his eyes but not his thin, pointed nose.

"Keep yelling like that, sir," I said, "and I shall be forced to gag you with one of my good dishrags, which would be a shame. Cassie, help me get him into the chair. Sadie, grab the rope."

Once we had him positioned in a sturdy wood chair we'd pulled out for the purpose, I held his arms behind his back and Cassie held his feet as he tried to kick Sadie, who firmly coiled the rope around his ankles and the legs of the chair.

"That's right, dear," I coached the maid. "Now his hands and waist. Just as we practiced."

It was a good thing we'd practiced, too, as our only spare clothesline had been appropriated by the holiday-enthused Miss Walterson to create an evergreen garland for the parlor. Though we'd managed to cut a good bit of the greenery off ahead of time, it was still awkward and sap-riddled to work with.

But Sadie did an admirable job. He was now well secured—even if he did smell somewhat like a Christmas tree.

He'd stopped struggling even before she'd finished, no doubt realizing the futility of it.

Sadie mopped her face and washed her hands in the sink. "Anything else, miss?" She gave our captive a cool look, and he glared in return.

I grinned. The young woman showed promise. "You go on to bed, dear, and thanks."

"All right, then—good night."

I nodded to Cassie. "You go ahead, too."

She frowned. "You're sure you don't need me to stay?"

"I'll be fine. I need to have a conversation with this—gentleman. Alone."

With one last dubious look over her shoulder, Cassie left and closed the door behind her.

I pulled up a chair in front of the man and gave him a long look. Even through the hair that fell over his forehead, I could see his eyes were dark brown and wide. He was clean-shaven, with a receding jawline that would have been unremarkable except for a deep-cleft chin.

I'd seen him before—I was sure of it. "Who are you?"

His expression turned defiant. "It's no concern of yours," he squeaked. "Let me go."

Ah, it came back to me. That high-pitched, whiny voice…"You're the judge's secretary!" I exclaimed. "Morris, isn't it?"

His shoulders slumped. "I'm in for it now," he muttered.

"You most certainly are. Why did you break into my house?"

"You know why." He took a breath. "I saw…him. The man who stole the necklace. He came here."

"And you're after the necklace? It isn't yours, either, you know."

Morris blew out a breath. "Actually, it is."

I blinked. "I beg your pardon?"

"I bought it at a pawnshop for a…friend," he said. "At the time, I thought it was just a nice piece of costume jewelry. Even so, it was pricey—everything I could afford—but I wanted her to have something pretty."

"A pawnshop?" My thoughts were reeling. Had Mrs. Crofton been killed by a garden-variety thief, after all? "The proprietor didn't know it was the genuine article?"

He shook his head. "I guess not. Neither did I, at the time. The owner's daughter, who was staffing the shop when I got there, was the one who sold it to me."

"If it was for your friend, how did Miss Rowe come to have it?"

He grimaced. "A few weeks ago, Judge Rowe and his wife were in a frenzy of preparations for an event they were hosting. Gifts were to be exchanged with some of the family's most prestigious friends and business associates. The rest of the staff was busy, except for me, so the housekeeper put me in charge of wrapping the gifts. I saw there was plenty of gift paper—quality stuff—so I decided to use some to wrap my friend's present as well."

I folded my arms. "You mean to tell me you *mixed up* the gifts?" This man could mess up a free lunch. It was a wonder Rowe kept him on, family relation or not.

He shrugged as much as his bonds would allow. "I wrote out all the name tags and had some of the boxes wrapped. Then I was called away. The housekeeper followed me back, chattering in my ear about the next task she wanted me to do…" He sighed. "I guess I lost track. I took what I thought was my lady friend's gift up to my room and left the others I'd wrapped— including Miss Rowe's—for the judge. The boxes were the same size," he added petulantly. The sharp whine made me cringe.

"Wouldn't Rowe have realized the mistake?" I asked.

"He never saw the piece to begin with. Mrs. Rowe picked it out and told him their jeweler had it set aside. He had only to call to have it boxed and sent over."

I waved an impatient hand. "The wife knew, then. What did she say when Allison opened the wrong gift?"

"I don't know. I wasn't there. Maybe Mrs. Rowe blamed the jeweler for the mistake?"

Possible.

"When I saw Miss Rowe wearing it later," he went on, "you could have knocked me over with a feather. But the young lady seemed mighty pleased with it, and no one said anything to me."

"Where's the necklace she was supposed to receive?"

"I still have it," he mumbled. "I'm spending Christmas Eve with Miss— Well, best not to get her mixed up in this."

I shook my head. Either necklace was worth far more than Morris had paid.

"You wouldn't have tried to steal Miss Rowe's necklace if you still believed it was costume jewelry. What changed?"

He looked down at his shoes. "The pawnbroker sought me out later. He offered me triple what I'd paid for it."

The pawnbroker must have realized the mistake. "So you were going to steal it, sell it back...and then what? The household staff is the first to bear scrutiny after a theft."

"I hadn't decided *positively* to steal it last night," he said defensively. "I wanted another look at it first, and I thought it would be wise to test out the combination. I found the slip of paper wedged under the drawer of Mrs. Rowe's vanity."

"But you realized someone had gotten there ahead of you."

He nodded. "I knew he was hiding in the wardrobe, but I didn't want a physical confrontation. I pretended to leave, waited until he came out, then followed him here. Far easier to steal from a thief." He looked down ruefully at his evergreen-trimmed bonds. "Or so I thought."

"Who's the pawnbroker?"

He hesitated.

"You can either tell me or the police."

"Why do you want to know?" he demanded. "Are *you* going to sell it to him and take all the money?"

I winced again at the plaintive squeak of his voice. "No— and neither are you. I merely want to discover who sold it to the pawnbroker in the first place. So—tell me where you got it."

He gave me a long look before answering. "Fuller's, on Elston. What are you going to do with me?"

I could barely stand that whine a minute longer. He flinched as I grabbed the kitchen shears, then relaxed when I began freeing him from the rope. It was a shame to cut salvageable clothesline, but I'd apparently taught Sadie her knots too well.

"You're letting me go?" he asked incredulously.

"On two conditions—make that three. One, you return the necklace to Mrs. Rowe's safe." I pulled it out of my pocket and dropped it into his hand. "Two—you never say a word of this to anyone. Violate those conditions, and I will find you and turn you over to the authorities."

He stood and rubbed his wrists. "I-I promise." He narrowed his eyes. "What's the third condition?"

I suppressed a sigh. "Don't wrap any more Christmas gifts for the judge."

CHAPTER 10

I left before breakfast the next morning to visit Mr. Pinkerton. He knew every pawnbroker in the city and could advise me as to how to best approach Fuller. And since Pinkerton had a telephone, he'd be able to reach Phillip Kendall quickly so I could update him on developments as well.

I wouldn't be home to witness Miss Walterson's disappointment over her destroyed Christmas decoration, but I trusted Cassie to come up with a suitable story of its demise.

Pinkerton was already in his office with someone, so I sat in the waiting room. Twenty minutes later, much to my surprise, a scowling Frank Wynch walked out of Pinkerton's office.

"Frank? What are you doing here?"

His face lightened. "Pen! I could ask you the same."

"I need Mr. Pinkerton's advice on my case. Any word on Tilly and her baby?"

"Not yet, but I haven't had much time to spare from watching Dutch. Speaking of Dutch, there's been a new development. I was just reporting to Pinkerton about it. Someone shot at Dutch last night."

"Shot *at* him? He missed?"

Frank nodded. "Lying in wait for him in the stairwell that

leads up to his flat. Dutch is usually the last to leave the store, you see. Temple put him in charge of locking up."

I raised a skeptical brow. "And the gunman missed at such close quarters?"

"Well, it was dark, and he couldn't see more than an outline. Bert heard the shot and came running, but whoever it was had already escaped out the back door." He narrowed his eyes. "You don't believe it to be a genuine attempt?"

"It might have been a genuine attempt to scare him, but killing Dutch accomplishes nothing for those wanting to know where he hid the stolen bonds. Where is he now?"

"Packing his things. The grocer's offered to put him up at his house for a while, until Dutch can make other arrangements."

"That's surprisingly kind of him," I said. "Not many people would hire a former convict to begin with and rent him a place to live—and now offer his home as a refuge."

Frank shrugged. "We looked into Robert Temple when Dutch started working for him. An upstanding fellow. He's a Quaker—takes his charitable deeds very seriously."

"How, *um*, refreshing." One can get jaded after working with the criminal element.

He frowned. "The unfortunate side effect of the entire incident is that our cover's blown. O'Neill's running in to render aid took care of that."

The cynic in me wondered if that was, indeed, a side effect —or the primary purpose. "Was the gun found?"

He nodded. "Tossed to the bottom of the stairwell. An unremarkable Army revolver."

"What are you going to do now about keeping an eye on Dutch?"

Frank inclined his head toward the office. "Pinkerton's considering our options."

"So you have free time on your hands to look for Tilly?" I asked pointedly. "They won't have gone far if they're still monitoring Dutch."

He sighed. "I'll do what I can."

"What did you learn from the police about Tilly and the Mosers?"

"Tilly had a couple of incidents in her younger days, but not recently enough to justify locking her up when she was caught shoplifting this last time—especially with a baby involved. Nothing on the Mosers. The store dropped the charges, provided they never set foot on the premises again."

Pinkerton leaned out of the doorway. "You wanted to see me, Mrs. Wynch?"

Frank pressed my hand in goodbye, and I went in.

Pinkerton closed the door as I seated myself.

"It's looking as if my case isn't much of one, after all," I began, relating what occurred over the past two nights. Pinkerton's brows shot up at mention of Kendall's safe-cracking. I went on to include what I knew of the path the necklace had taken, based on Morris's account.

Pinkerton leaned back and laced his fingers across his waistcoat. "It bears out the original theory of a professional burglar killing Mrs. Crofton."

"It does. However, Morris said that the necklace had just come to the pawnshop when he purchased it two weeks ago. But almost a year has passed since the woman's murder. Why the delay?"

"Probably for that very reason—it's a distinctive piece. A thief selling it would be hesitant to be connected to a murder. He'd lay low for a while."

"There wasn't any danger. The police report didn't list the necklace among the stolen items."

"No doubt an oversight, because Mrs. Lockwood had lent it to her friend." Pinkerton shrugged. "But the thief wouldn't have known that."

"Even if a common thief killed the poor woman, we should find him and bring him to justice." For some reason, this case was pricking my stubborn streak.

"In a perfect world, of course," he said. "But our client engaged you to determine whether Judge Rowe was her friend's killer. The evidence seems to clear Rowe."

"There's another possibility."

He listened intently as I outlined the content of Eileen's letters. "It's suggestive that Rowe kept them," he said.

I nodded. "As if he was collecting evidence on the Widows' Benevolent Society. Can you get me more information about the organization? Especially any financial irregularities by its board members. Mrs. Crofton focused her suspicions on Richard Cartwright in particular."

Pinkerton tapped his chin thoughtfully. "I don't recall him on the list of neighbors interviewed by police."

"Their mansion was being built at the time. He didn't live there yet, but it's not impossible for him to have done it."

Pinkerton frowned. "How would he have gotten into the Crofton mansion?"

"I don't know—that's why I want to trace the necklace's path while you're retrieving background information. I'd like to start with the pawnbroker and find out who sold it to him."

"Who's the broker?"

"Fuller, on Elston Avenue."

He narrowed his eyes. "Claude Fuller—he *is* a bit on the shady side, that one. Never gets into outright trouble, mind you, but there've been some questionable transactions."

"Any ideas for getting him to tell me who sold him the necklace?"

He shook his head. "He's as close-mouthed as they come. All the successful ones are. Nobody wants a gossipy pawnbroker divulging their secrets."

I recalled something Morris had said. "What about his daughter? She's the one who sold it. I assume she's helping her father?"

"That's right." Pinkerton brightened. "I heard Fuller has

turned over much of the day-to-day operations to her. Anne is her name."

I sat back. How William Pinkerton kept the names and circumstances of so many people at the ready, I'd never know. But I was certainly grateful for it. "What else do you know about her?"

He turned his unfocused gaze to the filing cabinet. I waited.

"She's twenty-three now—no, twenty-four," he corrected. "Unmarried. Polio crippled her with a limp, poor thing. However, she's a kind, obliging young lady. With the gentlemen, that is," he added. "Doesn't care much for female customers."

That didn't bode well for my efforts.

Pinkerton must have noted my crestfallen expression. "What about Phillip Kendall? I'm sure he can make headway with her."

I'm sure he could.

"Good idea," I said.

Pinkerton reached for the telephone. "I'll have him come in."

Kendall arrived within the hour, and he listened raptly to my account of Morris's break-in and how we subdued him.

I have to admit, I felt a flush creep up my cheeks in the face of his praise, though I didn't feel I quite deserved it. "Morris is a meek, quivering fellow. Between the three of us, we had no trouble. And my maid's knots were an impressive sight to see," I added.

Pinkerton smiled. "Perhaps we should recruit her and expand our female complement of agents."

Kendall let out a chuckle. "You could do worse, sir."

"Her eavesdropping skills need work," I said dryly. "So we're agreed—Mr. Kendall and I will approach Fuller's shop when the daughter is staffing it? I'll report our findings."

Pinkerton stood to usher us out. "Excellent."

After some inquiries, Pinkerton's secretary Mary learned that Anne Fuller manned the pawnshop on weekday afternoons.

"Perfect," Kendall said. "I have only to make a quick stop to change clothes and we'll go. I can hardly play the part of a customer in this attire." He gestured to his impeccably tailored morning jacket and silk cravat.

I raised a skeptical brow. "I have difficulty believing your wardrobe contains a single scuffed or threadbare item. Beyond your reconnoitering outfit, that is."

"It's always wise to have variety." He looked over my own serviceable pleated shirtwaist and dark-green wool checked skirt. "I seem to recall a very becoming blue-green gown that you wore only a few days ago, for example. Quite a contrast to your current attire."

"A pity we cannot all wear our best finery on a daily basis," I said wryly. I checked my watch. "If you would hail a cab? We'd better get going."

We reached Kendall's hotel, and I waited in the hansom while he made a quick change. When he returned, I had to admit he looked the part of a man of strained financial means who was doing his best to maintain respectability—from the shoes, clean and polished but worn at the heels, to the sturdy brown-tweed jacket, fraying at the cuffs and missing a few buttons. Topping off the whole was a dark bowler with a faded brim.

Fuller's pawnshop was on a street front right off the north branch of the river, a location not typically patronized by the genteel lady shoppers of the downtown district. I wrinkled my nose at the river odors that wafted by and gratefully passed under the low-hung sign—Claude Fuller, Pawnbroker. Gold, Jewelry, Watches—to head inside.

Once my eyes adjusted to the gloom, I could see the shop was a jumble of dusty knickknacks, forgotten trunks, abandoned baby-dolls, and racks of clothing. The jewelry section, however, was neatly arranged, designed to attract the eye toward the glass cases that stretched along the length of the store.

A petite, curly-haired young woman standing behind the

counter called out a greeting as we walked in. Kendall made his way toward her as I veered off to a nearby garment rack to browse—and listen.

"Good afternoon, miss." Kendall leaned over the counter toward the shopgirl and murmured, "How is it that such a pretty young lady is stuck back here with these dusty old things?"

"Oh, sir—you are too kind," she said. "My papa owns the place. Since he's getting on in years, I help him out most days."

"What a kind-hearted girl—what's your name?"

"Anne."

"Well, Anne, it's a pleasure to meet you. I'm Mr."—he hesitated—"Hamilton."

I rolled my eyes and moved on to another rack. We were the only customers in the store.

"But do call me Phillip," he added warmly.

She tittered and dropped her voice to a barely audible murmur. "Your wife doesn't mind?"

"Oh, I'm not married," Kendall said smoothly. "The lady with me is my sister."

She brightened. "Ah! Well, that's all right, then. Are you looking for something in particular—Phillip?"

"An item of jewelry—a Christmas gift for our dear mother," he said.

I shifted over to the section loosely organized as ladies' hats. Now I could see Anne's face, which at this point had creased in perplexity.

"Shouldn't your sister be in charge of shopping for gifts of jewelry?" she asked.

Kendall waved a careless hand in my direction. "Her? She calls them fripperies. I'm the jewel expert in the family."

I turned my snort into a cough as I reached for a black straw hat adorned with a single peacock feather twined around its brim.

"Well, now, isn't that sweet of you," she said. "You've come to the right place. We're known for having the best second-hand jewelry in the area. Let me show you our loveliest collection— most of them are costume pieces, you understand—"

"Actually," Kendall interrupted, "I had a specific item in mind. A friend of mine—Morris is his name—was in here a couple of weeks ago. He showed me a stunning necklace that he'd purchased here for his lady friend. Red and clear sparkling stones, set in gold filigree?"

"I remember that," the girl declared. "I'm afraid we don't have another like it, though."

Kendall let out a mighty sigh. "Such a piece would have gone perfectly with the garnet gown Mama is to wear to Christmas Eve service."

Her eyes softened in sympathy. "I'm sorry, Phillip."

"Is there any way—if I might presume upon your kindness," he said earnestly, clasping her hand. "Can you tell me who sold you the piece? He may have another like it I could purchase."

She hesitated, but did not withdraw her hand. "Well, I don't know..."

"I would, of course, still purchase something from *you*, my dear." He let out a low chuckle. "Perhaps I should buy my sister something pretty. Ladies like to protest they do not care for something when they actually do—haven't you found it to be so?"

I pretended not to hear, keeping my face averted in case Anne looked my way. I had to bite my lip to keep from laughing. *Ladies like to protest*...he was holding nothing back.

No need to overhear the rest of the interchange—I had no doubt he'd be successful. I moved toward the front of the store and browsed the book section.

Within minutes, I felt his touch upon my arm. "Shall we go?"

Once he'd helped me into a hansom and we pulled away from the curb, Kendall presented me with a small, ribbon-tied box. "For you, Pen. A souvenir, a gift—call it what you will."

Inside was a small, silver brooch shaped like an ornamental key, the curved filigree of its head accented with pale blue stones.

"A key seemed appropriate somehow." He smiled. "Finding our way through obstacles, unlocking secrets—that sort of thing. Do you like it?"

"It's lovely," I said in a tight voice. I don't know why it touched me so.

"Allow me." He freed it from the cotton and reached for my collar. His gloved fingers brushed my throat lightly as he pinned it in place. "Perfect."

I ignored my warming cheeks as I nodded my thanks. "She gave you the name and address?"

He handed me a slip of paper.

Jon Anders, Purveyor of collectibles, 76 Clark Street

"Shall we go there now?" he asked.

"May as well." I was trying not to get my hopes up. If this was the thief we sought, would he really give his name and where he could be found? "Did you get a description?"

He grinned. "Indeed. A young, skinny fellow, medium height, sharp Adam's apple. Pale hair that he likes to slick back with too much pomade. And it seems he hasn't been entirely successful at growing a mustache." Unconsciously, he stroked his own glossy black mustache as he spoke.

"Anything else?"

"Well, he's a bit of a dandy—likes to wear ornately embroidered waistcoats, silk cravats...you know the kind."

Indeed I did.

"Carries a walking stick," he added.

"Not exactly the rough-and-tumble sort of man I imagined," I observed.

He tucked the paper back in his pocket. "Thieves come in all shapes and forms, my dear."

Don't I know it. I didn't say that aloud, of course.

~

Kendall and I turned away from the third establishment on Clark Street where we had inquired of Jon Anders. No one had heard of him.

I tucked my chin in my scarf against the chill of the wind. "Such a waste of time."

"Well, we wouldn't want it to be *that* easy, would we?" He raised his hand for our third cab of the day. "Where to next?"

"What time is it?"

He fished in his waistcoat pocket for his watch. "Four o'clock."

"The Cartwrights' auction starts in a few hours. I should go home and get ready."

"What exactly is our plan for this evening?" he asked.

"I want a look at Cartwright's personal correspondence. Even an old appointment book could be illuminating. Anything to indicate what sort of dealings he might have had with Eileen Crofton."

He flashed me a skeptical look. "Tall order."

"I know. Chances are slim I'll find anything of use in so short a time. But it's all I can do while I wait for Mr. Pinkerton to find out more at his end."

"How can I help?"

Bless the man for not trying to talk me out of it. "I seem to be in need of your help a good bit lately."

He smiled. "That was the plan, you know—to make myself indispensable."

I chuckled. "I should have known."

"Seriously, though, any time you find yourself in a spot, you can count on me. Room 35 at the Tremont." He clasped my hand. "I plan to stick around for the foreseeable future."

I wasn't sure what to make of that.

He let go of my hand. "So, what do you have in mind?"

CHAPTER 11

*a*unt Lou sent her carriage early to bring me directly to the Cartwrights' mansion, where I was to meet with her and the other ladies—Mrs. Cartwright, Mrs. Rowe, Allison, and Susannah—to help set up the auction.

I wasn't quite prepared for the sheer size and solidity of the Cartwrights' three-story mansion—or perhaps *fortress* would be the better term. Its face was entirely constructed of rusticated granite blocks, the severity alleviated only by the arched stone doorway and the mullioned upper-story windows. Aunt Lou was right—it was hideous.

After gawking at the hand-carved dark walnut staircase that stood in stark contrast to the circular vestibule's pink marble floor, I followed the maid to the ladies' parlor.

"Ah, Penelope," a harassed-looking Aunt Lou greeted me. "I'm glad you're here. We're behind schedule already. Can you help the young ladies affix tags to the candlesticks?" She brushed back a damp lock of graying brown hair as she gestured toward her daughter, huddled with Allison Rowe and whispering in her ear. Not much seemed to be getting done.

"Of course." I inclined my head toward Gladys Cartwright, who'd just finished giving instructions to a footman carrying an enormous hookah. "Your home is magnificent, Mrs. Cartwright."

She gave me a thin-lipped, condescending smile. "Yes, indeed it is. It has been quite the ordeal, having the place built exactly to our requirements. We were supposed to move in this time last year, but the interior decorator made a complete mess of my instructions. He had a mahogany staircase installed when we'd *clearly* ordered walnut, and he confused the wallpapers—I had specified *Acanthus* in the dining room and *Strawberry Thief* in here and he reversed them. Can you imagine?" She waved a hand at the walls in exasperation. "Everything had to be ripped out. It added another three months to our timeline."

Behind Mrs. Cartwright's back, Aunt Lou grimaced.

I, on the other hand, wondered about the possibilities such information presented. The house had been built by the time Eileen was killed. And, even though the wallpapers were not up to standard, the place was habitable. Had Richard Cartwright stayed here on occasion to oversee the work? That would put him right nearby.

"I can only imagine the inconvenience," I murmured sympathetically. "How fortunate that your husband was monitoring their work."

Her dark eyes glinted. "Not closely enough for my liking," she snapped. "Not until he realized the grievous mistakes being made." She put her hands on her narrow hips. "Men."

As she moved away to give instructions to the housekeeper, Aunt Lou leaned in and murmured, "If you value your sanity, do *not* mention the Hammersmith carpet in the parlor."

"Why, is something wrong with it?"

Her lips twitched. "She could not procure the seventeenth-century Persian medallion pattern and had to settle for the more common floral design."

"Oh dear." I smirked. "I'll keep that in mind."

Allison and Susannah looked up as I approached, their eyes wary. Here was another adult ready to order them about.

"Hello, ladies." I pulled up a chair and reached for a stack of tags. Susannah's double-stranded pearl bracelet glinted in the light.

"How pretty," I said.

Susannah smiled and nodded toward her friend. "Allison offered to lend me either this or her gold braided necklace when I realized I'd forgotten to put on any jewelry before leaving the house. I was in a hurry to change," she added apologetically. "My latest ceramic piece took longer than I'd anticipated."

Allison reached for a pencil. "A lady should never forget to put on jewelry before going out *anywhere*." She clucked her tongue. "You're still such a child, Susannah."

Susannah stiffened at the rebuke.

I could sympathize with the younger girl, as jewelry was rather low on my list of essential accoutrements. The only adornments I was wearing at the moment were my lapel watch and the key-shaped brooch from Kendall.

"Well, then," I interjected, before a quarrel ensued, "how fortunate that you had an item to spare, Miss Rowe." My gaze drifted to her chain necklace. "Both pieces are lovely. Would you pass me the price sheet, please?"

Once all of the items were tagged and set out for attendees to view prior to the auction, I was free for a while—at least until the auction itself, when I was assigned to act as cashier.

I watched Kendall from a distance as he perused the tables and struck up conversations. When he finally drew Cartwright aside, I knew it was time to move. I had about twenty minutes before I'd be missed.

I had already established that Cartwright's study was on the second floor, tucked at the back of the house and sporting a balcony that overlooked the garden.

No one was about. I tested the knob, and it turned easily. Giving mental thanks for Kendall saving me time, I slipped in.

The room was dimly lit by a single wall sconce and the glowing embers of a banked fire. I'd have to take a chance and switch on the desk lamp.

After ten minutes of sifting through receipts, business correspondence, and bank statements—showing the man to be perfectly solvent—I had to concede the search wasn't getting me anywhere. No personal letters, appointment book, or diary had turned up. I had time for one more item—the strong box in the desk's deep drawer. I'd brought a single lockpick with me, concealed in the top of my stocking. It got the box open easily.

Inside was a stack of canceled checks, not from any of Cartwright's own accounts, but from the Widows' Benevolent Society. I riffled through them quickly. One noteworthy pattern emerged. Over the last three—no, four—years, numerous checks had been made out to Osage Ladies' Employment Bureau, care of S. Parker. Yet another name for Pinkerton to inquire into.

I checked my watch. Time to go. I restored the strong box, turned off the lamp, and made my way downstairs.

There'd been no quiet opportunity for catching up Aunt Lou on what we'd learned of the necklace, so I decided to visit the following day. I climbed aboard the streetcar at Wells Street, paid my five-cent fare, and took a seat on the wooden bench next to the *No Spitting* sign.

I typically enjoy observing other passengers—young wives who clutched bulging mesh bags filled with apples and tinned beef in one hand and restless children in the other, workaday fellows who hid behind their newspapers, ignoring the squeals of the aforementioned youngsters, and elderly women, too vain to wear spectacles, who squinted in bewilderment at the street signs and inquired of no one in particular the name of the stop we'd just passed.

Today, however, my mind was occupied with weightier

matters. How much should I tell Aunt Lou? I'd recount the path of the necklace, of course, but should I reveal my suspicion of her husband's affair with Eileen Crofton? Such news would be devastating.

After a couple of transfers, I got off the Indiana Avenue line and walked the few blocks to the Lockwood mansion. I'd half hoped she wasn't home, but she was.

The maid ushered me in. "Ooh, miss," she exclaimed, "let me help you out of your coat. Mighty cold today, isn't it?"

Mighty cold, indeed. My fingers were tingling inside my gloves.

"If you'll wait in the library?" she went on. "The missus is giving instructions to the butler."

I hadn't been in the library before and was entranced by the leaded glass skylight and the columned pillars flanking the broad fireplace, which had a cheery fire going.

It felt a bit drafty, though, even with the fire. A window must be open somewhere. I walked over to a deep, bay window seat tucked in a corner of the L-shaped space. Curtains had been drawn around it but were fluttering. I drew them apart, then quickly jumped back.

Susannah Adair, half leaning through the wide-open window, was ardently embracing a thin, blond-haired young man who looked familiar. Then I remembered—he was the one I'd seen peering through the parlor window the last time I'd visited. An admirer of the Lockwood windows, apparently.

The youth saw me first, grunted, and stepped out of Susannah's arms. The girl whipped around.

"I beg your pardon," I said.

She gaped, then fled the room without a word.

I turned back to the youth, who stood there, bold as brass, grinning up at me. Cheeky fellow. Young, skinny, much shorter than I, with a sharp Adam's apple, light blond hair slicked back, and a negligible bristle of hair on his upper lip.

I stiffened. Not unlike the description of the fellow who'd sold the Margharita necklace.

"What's your name, young man?"

He gave a sly smile, touched his walking stick to his hat in salute, and walked briskly away.

I'd hitched up my skirt and was about to straddle the window sill in pursuit of the miscreant when Aunt Lou walked in.

"Penelope!" she cried. "What on earth are you doing?"

I squinted for one last look at my quarry, but he was through the gate already. I scrambled down in as dignified a fashion as my position allowed.

"A young man was at the window, engaged in a—conversation—with Susannah. I thought I observed him peering through the parlor window the last time I was here." My gaze dropped to her clenched hands. "This is not news to you, then?"

"Sadly, no." She sat down and waved me into a chair. "Susannah is a very headstrong young lady. It's been difficult—especially after my remarriage—to control her. Edgar and I have discussed enrolling her in a ladies' academy in Philadelphia, just to keep a check on these antics."

"She sneaks out?"

"There's a great deal of sneaking behavior, I'm afraid. I don't wish to keep her a prisoner in her own home, but it's difficult to trust her these days. She's convinced herself—at fifteen, mind you!—that she's in love with this fellow. Edgar believes the youth has designs on her fortune."

"What do you know about him?"

"His name is William Cartwright—or 'Willie,' as his friends call him." She made a face.

"Richard Cartwright's son?" I asked, startled. "I didn't see him at last night's auction. Or the Rowes' affair on Saturday."

"He'd rather associate with his own friends than attend the 'stuffy affairs' of his elders."

"Why do you say he's after Susannah's fortune? The Cartwrights are wealthy in their own right."

"Not *quite* as wealthy, though we don't flaunt it as they do. Susannah's portion is worth millions. Far more than Willie can make as a clerk in his father's company, which is where he is now. He'll inherit his father's money eventually, but I cannot bear the thought of Susannah's fortune subsidizing such a profligate."

"How old is he?"

"Twenty, and with all the sense of a spoiled schoolboy. His father keeps paying off his gambling debts rather than taking a switch to him, as he should have long ago."

"How do you know so much about him?"

"Gladys confides her woes to me." She shrugged. "She has no one else who tolerates her."

"Imagine that," I said dryly. I had to wonder—what if Richard Cartwright didn't pay off *all* of his son's debts? Maybe the youth stole jewelry on the side and sold it in out-of-the way pawnshops. But how did the necklace get into his hands to begin with?

One ugly possibility presented itself. "Did Willie know Eileen?" I asked.

Aunt Lou blinked. "Only as another tiresome associate of his parents' generation. The family wasn't even our neighbor until well after Eileen's death. You remember Gladys going on about the wallpaper fiasco last night."

And Willie certainly wouldn't be staying at the mansion to oversee workmen as his father might have done, I reflected. It might not be the same fellow, after all. Who knew how many young, gawky-necked dandies lived in this town who wore their blond hair parted in the middle and slicked it down with excessive pomade.

"Penelope?" She broke into my thoughts. "You didn't come to discuss my trouble with Susannah. Do you have news?"

"Yes. We've traced the path of the necklace—to a certain

point." I explained the odd combination of circumstances by which the Margharita necklace had traveled from a pawnshop to Allison's neck.

"My word, that's extraordinary," Aunt Lou breathed.

"But of course, the missing piece of the puzzle is a significant one. Did the man who sold it to the pawnbroker—the broker's daughter, actually, who mistook it for costume jewelry —kill Eileen? The necklace wasn't brought to the pawnshop until a couple of weeks ago. Ten months after Eileen died. It could have changed hands several times before that."

"True. What are you going to do next?"

I wish I knew. I didn't want to say anything yet to Aunt Lou about the possibility of it being Willie who'd fenced the necklace. I still wasn't sure about that, now that a direct connection between him and Eileen had been ruled out. Susannah might never see the light of day again.

"I have several possibilities to consider. I'll contact you as soon as I know more."

There was a tap on the library door, and a maid stuck her head in. "Mrs. Lockwood? Cook wants to confer with you about the menu for Saturday."

Lou nodded. "I'll be there in a minute." She turned to me. "Excuse me, dear. Do you need a ride home?"

The question was punctuated by the wind rattling the windows. "If you would."

"Of course. I'll have my driver bring the carriage around. It will only be a few minutes."

Once she left the room, I decided to make good use of the time and look in on Susannah.

Though the mansion was large, I had little trouble finding the girl's room. I only need follow the sounds of pillows being thrown against the door. Who knew a young lady could possess so many pillows? Taking a deep breath, I knocked.

The thuds ceased, replaced by a sniff and a peremptory "Come in!"

No doubt she expected the maid, because she stared for nearly a minute at me standing in her doorway.

I took advantage of her confusion by stepping over the pillows and closing the door.

She recovered her composure and tossed her head defiantly. "I suppose you've told my mother all about Willie and me?"

"I left out the more salacious details," I replied, "but I had to give some accounting for myself, as she'd come upon me preparing to scramble out the window and give chase."

She blinked. "You were going to climb out the window after him? Why? He's nothing to you."

I folded my arms and considered the girl. Even red-eyed from crying, her piquant face had the freshness and energy of youth, and the wide forehead and round cheeks gave her an approachable quality. The young lady was formed for impish smiles rather than sulky scowls.

How much should I tell her? I was no parent, nor would I ever be now, but I'd noticed that the older generation invariably sought to shield their progeny from the problems going on right under their noses. Prevarication and evasion don't win the respect of a young person. Plain-speaking, however, often can.

"Well?" she demanded.

I took a seat, even though I'd not been invited to do so. I was about to cross a line in sharing information with the girl—information her mother may not wish her to know. "Your young man —Willie, is it? He seems quite attached to you."

She blushed. "Yes. And I feel the same."

"It's a rare and special feeling. You must be quite protective of him."

Her eyes blazed. "Mama and Edgar are always ready to think the worst of him! It's maddening."

"If he was in trouble, would you help him?"

Her eyes went wide. "Of course."

"When a young man finds himself in financial difficulties, he may deem it necessary to sell a few valuables to raise money—perhaps to pay off certain debts?"

She stiffened defensively. "So? Sometimes that happens. It's honorable to pay one's debts."

I heard voices on the stairs. Time was short. I had to take a bigger risk.

"Have you heard of the Pinkerton Detective Agency?"

She nodded. "Mama has started allowing me to read the newspaper."

At least the Lockwoods' protective measures weren't completely draconian. "Well, I'm a detective at the agency."

"A lady detective?" She looked me up and down doubtfully. "I didn't know there was such a thing."

"There aren't many of us, but we serve an important purpose. I'm sure you can imagine the kind of circumstances where only a woman's presence would be tolerated and yet be absolutely essential to the solving of a sensitive case."

A frown tugged at her brow. I could almost see the thoughts turning in her mind as she considered it. "Yes. Yes, I do see your point."

"I'm here to trace a certain valuable ruby-and-diamond necklace that was stolen from a dead woman," I began. "It's set in gold filigree, with a little scuff at one edge." I stopped in surprise as I saw her blanch. "You have seen such a piece?" I hadn't been expecting this. Had Willie shown it to her before selling it?

A voice called for me on the stairs. "Miss Hamilton! Miss Hamilton! Where are you?"

I stuck my head out the door. "Yes?"

It was the parlor maid. "Oh, miss! Ah've been looking all over for ya! The carriage is ready."

"Thank you. I'll be right down." I closed the door before she had a chance to reply.

Meanwhile, the girl had gotten out of the bed and was pacing the room.

"Susannah."

She stopped, eyes filling with tears, and looked at me. "Are we in trouble?"

We? I sighed. "I have to go. Is there somewhere we can meet tomorrow? Would your mother allow you to visit the Atheneum, perhaps?"

The girl shook her head. "I'm not permitted to go anywhere without her, except for my riding lessons. I have one tomorrow. The Palmer House stables. I'll find a way to end the lesson early, so we can talk before the carriage returns for me. Could you meet me there? About two-thirty?"

"All right. I'll be there." I clasped her trembling hands. "Don't give in to conjecture. No one is saying that you and Willie are in trouble, okay? Chin up."

She gave me a shaky smile as I left her.

The sharp scents of apple, cinnamon, and allspice filled the hall as I let myself in. I smiled as Sadie helped me out of my coat. "Smells wonderful. Cider?"

She nodded but didn't seem very happy.

"What's wrong?"

She passed me an envelope. I recognized Frank's scrawl —*Pen*—on the outside.

"He couldn't stay," Sadie said, watching me slit it open. "He looked mighty worried when he left. Bad news, miss?"

I scanned the page. "Frank's case. He's trying to find a young woman and her baby. We believe they're being held by unscrupulous people."

"That's terrible!" she exclaimed.

I continued reading. He'd staked out Munger's Laundry, learning that Tilly had been expected to pick up an order today. He'd lost her trail afterward when she'd changed conveyances.

We were so close. I'm sorry, Pen. I'll keep trying.

"Oh, another thing, miss," Sadie said. "On his way out, he

K.B. OWEN

wanted me to tell you something he'd forgotten to write down."
She closed her eyes to concentrate. "He said, 'Moser is not
Brinkerhoff.' That you'd know what he meant."

It meant we weren't making progress. I gave a wan smile.
"Thanks."

CHAPTER 12

I woke the next morning determined to find out what I could about Tilly Sohren. There was one lead that hadn't occurred to me before, and I was going to pursue it today. I had plenty of time before Susannah was expecting me at the stables.

"Where are you going?" Cassie asked, as she watched me put on my coat and hat.

I reached into the closet for one of our market bags. "I'm off to the grocer's. See you later." I was out the door before she could answer.

Temple Grocers occupied a double-storefront along well-trafficked Madison Street and obviously enjoyed a large clientele. After browsing the full vegetable bins and the clean, orderly shelves, I could see why. I lingered over the Valencia oranges. "Imported from Spain," the sign proudly declared. "Lowest price of the season." Had Cassie bought any yet for our Christmas stockings? It wouldn't hurt to get some. I gently set them in my net bag.

"Finding everything you need, miss?" a soft voice asked. A young man in a twill apron had paused in his sweeping.

"Yes, indeed, thank you," I said warmly. "My friend told me about your shop, and I can see why she likes it so."

He smiled. "I thought you were new here. I'm Robert Temple—junior. My father owns the store."

"How delightful to keep it in the family. You know, I *could* use your help with something."

"Of course."

"The friend who told me about your store—her name is Tilly—have you heard from her lately?"

He frowned. "I'm afraid I don't know that name."

Then I remembered. "Oh! My mistake. I was thinking of another friend. I meant to say Abby."

Temple brightened. "Abby, yes—a sweet lady. She does some odd jobs for us. Why do you ask?"

"It's been a week since I've seen her, and when I went to pay a call to her last address, she'd moved out, with no word. I'm concerned she's in some kind of trouble."

"He might know." He jerked a thumb toward a rough, grizzle-bearded man by the meat counter, shifting pickle barrels. "Abby did some cleaning for Dirksen there, but I haven't seen her in days. That's probably just as well." He leaned closer and dropped his voice conspiratorially. "We had an incident a few nights ago. Someone tried to shoot him, just after he closed up. The rest of us were gone by then."

"Heavens," I said. "How frightening."

He straightened his shoulders. "I'm sure it would seem so to a well-bred lady such as yourself."

I said nothing, though the weight of the double-barrel derringer in my coat pocket might have said otherwise.

"Wish I'd been here," he went on, puffing out his thin chest. "I would have taught the miscreant a lesson he wouldn't soon forget. Waving a gun around on *our* premises? That is not to be tolerated."

"No one was hurt, I take it?"

He shook his head and flashed a look again at Dutch. "That

one brings trouble with him wherever he goes. I wish Father wouldn't get involved with his sort."

"Why does he, then?"

"They're friends from childhood. And whenever Dirksen gets into trouble, he buys Father something as a peace offering and good will is restored."

I perked up. *Buys him something.* "Is that why your father hired him again when he got out of prison?"

Temple narrowed his eyes. "How'd *you* know he got out of prison?"

"Abby told me," I said quickly.

"Well, she really shouldn't be spreading that around. Bad for business. Father is a good Christian and acts according to his beliefs. A mantel clock wouldn't be enough to bribe his good will."

"A clock?"

"The one he sent to Father and my stepmother as a wedding gift. Just before he got in trouble last time."

My pulse quickened, but I affected an air of nonchalance. "I'm sure your Father and stepmother enjoyed the gift nevertheless."

He snorted. "Jane—Father's new wife—considers it garish and has it tucked away somewhere. Father's been pleading with her to pull it out, just during Dirksen's stay, so as not to offend him."

"It sounds as if your father is a considerate man." I gleefully considered Dutch's predicament. He finally had a legitimate reason for entrée into the Temple household —I was even more skeptical of the so-called gunman in the stairwell now—and yet Dutch didn't know where the clock was.

It also gave me an idea. I might not have a lead on Tilly yet, but *maybe* I finally had something to bargain with.

The problem was I had to get to the clock before Dutch did.

～

Palmer House Stables, located close to Lake Park, served a high-class clientele. Even if I hadn't known the sort of patronage the establishment drew, the roomy, heated stalls, numerous stable hands, and well-maintained equipage would have made it clear. There was even a section dedicated to thoroughbred horses, whose monthly upkeep likely cost more than I earned in a year.

There was no sign of Susannah—she must still be out on the bridle path for her lesson. I was a little early. As I was searching for a bench to sit upon and wait, I recognized the man and woman preparing to mount a pair of saddled horses. John Crofton and Allison Rowe.

Crofton spied me right away. I frowned as he touched his companion on the arm in a familiar gesture.

The young lady's eyes widened. "Miss Hamilton? What are you doing here?" She peered at me in confusion, no doubt because I wasn't in riding attire. Then she caught herself and remembered her manners. "Mr. Crofton, you remember Miss Penelope Hamilton, Mrs. Lockwood's friend from the Christmas ball?"

"I don't believe we were formally introduced then." He bowed. "A pleasure."

I inclined my head. "Likewise. I'm here to see about…suitable arrangements for a mare I just purchased." I thought frantically for a name. "Sadie." I prayed my long-suffering and underpaid maid would never learn I'd given her name to a fictitious horse.

"Ah." Crofton lost interest immediately and turned back to his horse.

"Indeed?" Allison came closer. "A mare? Pure-bred?"

"Yes. Arabian pedigree," I said recklessly.

"How exciting! I should like to see her, when she's settled."

I'd had enough of horse talk and didn't want to embroil myself further in lies I'd quickly lose track of. "Did your father find anything of interest at the auction the other evening?"

She tossed her head and laughed. "Some contraption to

light his cigars more easily, I think. Nothing that Mother and I wanted." She glanced back at John Crofton. "Mr. Crofton, on the other hand, took my advice on a watercolor that I believe is well suited to his library."

He shot her a quick look, and no wonder. Even if her knowledge of what his library looked like had a perfectly innocent explanation—a family visit while Eileen Crofton was still alive, for example—such a level of familiarity was unseemly. I wondered what Judge Rowe would think of his daughter showering her attentions upon the recently widowed man.

But that was their problem, not mine.

"Sometimes it's good to make a change," I said, "particularly after the loss of a loved one. I'd noticed you donated quite a few items to the auction, Mr. Crofton," I added, remembering the brassware inventory sheet.

Crofton nodded. "Most of those were originally Eileen's. I never cared much for bric-a-brac, but I hadn't the heart to let go of the things she loved before now. Too painful, you know."

Allison looked down and fiddled with her riding crop.

"The upcoming auction seemed like the right time to finally do so," he went on, "so I had the staff sort through everything. My wife's more personal items I decided to give away to friends, such as Louisa Lockwood."

A tired-looking riding instructor was approaching, his boots muddy from a previous lesson—perhaps Susannah's, though I had yet to spot her. The horse he sat upon was even muddier.

"You're early, Miss Rowe!" the instructor called. "Give me a few minutes."

"Well, don't let me keep you," I said to Allison. "I'm just going to look around."

Susannah emerged from the path soon after, charmingly flushed from her exertions, wisps of dark-brown hair curling at the edges of her riding cap. A stable boy hurried to help secure the bridle. She dismounted without help and with far more grace than I could hope to achieve.

"Miss Hamilton!" she exclaimed breathlessly. "I'm so glad you're here."

I eyed the boy as he led the horse away. "Let's walk, shall we?"

Once we'd put a little distance between us and the stable, I asked, "Tell me what you know about the necklace. How did Willie come to have it?"

She perched upon a hay bale, and I gingerly followed suit. "I gave it to him."

"*You* did?"

"I found a bag with the necklace and other jewelry pieces partially buried in the topiary garden."

"When was this?"

"Ages ago. Near the end of January." She reached into a small leather riding satchel and pulled out a dirt-stained, red-velvet sack. "Here's what's left. I don't know whose they are or how they got there."

"And Willie's role in this was to sell the jewelry at pawnshops on your behalf?"

"That's right. He'd sold several pieces for me these last few months. The necklace you described was the most recent of them."

"What did you need the money for?"

She shrugged. "I didn't keep it all—I let Willie have most of it. I just wanted funds of my own to do with as I wished. Edgar had cut off my allowance." She looked down at her hands. "I must admit, there was a time when I thought I wanted to run away. I knew I'd need money for that."

"Well, I'm glad you don't feel that way anymore."

She nodded. "Even though Edgar is still difficult, it helps that I have my pottery now. It's a soothing occupation."

I looked inside the sack. Several items remained—a pearl strand, a pair of gold earrings, a gold chain bracelet, a number of colored-stone brooches, and an opal scarf pin. I stood and began to pace, still clutching the bag. What to do next?

Three riders were heading toward the far end of the grove where the bridle path began—Crofton, Allison, and the riding instructor. They glanced our way. Quickly, I stuffed the pouch in my reticule and turned back to Susannah.

"Do you have any idea how the bag got into the garden?"

She shrugged. "Not really. I figured someone had thrown it over the fence to avoid being caught. Edgar's always complaining about how most servants are trying to rob their masters blind."

I mulled over her account on the streetcar to the Pinkerton Agency, awake to the irony of carrying enough money in gems to have hired a more comfortable conveyance many times over.

To my disappointment, William Pinkerton was out.

"Why don't you leave him a note?" Mary, his personal secretary, suggested.

I didn't want to take the time to compose one. Instead, I handed her the sack of jewelry. "Be sure to lock it up in the safe —it's evidence. Tell him a report will follow on the Louisa Lockwood case."

She'd seen too much in her day-to-day dealings at the agency to be impressed with such a cryptic remark, merely nodded, and set it aside.

"Where's the business directory?" I asked.

She pointed to the writing desk in the corner. "Help yourself."

I looked up Robert Temple. Below the business address was his personal one—150 S. Robey Street. I closed the book, thanked her, and left.

I would have preferred to break into a private residence when everyone was sleeping rather than the middle of the afternoon. However, I very much doubted Dutch Dan would be sleeping tonight. He would be tearing the house apart in search of his clock.

I bit my lip. If he hadn't already found it. He'd stayed in Robert Temple's home these last two nights.

No, I reassured myself. Judging by his actions thus far, Dan Dirksen had learned the importance of patience. He'd already waited weeks after getting out of prison to make a move. His first few nights in an unfamiliar house, with a host solicitous of his welfare—Dutch Dan would expect to be checked upon during the night. He would have stayed put.

If I were Dutch, tonight would be the earliest I'd make the attempt, which was why I had to proceed this afternoon. At the moment, the men of the household were all working at the grocery store. The wife, perhaps an infant, and a maid-of-all-work would be the only ones home. I didn't expect more of a staff than that, even for a prosperous grocer's family.

I groped in my left coat pocket and felt the reassuring shape of my set of lockpicks. The other pocket held my derringer. I didn't expect to need that, but I never went anywhere without it these days if I could help it.

As I crossed the street to head for Robey, I considered where a housewife might relegate an unwanted gift. Not many of those came my way, but I remembered one garish monstrosity Cassie and I were gifted with by a departing lodger. It was a stuffed mongoose, so hideous Cassie couldn't bear to look at it and so odiferous I couldn't bear to smell it. Before we'd finally donated it to the church's jumble sale, it passed the time in a dark corner of the cellar, beside the canned preserves and disused tools.

I felt my spirits lift. It was a good place to start and sufficiently out of the way that I might slip in and out unseen.

The house was situated on a coveted corner property, proudly bordered with arborvitae and sporting a flagstone path to a gated backyard garden. I grimaced. This part of the path was in clear view of the street. I turned the corner and considered my options. The sidewalk was well-populated today with nannies airing their charges before the evening meal. No opportunities there.

I kept walking until I spotted a gap in the fences between properties. I slipped in—not an easy task, as it involved stepping through brambles and tall, neglected grass—but eventually I came to the back gate of the Temple yard without being observed. Expelling a breath, I cautiously creaked it open.

Though I didn't take the time for a good look at the space, I saw enough to know that Cassie would have been elated to tend such a garden. Maybe someday.

I quickly scooted to the well of the cellar's transom window, pulled out my picks and a sturdy file, and set to work. It was slow going—even through my thick gloves, my fingers grew numb from the chill of the ground. When the chisel slipped yet again, I took off my gloves, flexing my fingers and breathing upon my hands before putting the gloves back on.

After what seemed an eternity, the latch finally gave way. I lifted it as silently as possible, which is to say—not so silently. The cold wood groaned in protest as I swung the casement out of the way. I paused, listening. No running footsteps, no outcry.

I exhaled and tucked my tools away, hid my bag of oranges in the shrubbery, and climbed through the window. I had to hang by my hands briefly to get a sense of how far I was from the floor before I dropped down.

After the brightness of a winter afternoon, the gloom of the basement made it seem like night-time. I dearly wished I had a lantern.

I tried to be patient, taking slow breaths to still my racing heart, waiting for my eyes to adjust. Eventually I felt more confident in maneuvering the space, dodging crates stacked beside the furnace, exploring boxes, trunks, and a series of shelves built into the length of a long wall. If I'd cared to take the time, I could have told you about the sensibilities of the current Mrs. Temple by relating the kind of items which had been banished.

However, my overarching concern at the moment was locating the forsaken mantel clock.

At last I found it, shoved behind a large box of old nails. It was garishly bulky—about the size of a breadbox, and heavy. I grunted from the exertion of pulling it down.

I was about to bring it closer to the light when I heard footsteps on the stairs. Frantically I cast about for a place to hide—I really should have planned that ahead of time, *drat it*—and, hugging the ugly clock to my chest, crouched behind a large, well-worn hobbyhorse in the far corner, no doubt once beloved by Robert Temple, Jr. I stuck a finger under my nose to keep the tickling horsehair mane from setting off a fit of sneezing.

"Are you sure we have another jar down here, ma'am? I didn' see none," came a young girl's voice.

"You need to keep a better inventory, Nan," said another female, this one more severe in tone. Undoubtedly the mistress of the house. "I know we have more. Pickled beets are his favorite, after all. Now, open your eyes, stupid girl, and look!"

"Yes'm," she said meekly.

Silence. I waited, the blood pounding in my ears.

"Ah, here's some!" the girl said. "But only two jars left."

I heard the older woman's mighty sigh. "All right. Make sure the master knows he needs to bring home more tomorrow."

Next came scraping noises, followed by the tread of feet on the wooden steps, and the rasp of the door closing.

I let out a breath and carried the clock over to the window. The wood casing was painted black in a fashion intended to imitate onyx but failing utterly. The feet, molding, and handles were done in bronze, with dragons' heads at the top of the handles. *Ugh.* No wonder Jane Temple hadn't wanted it within sight of her furnishings.

I turned it over and pried open the back.

Inside were an envelope and a pouch containing a key. A safe deposit key for—I squinted at the embossing. "First National Bank, Edgewater." After a quick scan of the envelope's contents, I could see it identified the bearer as authorized to access the box.

Dutch must have realized he might be seized at any moment. When he'd gone to get the bonds appraised, he'd first opened an account in a fictitious name. I checked the document. Robert Temple, Sr. *Nice touch.* Then, he'd placed the money and bonds—except for a sample few to bring to his dealer—in a safe deposit box. After that, it was simple enough to conceal the key and document in the clock, wrap it as a gift, and send it off to his good friend Robert Temple, on the occasion of his marriage.

I pocketed the pouch, key, and paper. What to do now? This was the trickier part of my plan. The safety of Tilly and her baby depended upon making the right choice. I pulled out my small memo pad and pencil and began to write.

What you're looking for will be restored when you tell me where I can find your former partner, Olivia. I'll be waiting at...

I hesitated. I didn't want to provide our lodging address and risk the safety of Cassie and the others. It is one thing to put oneself in danger, and another matter entirely to jeopardize others.

Frank's address? I grimaced. He'd be bound by Pinkerton rules and those of the client employing the agency. The express company that had been robbed would not take kindly to negotiating with a criminal for the discovery of another criminal. Frank would eventually find out, of course, but it would be too late to stop it then.

So...who? I let out a low chuckle. Phillip Kendall. I was sure he'd be up to the challenge. Besides, he'd offered to help if I was in a spot.

Tremont House, Room 35.

I left the name blank. Let Dutch speculate who'd bested him.

I put the clock where I'd found it, climbed back through the window—it was more difficult to get myself out than it was to get in—and closed the sash. Some of the frame had splintered, but I hoped it wouldn't be noticeable.

I retrieved my bag of oranges and successfully gained the sidewalk. *Whew.*

I felt a grip on my elbow. My heart froze.

"What are you up to?"

It was Frank, his expression ready to spit nails.

CHAPTER 13

"*W*hat are *you* doing here?" I asked instead.

"It's my turn on night shift. I came ahead of time to learn the layout of the place before Dutch settles in for the night." He kept a firm hand on me as he flagged down a cab, gave the address for the Pinkerton Agency, and helped me in.

"Why are we going to the office?" I asked.

"We have to figure out how to proceed from here, now that you've broken into a private residence. I don't want to get you in trouble, Pen, but I suspect you've jeopardized our operation."

"Hardly," I retorted, drawing out key and letter and shoving them into his hands. I blinked to fight back tears. How would I get Tilly and her baby to safety now? They could already be dead, if Olivia and Moser had decided her usefulness was over.

He stared at the items for a good long minute. "The stolen bonds and money have been *in a bank* all this time?"

"Ironic, isn't it?" I snapped.

"How did you know?"

"I didn't know that part until I found what was hidden in the clock Dutch had sent to Temple." I leaned back wearily against the seat cushions. "As to the rest of it, I'd prefer to tell you and

Mr. Pinkerton at the same time. Then I want you to do something for me." They weren't going to like it.

Pinkerton was in his office this time, and he stood in surprise as Frank and I walked in. "I wasn't expecting you back so soon, Mrs. Wynch. I've seen the gems. Good work. Are you here to explain how you got them?"

I shook my head. "We're here about Frank's case."

Frank pulled out the chair for me, closed the door, and perched on the deep window sill.

Pinkerton glanced between the two of us. "I didn't know you were assisting with his case. How did that come about?"

Frank shifted uncomfortably, and I flashed him a smug look. He hadn't bargained on a full accounting of what had brought me in to begin with.

"I think he'd better tell you that part," I said.

Pinkerton's brows lowered as Frank described the encounter he'd seen between Bert and Dutch's maid, and the subsequent request made of me to learn more about her.

"That's a serious breach of procedure. You should have reported it right away. Where's Bert now?"

"It's his shift watching Dutch at the grocer's," Frank said.

Pinkerton reached for the intercom button.

Mary stepped in promptly. "Sir?"

"See if Stan's still around. Ask him to go to Temple's grocery to take over for Bert O'Neill and have him tell Bert to report to me right away."

"Yes, sir." She closed the door on her way out.

Pinkerton's attention shifted to me. "And what did you learn when you followed her?"

"Quite a lot." I proceeded to explain the developments thus far.

Pinkerton shot Frank a look. "And you didn't see fit to put any of this in a report to me? Not even the fact that the person who tried to kill you was a woman who likely conspired with

Dutch Dan and Samuel Brinkerhoff to rob the bond shipment?"

Frank looked down at his shoes. "I wanted to locate them first."

"It's urgent that we find Tilly and her baby," I said. "I believe her sister has been forcing Tilly to cooperate—searching Dutch's quarters under the guise of a maid—with threats that her infant would come to harm otherwise. And now they're holed up somewhere after the attempt on Frank."

"Unless Tilly already found what they were looking for," Pinkerton said, "and they've left town."

I looked at Frank. "Show him."

"Pen found this, just this afternoon." Frank laid the envelope and key on his desk.

Pinkerton's slow smile lit up his eyes as he glanced at me. He stood. "If you'll excuse me, I'll send a wire immediately to make sure the box is secured. Then I want the whole story of how you retrieved it."

It was past eight o'clock that night when Frank and I finally arrived at my doorstep. I was bone-weary from my day traveling hither and yon across the city, but I wasn't done yet. "Why don't you come in for some dinner? We still have to discuss what happens tonight."

Frank checked his watch. "Sure. I have a couple of hours before I take over. I'd welcome something to eat."

Cassie's eyebrows nearly met her hairline when she saw me bringing Frank into the kitchen. Without a word, she set down her dishrag and brushed past us.

Frank watched her leave. "Touchy."

"Don't worry about her. I'll explain it to her later." I rummaged in the pantry for what remained of the ham and passed the platter. "The person you really have to watch out for is Sadie. I've discovered she's remarkably cool under pressure." I waved a hand at his inquiring look. "Never mind. Long story."

"I look forward to hearing it some time," he said, setting plates and cutlery on the table. "There. Ready."

Over a cold meal of ham, bread, cheese, and pickles, we talked about what Dutch Dan would do once he found my note.

"I see three possibilities," I said. "First, he's wide-awake to this being a trap and simply cuts his losses and skips town."

"That would be the cautious approach," Frank said. "I don't think he'll be scared off so easily."

I nodded. "Mention of his former partner in the scheme might pique his curiosity."

Frank pushed aside his now-empty plate. "And being the two-timing crook that he is, he'll probably go to the address and try to con his way into getting back the key and letter without divulging anything useful in return. Where are you sending him? Not here, I hope."

"Of course not. It's the address of a colleague—Phillip Kendall. Pinkerton hired him to help with my case."

He shot me a look. "A colleague, eh? I don't believe I know anyone named Kendall."

"He's not from around here." At the sight of his frown, I added tartly, "Jealousy doesn't look good on you, Frank."

He blew out a breath. "No. I suppose not." He reached around the plate to clasp my hands. "But you know how I feel about you."

I gently withdrew from his grip. "I do. But back to the matter at hand. If Dutch leaves Temple's house, you'll follow? We might need assistance if he gets…rough."

Frank stood. "You can count on me."

Cassie returned to the kitchen almost as soon as he'd gone, sat down, and folded her arms. "Are you going to tell me what's really going on between you and Frank?"

I got up to clear the plates. "I'm helping him with a case. That's all."

"I'm worried about you, Pen. I don't want him to hurt you again."

I ran water over the dishes, dried my hands, and turned back to meet her eye. "I don't want that to happen, either. But the case has gotten complicated. A young mother and her child are at risk now."

"Oh." Cassie frowned as she peered at me closely. "You're terribly worried, aren't you?"

I nodded, not trusting myself to speak.

She got up and encircled me in her arms—as high as she could reach, at least, as I was a good head taller than she. I bent down and hugged her back.

I disentangled myself from her embrace and draped the dishcloth over the drying rack. "I brought us oranges. Can you find a place for them to keep? I have to get ready to go."

"Again? You've barely been home all day. Miss Walterson hoped you could help her string the popcorn-and-cranberry garland."

I grimaced. Pricking and staining my fingers wasn't my favorite activity on the best of days. "I'm sure she can manage. Don't wait up for me."

As I walked briskly to the cab stand in the cold night air, I reflected that I did miss being home.

It was a short drive to Tremont House. Kendall knew to expect me—Pinkerton had called ahead this afternoon. It wasn't the most decorous situation for a woman to visit a man in his rooms alone, but I didn't care at this point. I wouldn't take an easy breath until Tilly and her baby were safe.

I stepped into the elevator as if I lived there myself, told the operator what floor I wanted, and ignored his attempts at conversation. I stepped out into a plush-carpeted hallway and found Kendall's door.

He opened it before I had a chance to knock, looked up and down the empty corridor, and quickly ushered me in.

"Let me take your coat. Come, sit by the fire to warm up. Tea?" He held up the pot, but I shook my head.

"So what's this all about? Pinkerton said precious little over the telephone."

"He couldn't risk anyone else being on the line. I'm here to fill you in on what role you are to play in a little charade to get an ex-convict, Dutch Dan, to tell us what he knows about a woman named Olivia Moser." I recounted the bare outlines of Frank's case thus far—the robbery, Dutch's capture, Tilly's involvement, and what we conjectured about her sister's scheme.

"What is it you want from Dutch?"

"Since he and Olivia have a past association—enough for her to know he's secreted the bonds and cash somewhere and has been trying to lay her hands on them—he's likely to know where she could be hiding out. And where *she* is, Tilly and Henry are sure to be."

"I see." He plucked an invisible piece of lint from an impeccable trouser leg as he sat back. "And what have I to bargain with?"

I passed over the pouch and the envelope. He raised an eyebrow.

"This isn't the actual key. Mr. Pinkerton substituted a dummy key close in appearance. Dutch hasn't seen the key in nearly two years, so we're counting on it passing muster. We don't need the pouch or letter. He can have those. The box has already been secured at the bank."

"How did you come into possession of these?" he asked.

For the second time that day, I explained what I'd learned from the grocer youth and my subsequent break-in at the Temple home.

He flashed me a wide grin. "I'll make a second-story man out of you yet, Pen."

Under normal circumstances, I might have bristled at such a

remark. However, it had been a long day. The incongruity of it all bubbled to the surface, and I couldn't resist a laugh. "I haven't your steely nerves. It was enough of an adventure to last me into next year, at least."

Kendall's glance flicked to the clock. "Ten-thirty. If he comes tonight, when should we expect him?"

"I imagine a grocer's household keeps early hours. Everyone has likely retired by now. Assuming Dutch waits a couple of hours more—then he'll have to locate the clock…" I shrugged. "It could be a while. If he leaves the house, Frank will trail him, so we'll have assistance if things turn violent."

"Let us hope not. Are you waiting with me?"

"If you don't mind. I can hide in the bedroom when he comes. I'd like to listen in." Though I doubt Frank or Pinkerton had that in mind when they sent me here to drop off the key.

Kendall grinned. "Don't mind at all, but I insist on you having some tea in the meantime." He reached for a spare cup. "Shall I pour?"

No amount of tea could keep us from dozing in our chairs by the fire, but the sound of stealthy footsteps in the corridor awakened us around two o'clock.

I quickly got up and hurried over to the connecting door to Kendall's bedroom.

"Hsst," came Kendall's low voice. He thrust my empty teacup at me.

Heavens, I'd missed that. I retreated with the cup just as a low knock sounded upon the door.

After I was safely out of sight, Kendall said, "Who is it?"

I strained to hear the answer through the closed bedroom door. All I could pick up was the barest murmur.

Kendall let him in. I put my eye to the keyhole. A wingback chair in the sitting room partially blocked my view as the visitor crossed the room, but I saw enough of the grizzle-bearded man to know he was Dutch Dirksen.

"You have what I want," the man growled. "Give it to me, now." He lunged at Kendall.

I stifled a gasp when I caught a glint of metal in his hand. Kendall parried the thrust with—were those sugar tongs?—grabbed Dutch's wrist, and twisted. The knife clattered onto the tea tray. It happened so quickly, I wasn't quite sure how he'd done it.

"Now look what you made me do," Kendall *tsk*ed. "The creamer is knocked over. What a mess." He shoved the man into a chair, wiped milk off the knife, and put it in his pocket.

Dutch clutched his wrist. "You could have broken it!" he whined.

"I could have if I'd wanted to." Kendall's voice was steely. "And it would have been no worse than you deserve."

I blinked. Kendall was full of surprises.

"However, I want us to be friends," he went on smoothly. "I have something you want, and you have something I want, correct?"

Dutch continued to look down at his hand.

"For heaven's sake, man, don't tell me you haven't suffered worse than that." Kendall went over to the credenza and poured a tumbler of amber liquid that he thrust at Dutch. "Here—this will fix you up."

The man downed it in one gulp. "*Whoo-oo.*" He cleared his throat. "That's good stuff."

"More?" Kendall held up the bottle. Taking Dutch's grunt as assent, he refilled his glass, sat down across from him, and waited.

Finally, Dutch set down his glass and looked over at Kendall. "Yer not such a bad fella. I didn't have yer measure a'fore now. I guess I shouldn't've come at you with the blade," he added grudgingly. "Bad habit o' mine."

"Well, then, we understand each other." Kendall went over

to the desk, pulling out pouch and envelope. "Is this what you want?"

Dutch leaned forward eagerly. "Were you the one to leave the note?"

"Does it matter? Where I can find Olivia Moser?"

He let out a bark of laughter. "That's what she's calling herself these days, eh?"

"What other names does she go by?"

Dutch reached out with his good hand. "Lemme look inside the pouch first. I want to be sure my key's there and you're not trying to trick me."

"See for yourself." Kendall tossed it to him casually.

Dutch took out the key and turned it toward the light. I held my breath.

He gave a grunt and tucked it in his pocket. "All right, you kept your word, I'll keep mine. But first, tell me—what's Olivia to you?"

"We had a job together. She double-crossed me. That's all."

Dutch squinted at Kendall for a long interval. "What's your name?"

Kendall shifted impatiently. "Why all the questions? You have what you want."

"You're forgetting the envelope. I want that, too."

Kendall held it up. "First, locations and aliases for Olivia. And don't lie to me. I know where you're heading next." A smile touched his lips.

"All right, all right! What do I care what happens to her? She's gone by lots o' names over the years, but at the time I was sent up, she was known as Brinkerhoff."

Ah, now it was starting to come together.

Kendall came to get me when the coast was clear. "You heard everything?"

I nodded. "And saw a good bit. That little maneuver to

disarm Dutch was quite impressive. I didn't realize you were so formidable with a pair of sugar tongs."

He shrugged. "It was nothing."

Was that a flush of modesty I saw? Surely not.

"There aren't any trains at this hour," I said, "but I'm sure he'll leave for Edgewater at his first opportunity. Frank will follow him long enough to establish when he gets aboard. The authorities will be waiting at the bank when it opens on Monday and take it from there."

Kendall frowned. "You're sure Frank followed him here? I didn't see or hear anyone else in the corridor."

I smiled. "Frank's very good at what he does."

Kendall turned to the writing desk. "Let me write down the addresses while they're fresh in my mind."

"Good idea." I paced the room. "It's quite telling that Brinkerhoff is one of her names."

Kendall shook his head, keeping his gaze upon his writing. "How is Brinkerhoff significant?"

"Samuel Brinkerhoff was the express driver for the bond shipment. He was never found, dead or alive."

"So Olivia is Brinkerhoff's widow?"

"It seems likely."

Kendall passed me the paper. "Maybe he isn't dead but in hiding. She could be acting on his behalf to find the bonds Dutch cheated them out of."

"Possibly. However, the man she's been associating with lately isn't Brinkerhoff—Frank confirmed that his name's Clement Moser. No known record, but he was the fellow helping the hoisters I caught, and he paid the rent on the house they lived in for a time."

I looked down at the page. Dutch had provided three addresses. "I'll bring these to Mr. Pinkerton as soon as he gets in tomorrow—today," I amended. I looked into Kendall's dark eyes and felt a surge of gratitude. I would never have been able to get Dutch to cooperate alone.

I extended a hand, forgetting I hadn't put my gloves back on. "Thank you," I said earnestly.

Kendall clasped it—he wasn't gloved, either—and I felt discomposed by the warmth and strength of his grip. He pulled me close, and I went willingly.

"Pen," he breathed into my hair. Still clasping my hand, he circled his other arm around my waist.

Every mama will tell you—this is why a woman doesn't go into a man's room unaccompanied. And yet I'd done it. My thoughts swirled as his hand traveled up to caress my back. I closed my eyes and breathed in his scent. Had I hoped for this?

My thoughts turned to Frank, following Dutch Dan alone on a frigid night. I gently pushed away and gave Kendall a rueful smile. "I think it's time for-for me to head home."

CHAPTER 14

*E*ven though it was a Saturday, I knew Pinkerton would be in the office bright and early. He was standing at Mary's desk when I arrived. "Ah, Mrs. Wynch. Success, I trust? I have yet to hear from Frank."

"He may be trailing Dutch to the station even now," I said.

Pinkerton nodded. "Dutch will have to cool his heels until the bank opens Monday morning, but the authorities will be waiting for him. Did Kendall say if Dutch seemed suspicious of the key I substituted?"

"All went smoothly." I refrained from volunteering the fact that I'd witnessed it for myself. I handed him the addresses Kendall had collected. "You'll have to proceed quickly. If Olivia has been keeping as much of an eye on Dutch's movements as we have, she'll soon know he's on the move."

"Right." Pinkerton passed the paper to his secretary. "Contact Stan and have him gather several men to search these locations. We're looking for Olivia Moser, Mathilda Sohren, and her child, Henry."

"There could be a fellow named Clement Moser with them," I added. "And Olivia used to go by the name of Brinkerhoff."

155

Mary nodded and reached for the handset.

"Indeed?" Pinkerton led me into his office and closed the door. "How did that come to light?"

"Dutch told Kendall that he and Olivia had known each other for years, and she was going by that name when he was sent to prison. Likely Brinkerhoff's wife, don't you think?"

"Safe to say. I appreciate you spending so much time helping Frank." He paused, a gleam in his eye. "Maybe I should assign you two together again."

I suppressed a snort. "I'm fine with the arrangement we have."

"It's a shame it's taken you away from your own case. How is that progressing? We'd had no time to discuss it yesterday."

"I've traced the necklace as far as Louisa Lockwood's daughter, Susannah. By her account, she found the sack of jewelry—you have what remains of the stash after she sold off the other pieces, including the Margharita necklace—buried in the bed of their topiary garden late in January."

"Shortly after Mrs. Crofton's death," Pinkerton mused. "In the Lockwoods' garden… How trustworthy is the young lady?"

I grimaced. "That is open to interpretation. She's a headstrong fifteen-year-old girl, with all of the stormy emotions inherent to her tribe. Acts on impulse, engages in sneaky behavior…oh." I stopped and looked at him in surprise. "You mean—could she be lying about *finding* the jewels? That she got them by some other means?"

He shrugged. "She lives just next door. And how did she sell them? No proprietor is going to buy from a young girl."

I explained the role Willie Cartwright had to play in this little drama.

"Sounds like an unsavory fellow."

"Her parents don't want her associating with him, but he will come into wealth someday. His father is the real estate mogul, Richard Cartwright." It's amazing how poor behavior is excused in the privileged few.

"It's unlikely the girl had anything to do with Mrs. Crofton's death, but what about Willie? He sounds like just the sort to try robbing the lady, thinking it an easy job, and then things went wrong."

"The Cartwrights moved into the neighborhood several months after the incident, but I wondered about it myself. The house was habitable though not yet lived in then. Richard Cartwright could have stayed there on the night in question. But Willie? Doubtful. And he didn't care to socialize with his parents' generation of acquaintances."

"I see."

"Anything yet on the finances of the Benevolent Society?" I asked.

He shook his head. "Nothing suspicious so far. I still have a couple of inquiries out."

"I discovered a strongbox of canceled checks from the Benevolent Society in Cartwright's desk. Many of them were written out to the Osage Ladies' Employment Bureau, care of an S. Parker."

"I'll add that name to the inquiry and see what we come up with. But back to the sack of jewels. Several possibilities present themselves." He tugged on a finger. "One, an actual thief broke in and stole them, then panicked and threw them over the Lockwoods' fence into the shrub bed. The Lockwoods and Croftons own adjacent properties, correct?"

"That's right, but Susannah said the sack was 'half-buried' in the dirt and leaf debris."

He shrugged. "It's not uncommon for young ladies to add spurious details for the sake of drama."

I let that one go uncontested.

He held up another finger. "A second possibility—Lockwood killed Mrs. Crofton for unknown personal reasons, took her jewels to make it look like a burglary, then buried them in the garden until such a time as he could dispose of them safely. After all, one doesn't expect a garden in winter to be scrutinized closely. But Susannah inadvertently thwarted his plan when she found the bag and took it."

"True." I thought back to the police report of Eileen's death. "Lockwood told the police he was working in his study all evening. No one could corroborate that, as the ladies were out late at a concert and retired immediately upon coming home. The latest hour anyone saw Edgar was"—I closed my eyes briefly to remember the detail—"when the footman brought him brandy at eleven o'clock."

"Plenty of time," Pinkerton said. "I seem to recall the coroner's report concluded that Mrs. Crofton had died within three hours of her maid discovering her at six o'clock that morning."

"What about Eileen's husband, John Crofton?" I asked. "He had motive, if he'd grown tired of her extramarital affairs. I know the police report said he was at his mother's in Cincinnati that night. Are we certain of that?"

He gave a nod. "That occurred to me as well. I talked to the man in charge of the case last year. Four servants, in addition to the mother, corroborated Crofton's presence."

"Oh. That does seem definitive, then."

Pinkerton narrowed his eyes. "You seem rather desperate to avoid considering Lockwood a viable suspect. Why?"

I shrugged. "It's more a matter of eliminating the other possibilities before exploring Lockwood's role in depth. I've turned up additional information that entangles him further with the murdered woman, in fact." I explained the letters we'd found from Eileen to Judge Rowe, her mention of Rowe doing a favor on behalf of a man she referred to only by initial—E— and wanting the rumors of her relationship with E suppressed so as not to hurt her husband.

Pinkerton leaned forward in interest. "A relationship...you mean an affair?"

"I believe so. What else would hurt her husband?"

"And what was the nature of this favor?"

"Rowe was to help E secure a board position with the

Widows' Benevolent Society. It was to lead to an eventual appointment as chairman. Edgar is about to become chairman of the charity board. I learned of it while visiting the Lockwoods."

"It cannot be a coincidence," he agreed. "How did you come upon the letters? One wouldn't expect them to be carelessly lying around."

I bit my lip. May as well get it over with. "It was in a safe in the judge's study."

He rubbed his temples as if he felt a headache coming on. "Breaking into *one* safe wasn't enough for you and Kendall...you had to break into a second one?"

I made a face. "That was the first one, actually. We thought the necklace might be there and found the letters by accident. But we weren't caught," I added quickly. "And Kendall put them back later."

He shook his head in disbelief. "You were lucky. Searching a man's desk is one thing, but to break into a safe...it could have gone quite badly. I wouldn't have been able to protect you. You must be more prudent in the future."

"Yes, sir," I said meekly.

He was quiet for a while. "What's your next step?" he asked finally.

I lifted a shoulder. "The entire situation is...awkward. It would seem I should be investigating my client's husband for the murder of her best friend. But even if what I discover clears him of guilt, the process will expose some ugly truths she would never have wanted to know."

"What does she know at the moment?"

"Only that I've confirmed the necklace Allison owns was indeed her missing one and that we'd traced it to a particular pawnshop. I told her we were still trying to discover who originally sold it to the pawnbroker. Which was the truth at the time she and I last spoke," I added. "I hadn't yet talked to Susannah."

"But you already knew about the letters. You withheld the connection to Edgar," he said.

I looked down at my gloved hands. "Yes."

He gave a mighty sigh and stood. "This line of work is not for the tender-hearted, Mrs. Wynch. You have a decision to make."

The last thing I wanted right now was to be alone with my thoughts, so when I returned home at midday, Sadie and I set to work on the long-overdue task of cleaning the pantry. We emptied it completely, disposing of cracked dishware, old, ripped flour sacks, and rusted tins. We fixed cabinet hinges, scoured shelves, and then put everything back. It helped keep my mind off my troubled case, though I still felt the weight of it.

Cassie came into the kitchen to admire our results, then shooed us out. "You two go and relax. Put your feet up."

"Is it all right if I go out?" Sadie asked. "I've some Christmas presents yet to buy. But I might not be back in time to prepare dinner."

Poor girl, she didn't have much free time to squeeze in her own errands. Thankfully, the stores had later hours, now that we were only a week away from Christmas Eve.

"Don't worry," Cassie said. "Miss Walterson has offered to help me cook tonight."

Sadie and I exchanged an amused glance.

Cassie folded her arms. "I know, I know—I'll make sure she doesn't start another fire. Go on, now."

Sadie went out almost immediately. I settled in the parlor to continue embroidering Frank's handkerchiefs. Where was he now? If Dutch had left town this morning, I would have expected word from him by this point. Unless...had Frank joined the hunt for Olivia Brinkerhoff? I prayed the search would lead to finding Tilly quickly.

I must have dozed in the quiet of the room. Mercy, I'd been

doing that frequently these days. I was disoriented when I first awoke—*was* I awake?—for, standing before me, was Tilly Sohren clutching her child.

I rubbed my eyes, and then I knew it wasn't a dream, for there was Frank standing behind them, grinning from ear to ear.

"I knew you'd want to see with your own eyes, Pen."

"Frank!" I jumped up—trailing embroidery thread, handkerchiefs, and heaven knew what else—and embraced him. His arms tightened around me briefly before he winced. "Something just jabbed me."

"Oh!" I laughed ruefully as I plucked the sewing needle out of his waistcoat. "Sorry."

I turned to Tilly and guided her to a chair. "Here—please—sit down."

Her appearance bespoke a hasty departure. She still wore a kitchen apron over her dress with only a light shawl thrown over herself and the child. No gloves. Deep fatigue was evident in the shoulders hunched protectively around Henry as she rested her cheek against his.

"You're unhurt, I hope?" I said. "Can I get you some water?"

She drew a shuddering breath and tried to speak, then gave up and nodded, her wide eyes holding mine for a long moment.

"Be right back." I hurried to the kitchen, where Miss Walterson was hard at work scraping carrots and Cassie was stirring something on the stove.

"Who was at the door?" Cassie asked.

I grabbed a glass. "Good news, for a change. Can you set two more places for dinner?"

Two extra places turned out to be one, because Frank was needed back at the office. Tilly had already told him the gist of Olivia's and Moser's scheme on their way to us, and the situation was unraveling quickly.

As anxious as I was to hear the story, I kept my questions to myself during dinner. Our other lodgers except Miss Walterson were out Christmas shopping, and Miss Walterson, bless her, was so preoccupied with cooing over Henry and feeding him pieces of cooked carrot that she didn't ask for a detailed explanation of their arrival.

Sadie returned from shopping as Tilly was upstairs settling a sleepy Henry in the spare bedroom we'd set up for them. I gave the maid an abbreviated explanation of the situation, and she promised to stay within earshot of the child in case he awoke. Tilly and I needed to talk.

Cassie joined us in the parlor as Tilly and I were settling in. "Is the child asleep?" she asked Tilly.

"He is." Tilly's deep-set brown eyes grew misty. "Thank you for allowing us to stay. I hope Henry and I won't be an inconvenience."

Cassie waved a hand. "Not at all. We have plenty of room and not many lodgers at the moment." She glanced at me. "Pen has been quite worried about you."

Tilly flashed me a smile. "I'm also grateful to you and Mr. Wynch, miss. I only wish I'd been able to tell you the day you caught us in the department store. But I was so afraid of Olivia and what she'd do to Henry, even there." She shivered.

"You're safe now," I said. "Frank said she and Moser have been taken into custody?"

"Yes."

"Rather despicable behavior, to threaten you and the child," Cassie chimed in. "And your own sister."

"We used to be quite close. Olivia and I had to make our own way in the world from an early age, mostly by—well, um, thievery. We became quite good at it. I even learned to make cheap costume jewelry to swap out for good pieces." She looked down at her hands. "My early years were not worthy ones, I'm sorry to say."

Cassie looked up from her knitting. "Didn't you try to do anything else? Something more…honorable?"

She gave a sharp laugh. "Of course. And eventually, I did

break away from that life. Several years ago, I met a wonderful man—Carl Sohren. He was a machinist. We married. Just when we learned I was expecting, though, he was killed in an equipment accident, and I was left on my own."

"I'm sorry," I said. "Is that when Olivia found you again?"

Tilly nodded. "She'd married in the meantime, too. Her husband—Sam Brinkerhoff—seemed to be a good man. He welcomed me, and the baby when it came. But Olivia ruled the roost in that household. She has quite the dominant personality," she added. "You probably didn't spend enough time around her to really see it."

"I saw enough," I said dryly, remembering the woman's bravado in the face of certain failure. "So you lived with the Brinkerhoffs for how long?"

She pursed her lips. "I moved in shortly after Carl died, and the baby was born about five months later. Henry turns three next month," she added proudly.

"He looks to be a fine, sturdy boy," Cassie chimed in with a smile.

"So you were living there when the shipment was robbed and Olivia's husband disappeared," I said. "Do you know what happened to him?"

Tilly scowled. "Olivia had him killed. It was either Dutch or Clem who did it. I overheard Olivia and Clem discussing it in a vague, general way, nothing specific in terms of when or where. And now, of course, I know about Dutch's involvement. I'd never met him before Olivia put me up to working for him a few weeks ago." She sighed.

"Why didn't you try to warn Brinkerhoff?" I asked.

"He was out of town on business when I found out, then he went straight out early the next morning. I was sleeping." She made a face. "Babies are exhausting. I thought I'd have another chance to talk to him."

"Were Olivia or Moser aware of what you'd heard?" I asked.

She shook her head.

"Why did Olivia want him dead in the first place?" Cassie asked.

"They'd been arguing for months. Sam refused to do anything crooked, no matter how she pressed him. He took pride in the fact that he was entrusted with the safe transport of valuables. It was the one thing he wouldn't compromise, even as he gave in to her other demands."

"When did Moser come into the picture?" I asked.

"About a month before Sam died. I saw him hanging around whenever Sam was out. I knew Olivia was cheating." She grimaced. "I didn't want to get involved in a married couple's private business, though. I'd hoped she and Sam would work it out."

"What happened after the robbery?" I asked.

"I took the baby and left. Got a position at a local bakery and rented a room over the shop. We were managing. Then Olivia showed up unannounced, just this past November. I hadn't seen her in almost two years. She was so nice to me, and I let my guard down. She offered to make some tea. She must have put something in it. I passed out, and she kidnapped Henry." Her voice broke. "I woke up to a note that threatened harm to him if I went to the police and didn't do exactly as she said." She sank back against the cushions. "I'm so tired."

"I'm sorry to keep you," I said. "I have just a few more questions. So Olivia came back into your life last month and used Henry to coerce you to search through Dutch's belongings, correct? In the guise of his cleaning woman?"

She nodded. "Dutch didn't know I was Olivia's sister, and I was already known and trusted at the grocer's—I'd deliver goods from the bakery to their shop regularly. I went by my middle name, Abby. I had only to ask for the job, and Robert Temple hired me on Dutch's behalf." She met my eye. "I never found anything in Dutch's flat, though. And then you followed me home that one night." A smile touched her lips. "It was a shock to recognize you, even in male attire. But then as I thought about it, I knew you were a detective—I guess you have to go to extreme lengths sometimes to find out things."

I suppressed a grimace. True enough. "Was it Olivia who waited outside our house the next night, followed Frank, and tried to kill him?"

Tilly's eyes filled with tears. "I'm so sorry, Miss Hamilton. When I told her I'd recognized you, I was hoping it would scare her into giving up and fleeing—especially since I hadn't found out where Dutch had hidden the bonds and the rest of the cash. I had no idea she'd—well…" She couldn't finish the sentence.

"Make an attempt on Frank's life? I believe you. She must have had Moser waiting nearby with a conveyance." Idly, I wondered how Olivia had come to be such a good shot, but Tilly was drooping with fatigue and I didn't want to keep her longer than necessary. "So that's when you all packed up and went into hiding?"

Tilly sniffed into the handkerchief Cassie passed over. "It was obvious by then that Dutch hadn't hidden anything in his flat, and Olivia didn't want to risk you bringing the authorities down on us. But when she told me how you thwarted her attempt on Mr. Wynch, I realized how resourceful you are. I held out hope that you'd be able to find me."

"That's when you hid the items in Henry's crib," I said. "Very clever."

Tilly smiled as she dabbed at the last of her tears. "It almost worked when I went to pick up the laundry, but Olivia was waiting with Henry in a second conveyance that I was to take. Perhaps she suspected I would try something—"

There was a knock on the parlor door, and Sadie came in, holding the baby. "He woke up, and I can't seem to get 'im back to sleep." She passed him into Tilly's arms. "Guess I'm no good with babies." She shrugged.

I smiled. As long as she was good with intruders, we'd be fine.

CHAPTER 15

lthough I should have slept well that night, secure in the knowledge that Tilly and her child were safe, my rest was broken by disturbing dreams where I walked along garden paths that grew darker and colder. From indeterminate directions I'd hear the rustle of skirts, then catch glimpses of delicate hands in the shadows—one clutching a pistol, another gripping a knife, another holding a rope—ready to catch me unawares.

I awoke, jaw clenched, neck stiff, gripping the quilt. Tilly's account of Olivia's scheme had rattled me more than I'd realized.

By the time I got dressed that morning, I knew what I had to do about Aunt Lou's case. I couldn't withhold important information from her any longer. Tilly had brought home that lesson —if she'd only told us the truth when she was caught at the department store, we would have been spared much anguish.

I wasn't looking forward to telling Aunt Lou the painful truth about those she held dear—Susannah's sordid dealings in selling off Eileen's stolen jewelry, Edgar's affair with her best friend, and the possibility that he was the woman's killer.

But as my client, she deserved to have all the facts at her

disposal and decide how she wanted me to proceed. Susannah would have to be part of the conversation as well.

I stopped at the office on my way to the Lockwoods'. Pinkerton wasn't in, but that wasn't my purpose.

Mary raised an eyebrow at my request to borrow the sack of jewelry from the safe.

"It will aid in my interview of a witness," I explained. "I'll return it when I'm done."

Reluctantly she agreed, though she made me sign for it first.

It was a most unfashionable hour—not quite ten o'clock—to call at the Lockwood mansion, but the parlor maid was familiar enough with my visits that she let me in without a murmur. She did look askance, however, when I asked to see both Mrs. Lockwood and Susannah.

"Miss Susannah is still at breakfast. But I'll let the missus know you're here. Will you wait in the library?"

This time, the library was free of impetuous young ladies and their ersatz gentlemen friends—I checked, despite the maid's assertion—and I had the quiet space to myself. Heaven knows I needed it. Every time I thought I'd decided on one approach in breaking the news to Aunt Lou, another presented itself, and I was in an agony of indecision. The velvet sack of Eileen's jewels weighed down my reticule like a bar of lead.

"Penelope?" Aunt Lou stood in the doorway, still attired in her morning gown, the white, shaggy fluff of a dog at her heels. "How fortuitous! I was going to send for you later. I have some news to share."

The dog gave a low growl at the back of his throat as he took a few steps toward me.

"Plato!" she said sharply. "Go lay down." She pointed to a cushion on the floor by the hearth.

With one last glare in my direction, the dog trotted over to the cushion and settled himself.

She made a face. "Sorry about that."

I gave a wan smile. "At least he didn't bark this time." Maybe the beast was warming up to me. "So, what's your news?"

She crossed the room, looking intently at my face. "It can keep. Something's wrong. Tell me."

"Part of it concerns Susannah. I'd rather wait until she's here."

She swayed and gripped a chair back. "Susannah?"

I helped ease her into the chair. "Shall I ring for the maid? Do you require anything?"

She held my eye. "Answers, Penelope. I require answers."

"That's why I'm here—to provide what few I have. Is Susannah coming?"

"I'm already here." The girl walked in and closed the door behind her.

"Good," I said. "Please, have a seat."

She sat beside her mother and gripped her trembling hand. A surprisingly compassionate gesture from the usually sulky girl. She looked up at me. "You're going to tell her, aren't you?"

"I must." I took a seat across from them. "Aunt Lou, Susannah found this in your back garden last January, shortly after Eileen's death." I pulled the sack from my purse and set it on the table at her elbow. "Not everything is here that was originally. Your daughter sold off some things, including your ruby necklace."

Susannah flashed her mother a startled look. "That was *yours?*"

Her mother stared at the pouch in my hand.

"How did it get there?" the girl asked.

When it didn't look as if Aunt Lou was up to speaking—and no wonder, as she was trying to come to terms with the notion that her daughter had trafficked in stolen goods—I answered for her. "She lent the necklace to her friend, Eileen Crofton. When Mrs. Crofton died, it went missing, along with a good bit of

Eileen's own jewelry. The police determined it to be a burglar. That, however, is open to question. But let us proceed more methodically." I handed Aunt Lou the sack. "Do you recognize these pieces as once belonging to Eileen?"

As she pulled out her pince-nez, set the bag in her lap, and removed each item to lay it out upon the table, Susannah said, "I didn't know the necklace was yours, Mama. I've never seen you wear it."

Aunt Lou was absorbed in her task. She touched an opal scarf pin. "I gave Eileen this for her birthday one year." She half-heartedly waved her hand toward the array of items—the colored-stone brooches, the gold chain bracelet, the strand of pearls. "I don't recognize them all, of course, but enough to safely say they're hers."

"Mama?" Susannah prompted anxiously. "About the necklace—I didn't know. Honestly."

Aunt Lou patted her daughter's hand. "You were very young the last time I wore the Margharita necklace. It had been locked away in the safe for years."

"Oh," Susannah said in a small voice. She glanced at me. "Who has the ruby necklace now? Can you get it back?"

I shook my head. "Through a series of misadventures, your friend Allison now owns it."

Susannah put a hand to her mouth to stifle a shriek. "What do we do?"

Aunt Lou put the items back in the pouch. "I'm not interested in recovering it, dear." She fixed her with a stern look. "And it would be a kindness to never tell your friend where it really came from."

"Ladies, I must remind you—this is about something far more serious than a stolen necklace. A woman has been murdered."

Susannah's eyes widened. She looked at her mother. "You told me she died of an illness."

Aunt Lou made a face. "You were only fourteen. I didn't want to frighten you."

"Susannah," I said, picking up the sack, "would you show us exactly where you found this?"

As we put on our coats and followed her out—even Plato got up to keep us company—the parlor maid came rushing after us. "Miss Susannah! The pottery master's here for your lesson, and Miss Allison has just arrived as well."

Aunt Lou waved an impatient hand. "Have them wait in the salon. Susannah will be ready shortly."

The maid hurried away. At my inquiring look, she explained, "Francois is a highly sought-after master of ceramics. The young ladies are glazing their new pieces today." Aunt Lou shivered in the damp chill as we headed for the back gate. "Let's be quick about this."

Susannah led us to the back corner of the topiary garden, the evergreens still vibrant but the beds strewn with brown and withered leaves that had drifted in. The dog left us to sniff the perimeter and take care of business.

The girl pointed. "There."

I crouched for a closer look. "Against the fence?"

"That's right. Partially buried in leaf litter and loose dirt. Up to here." She touched the neck of the sack.

"Do you recall exactly when you found it?"

"January twenty-first." She glanced at her mother. "I remember, because it was the day before I was to go to Allison's house in the country for a skating party, but Edgar forbade it because I'd talked back to him at breakfast." She blew out a breath. "I took a walk outside to try to calm down. That's when I found it."

"Oh, my dear." Aunt Lou drew her close. "I admit there are times when Edgar is much too harsh with you. I'm sorry."

Susannah sniffed and returned the embrace. "I'm sure I deserve most of it." Her voice was muffled against her mother's shoulder.

I noticed movement in the window along the far side of the house. Allison was watching us. When she caught my look, she stepped back.

That made me wonder from where else we were visible. I surveyed the area. The Lockwoods' back windows opened to the garden, but then I spied the round, stained-glass window belonging to the Crofton mansion beyond. An upper landing window would be my guess. Was that how Edgar Lockwood and Eileen Crofton had covertly communicated and arranged their rendezvous?

I shook myself. The next part of my report was not for Susannah's ears.

"Thank you, dear," I said to the girl. "You've been a big help. Go ahead to your lesson. Your mother and I have more to discuss."

Susannah hesitated and leaned close to her mother. "You forgive me?"

Aunt Lou smoothed an errant strand from her daughter's forehead. "Of course. Now, you'd better go on."

With a last grateful look over her shoulder, Susannah hurried away.

I had to give Aunt Lou credit—she waited until we were back in the library, out of sight of Susannah and the servants, before she collapsed onto the settee and cried.

I passed her a clean handkerchief and waited. There wasn't much else I could do.

Finally, the tears passed, and she looked up with a rueful grimace. "I don't often succumb to such weakness. I apologize."

"No need. This has all been terribly trying."

"To have Susannah pawning jewelry, sneaking around, and yet feeling she had no one to turn to except... I suppose it was Willie Cartwright who sold the pieces for her?" At my nod, she added, "We were right to conclude he's a bad influence."

I sighed. She still didn't grasp the full import. "I'm afraid there's more."

"More?" She blinked in confusion. "But we know what happened now, don't we? It really was a thief who killed Eileen and then threw the bag of jewels into our yard because he panicked and wanted to get rid of them." She smiled through the last of her tears. "That was very good detective work, dear. Thank—"

I held up a hand. "Don't thank me yet. The bag wasn't simply tossed over the fence. Based on how and where Susannah found it, someone snuck in and buried it there. And there's something in Eileen's last letter to Judge Rowe that I haven't yet shared with you."

"Oh? What is that?"

"Do you recall I told you Eileen used a secret against the judge so he would grant her a favor?"

Aunt Lou nodded.

"That favor was for a man she referred to simply as 'E.' Judge Rowe was to use his influence to get this man appointed to the board of the Widows' Benevolent Society, with an eye toward the chairmanship eventually."

She blinked. "You mean…she was referring to Edgar?"

"It fits, doesn't it? He was appointed to the board only a year ago, shortly before she died. And he's just been elected chairman?"

"Yes—effective in January," she said. "It's to be celebrated at tonight's Society banquet. I thought it seemed a rapid advancement. This was Eileen's doing?" A frown tugged at her brow. "Why would she go to such lengths? She never said a word to me about it."

"Had Edgar been eager for the position?"

She shrugged. "Not really. He'd only recently joined the Riverside Club before being appointed to the charity board."

Interesting. Perhaps Eileen was the recipient of two favors— one from the judge, and the other from Edgar Lockwood, who agreed to take the position in order to search out what she suspected. I looked across at the frowning Aunt Lou.

I swallowed. Here was the hard part.

"It seems Eileen and your husband had a closer association than was generally known. She asked Rowe to put a stop to the rumors Cartwright had spread regarding their relationship. She was concerned her husband would be hurt to learn of it. But she didn't bother to refute its veracity."

Her lips whitened. "Eileen and Edgar...they both betrayed me?"

Pity twisted in my abdomen. "I'm sorry."

This profession isn't for the tender-hearted, Mrs. Wynch.

Truer words were never spoken.

We were quiet for a while, with only the sound of the grand-father clock beside the bookcase ticking out the minutes.

Her hands flexed in her lap. "Did he kill her, too?"

"I don't know. What do you remember of his activities that night? All I have is the police report to go on."

"He was still in his study when we returned from the concert around midnight. I went in to say goodnight to him. But that's all I know. Afterward, he told me he'd worked late and slept on the couch in the dressing room so as not to disturb me. Everyone else had retired. That makes him looks quite guilty, doesn't it? No one to account for his activities the night she died. And now an affair has come to light, along with her jewels buried in our very garden." She shivered and pulled her shawl closer.

"I grant you it looks distressing on the surface, but when we consider a motive, the theory begins to fall apart. *Why* would he kill her?"

"Some sort of lovers' quarrel?"

I suppressed a snort. "You'll find that sort of thing in penny dreadfuls, certainly, but consider how she died—smothered as she slept. Is it credible to believe that, in the midst of his anger, he waited until she fell asleep and then killed her in such a calculated manner? Your own motive would be much stronger, if you'd known of the affair back then," I added.

Her eyes flashed. "You're accusing me of killing my best friend?"

"Of course not. You wouldn't have hired me to begin with. Why dredge it all up again? Everything had settled down nicely for our murderer. The case was closed."

"Thank you for the vote of confidence," she rasped, then grew quiet again.

I watched her anxiously. Now that she'd learned her best friend had betrayed her, would she still care about solving the murder? No one would fault her for abandoning it.

Finally, she looked up. "As outraged as I feel, I do believe you're right. He didn't kill her. But he may be able to help find her killer."

"How so?"

"I was going to tell you earlier—I found something of Eileen's yesterday. An old appointment book."

I blinked at her for a moment before speaking. "Where? How?"

"John's housekeeper sent over Eileen's hats when they were going through items to donate for the auction. She thought I might like to keep some of them. And there it was, wrapped in tissue in one of her hat boxes."

I recalled John Crofton talking about clearing out his wife's belongings in anticipation of the auction. As to why it was there to begin with…perhaps Eileen feared a nosy servant would come upon it? Difficult to say. "Can I see it?"

She grimaced. "It's written in some sort of shorthand I don't understand. Only the dates and times are recognizable. I'd planned to show it to Edgar. He's quite clever with such things."

"Mr. Pinkerton has more resources at his disposal. Let me take it to him."

She frowned. "Now that I know of the affair, chances are there's something personal about my husband in the book. I can't take the chance."

From the set of her jaw, I knew there was no use pressing

her on the matter. "All right," I conceded, "then at least let me speak with Edgar. I want to get his account of his relationship with Eileen and what he might know—or suspect—about her death."

She stiffened. "Oh, he will give an accounting of himself, certainly." Her gray eyes hardened. "But it will be to *me*, not you."

Hell hath no fury like a woman scorned. I almost felt sorry for Edgar Lockwood. "What do you want me to do in the meantime?"

"Nothing." She stood. "You've taken this as far as you can. And much farther than I would have cared for, had I known."

I stood as well. "I *am* sorry," I repeated.

Her expression softened briefly. "You did your job well. I'll send a final check to Mr. Pinkerton."

So that was that. Throat burning and eyes blurred, I retrieved my coat and let myself out.

I paced the confines of my bedroom after dinner. Tilly and young Henry were charming the ladies in the parlor. Who could resist cooing over the furniture-clutching, giggling youngster? As happy as I was for mother and son—they'd certainly been through enough these past few weeks to deserve some light-hearted moments—I knew my presence would dampen the mood.

There was a tap on the door. "Pen?" Cassie called.

"Come in."

She was carrying a tray with two steaming cups. After setting it down, she perched upon the bed and watched me pace. "What's troubling you? I thought you'd be thrilled by the happy ending we're witnessing downstairs. Henry is delightful, by the way."

"I'm sure he is. But that happy ending belongs to Frank, not me. My own case is in shambles."

"Oh? What's happened?"

Tired of pacing at last, I sank into a rocking chair and rocked instead. "I can't tell you much—it's confidential."

"I don't care about the salacious details. Can't you couch it in generalities?" She passed me a cup. "Tilly made cocoa. Careful, it's hot."

I blew on it before taking a sip. *Umm*, very good. "Well, to start, I've been fired."

"You've been fired from cases before," she pointed out. "Including your recent department store assignment. That worked out in your favor—you ended up with a bigger fee than you'd expected."

I made a face. "I'd rather have been allowed to do my job."

"I don't suppose you can tell me who fired you this time, but can you tell me why? Was your client dissatisfied because you weren't making progress?"

"On the contrary. I *had* made progress. But my findings implicated a close member of the family. No one, including me, expected that."

"Oh. That must have been difficult."

I set my cup aside. "I nearly didn't tell her. But Mr. Pinkerton prevailed upon my better angel—or devil, depending on your perspective—to fulfill my duty."

"Duty—you mean to inform the client?"

"More than that—the duty to relate the unvarnished truth." Pinkerton was right, of course, but that didn't make it any less unpleasant. Aunt Lou was a kindly soul and didn't deserve such heartache. I wondered if she'd confronted Edgar yet.

"So she was angry, blamed you, and let you go?" Cassie asked incredulously.

I blew out a breath. "She wasn't angry at *me*. She was upset, naturally. But she couldn't imagine a private inquiry agent dealing in the personal details going forward. She's going to take it from here."

Cassie pursed her lips as she considered it. "Perhaps that's as it should be. In her position, I might prefer that."

"Maybe so, but we're talking about murder. I fear she may put herself in danger."

CHAPTER 16

$\mathcal{I}$ awoke Monday morning feeling uncertain what to do with my day. To abruptly go from juggling multiple cases to working on none, even during the bustle of the holiday season, left a gap I struggled to fill. I compiled an ambitious list of household tasks and settled down in my sitting room with sewing kit, button box, and a pile of clothes in need of mending.

"Miss Hamilton?" Sadie stuck her head through the open door before I'd gotten to my third button. "There's a young lady in the kitchen to see you."

"The kitchen? Not the parlor?"

Sadie shrugged. "The little boy's things are strewn all over. I thought it was better to put her in the kitchen."

"He needs a proper nursery to play in," I mused. I'd have to give that some thought, if they were going to be staying longer.

I was so absorbed in the problem of our limited space that I'd forgotten to ask who our visitor was, and the last person I expected to see perched upon one of our kitchen stools was young Susannah.

She jumped up at the sight of me. "Oh, Miss Hamilton,"

she wailed, "things have gone from bad to worse. I don't know what to do."

"How did you get here?" I asked in alarm. "Your mother and stepfather don't allow you to leave the house unaccompanied."

"I slipped out. Willie brought me. He's waiting in the coach outside."

I suppressed a groan. On top of Aunt Lou's other troubles, now she was going to panic that her daughter had eloped. It could also do irrevocable damage to Susannah's reputation if word got out. "Is it his family's coach or for hire?"

"His father's."

I rolled my eyes and called over my shoulder. "Sadie!"

She came running. "Miss?"

"There's a young man waiting outside. Send him on his way, in no uncertain terms." I was confident my maid was up for the task. "Then I want you to run to the cab stand and have a conveyance sent over right away." It would not do for Susannah to be seen arriving home in Cartwright's coach. Heaven knows who had observed her leaving in it.

Sadie sped off.

I turned back to Susannah. "Now then, young lady," I said sternly, "what is so urgent that you would take leave of your senses? I assume you went through your mother's personal files and found my address?"

She nodded. "I'm sorry—I had to come. Yesterday, Mama and Edgar had the worst argument I'd ever heard. And when we attended the Society banquet last night, people were treating Edgar quite coldly—even though he was the guest of honor— and whispering terrible things behind his back."

"Whispering about what? You must have heard some of it, to know it was bad."

"They were talking about the pouch of Mrs. Crofton's jewels being found in our garden."

My heart sank. Word had gotten out already.

"And some were speculating—the women especially—that it must mean it was Edgar who killed her."

"How did they learn of the bag?"

The girl looked down at her shoes. "Allison, I think. She was at the window when we were out in the garden yesterday."

"True—I saw her myself—but how could she know what was going on from that distance?" I scowled. "Unless you told her."

"She asked me point blank about it afterward," she said defensively. "It did look odd, the three of us out in the garden in the dead of winter. I couldn't think of what to say except the truth."

"Does she know about the necklace, too?"

"*Um*, well…"

I blew out a breath. "You were supposed to keep that private."

She met my eyes, her own filled with contrition. "She's my trusted friend and confidant. I felt so guilty about the necklace —I couldn't keep it to myself."

"What did she say?"

"She was exceedingly distressed that it's actually Mama's necklace, but she promised not to tell her parents." Susannah sighed. "Although she seems to have told a lot of people about the pouch itself."

"Or at least told her mother, who then told everyone else. Who was at the banquet?"

"The Cartwrights, including Willie"—she blushed—"Mr. Crofton, the Rowes, and some other men on the board whose names I don't know. And us, of course."

"I see."

"Oh, I wish I'd never found that bag!" she wailed.

"Let's get our coats." I led her down the hall. "What exactly is it you want me to do? I can't stop the gossip. Besides, Eileen's jewelry found on your premises doesn't necessarily indicate guilt. The conjecture will pass in time."

"Not when he had an affair with Mrs. Crofton," Susannah retorted. At my look, she added, "Yes, I heard, as did the staff. Mama and Edgar were arguing quite loudly." She gritted her teeth. "Allison's right—that Mrs. Crofton was no better than she should be."

"Let the dead rest unmaligned," I said. "The woman cannot defend herself now. Besides, Edgar took an active part. Did you tell Allison about the affair, too?"

"No." Susannah shrugged into her jacket. "But she hears the gossip. She's much less insulated than I am." She blew out a breath. "Her parents let her *go* places and *do* things."

I pulled on my gloves. "She's two years older and doesn't have a habit of sneaking around with a man."

"Oh, doesn't she?" the girl muttered.

"What?"

"Nothing."

Sadie came through the door, huffing from exertion. "Cab's here. You'll need an umbrella. It's starting to rain."

Once we were settled in and on our way, a terrible thought occurred to me. "You didn't tell Allison I was a detective working for your mother, did you?"

"Of course not," she said quickly. "I mean—I didn't tell her about *you*. I did mention that we had a detective looking into the discovery of Mrs. Crofton's jewelry in our garden."

I rubbed my temples. Lord save us from gossipy young ladies. "Why say anything at all?"

"I wanted her to know we're trying to get to the bottom of this—that we have nothing to hide."

I shook my head. Once people have hold of an idea, they tend to cling to it. Susannah was too young to have learned that yet. "Last night, at the banquet—was Edgar aware of what people were saying behind his back?'

"I fear so," she said. "He seemed ill at ease when he noticed the others were avoiding him. Mr. Crofton, in particular. I saw Edgar try to approach him on several occasions, but he'd walk away."

Edgar had no doubt wanted to reassure Crofton he was innocent of killing his wife. And what of the affair? Both were very awkward conversations. "So your stepfather never spoke privately with anyone last night?"

"Actually, he talked to Mr. Cartwright, just as the carriages were pulling up to take us home. It didn't seem to go well, though."

"How so?"

"I only heard a few words—Edgar said something about 'authority.' I'm fairly sure I heard 'audit,' too. Mr. Cartwright clenched his fists at that."

I could imagine. Once Lockwood officially became chairman in January, there wouldn't be much Cartwright could do to stop an audit. The time to destroy evidence was now. But why tip him off with the threat?

I glanced through the window. We were turning onto Prairie Avenue.

Susannah shifted in her seat to look me full in the face. "Miss Hamilton, I think the speculations are wrong. My stepfather didn't kill Mrs. Crofton. I want you to find out who really did it, and clear him."

"Your mother has dismissed me from the case."

"I know. I'd like to hire you back. I-I have a little money," she added lamely.

I blinked. To be hired by a girl who hadn't even had her come-out yet… "What makes you so sure he's innocent?"

"He's a smart man. Why would he hide a murdered woman's jewelry in his own garden? That's foolish. Someone wanted them found."

When the girl wasn't ruled by emotions, she had a good head on her shoulders.

"If I hadn't found the bag," she went on, "the gardener would have, eventually."

I had to agree with her. "Whoever buried it there must have been confused when it took so long to surface." But now that it had, the killer would take full advantage. The seeds of suspicion had been sown at last night's banquet.

"So? Will you resume the case?" she persisted.

I frowned at the eager young face tipped up at me. "Why do you want me to? Even if he's innocent, he cheated on your mother. And it's clear you don't like him much."

She tilted her chin in defiance. "Someone is manipulating us for their own purposes. I don't like it. No matter how I might feel about my stepfather or whatever else he's done, he's family and it grieves my mother to suspect him."

Having a stubborn streak will serve you well, Aunt Lou had told me. The same could be said for her daughter.

"The perfect place to resume your investigation," she went on, "is the musicale tomorrow night."

I blinked in surprise. "Your mother is proceeding with the event?"

"To cancel this late would give credence to the very gossip she wants to dismiss. It's to be the largest fundraising event of the season. And everyone from our immediate circle will be there—the Rowes, the Cartwrights, Mr. Crofton... Oh, and there's someone I haven't met yet, but I believe you know him—a Mr. Kendall."

"Yes, I know him," I said absently. When did Phillip Kendall become part of the Lockwoods' social circle? He did have a way of worming himself in wherever he went.

"Willie has decided to attend, too." The girl's cheeks pinkened.

I smiled to myself. I wasn't sure I'd recognize the fellow without a window between us.

"So are you coming? I know Mama invited you. And all the suspects will be there."

The carriage pulled up to the mansion driveway.

I gave her a startled look. "What do you know of *suspects*?"

She chuckled. "I'm only adopting Edgar's phrase."

Edgar's phrase? When had he talked of suspects?

Before I could ask the question aloud, the driver opened the door and Susannah hopped out, heedless of the rain. "Remember, nine o'clock," she called. She gave a little wave and ran to her front door.

"It's fortunate there have only been two evening-formal events to attend in connection with this case," I said to Cassie as I surveyed my reflection in the mirror. "I would have run out of gowns."

The aquamarine satin I had on tonight was my favorite of the two. The tulle underskirt was a pale ibis rose, with accents of the same color in the form of lace drapery that started at the top of one shoulder and tucked into the waist. Its smaller train made movement easier, too.

"You look lovely," Cassie said, adjusting the pearl-crusted comb in my hair. "So does this mean you've been re-hired?"

"In a manner of speaking. Susannah is clever enough to realize Edgar might have been framed. She wants me to continue." I was eager to get on with the case, not only for the sake of finishing what I started—though that alone was a powerful inducement—but because of what Susannah had recounted about the banquet. Whispered suspicions of Edgar were bad enough, but putting Cartwright on notice about an impending audit seemed foolish. And what of Edgar's talk of suspects? Where and to whom did he say that? It was as if he was deliberately trying to stir up a hornet's nest. Whatever plan he had in mind, I didn't want Louisa and Susannah caught up in it.

"And will the murderer be at the party?"

"Very likely," I answered, grimacing.

"Oh, Pen—do be careful."

I smiled at her furrowed expression in the glass. "Don't worry. It's a social function. Listening and observing will be my primary tasks tonight."

Unfortunately, the events of the evening were to prove me dead wrong.

CHAPTER 17

$\mathcal{T}$he traffic around Prairie Avenue tonight was as heavy as one might expect when the largest fundraising event of the season was being held, but at last we reached the Lockwoods' drive. I was probably one of the few to arrive in a hired conveyance. Even so, the liveried footman handed me out as gravely as if I were a duchess.

Bright brass lanterns lined the path. Adding to the festive look were wide red bows affixed to the wrought iron railings.

An attendant took my wrap, and I'd just turned toward the music salon in search of Louisa when I felt a light touch on my elbow.

I knew even before I looked up—I wouldn't soon forget the scent of his cologne—that it was Phillip Kendall. The memory of our last encounter brought a quick heat to my cheeks.

"Pen," he murmured, "what a delight to see you. And how lovely you look."

The compliment wasn't doing anything for my flushed complexion, I was sure.

"And you as well, Mr. Kendall." I kept my tone light and conversational.

"I was disappointed when I didn't hear from you about what happened to Dutch and his, *er*, associates."

"I apologize. I assumed Mr. Pinkerton had kept you informed."

"Oh, he has." Kendall liberated two glasses of champagne from a catering tray as it passed—quite a number of trays were circulating at the moment—and handed one to me. "I was gratified to learn that Tilly and her child were rescued from such a desperate situation. But, of course, I would have preferred to hear the good news from you."

I shrugged and brought the glass to my lips.

"And what of this case?" he asked. "Any progress?"

"Some." I grimaced. "I'm not supposed to be investigating further. Louisa dismissed me." I set down the glass.

"Ah. Then you must be here because you enjoy the featured soprano, Miss Stephens?"

"I always enjoy a good soprano." I met his eye. "I seem to recall your fondness for sopranos as well. Miss Joubert comes to mind." Or more precisely, the valuable opal around her neck.

Kendall, not to be goaded, merely grinned and spread his hands apart in mock innocence. "Who doesn't appreciate a talented young lady?" Dropping his voice and leaning in, he murmured, "Why are you really here? May I be of assistance?"

"Susannah asked me to come." At his blank look, I added, "You haven't met her yet. She's Louisa's daughter and Lockwood's stepdaughter."

"Ah, yes, Miss Adair. I met the young lady when I arrived."

"She's only fifteen." I wrinkled my nose at him. "Much too young for you."

"Indeed." His dark-eyed expression was inscrutable.

"Besides, you'd have to compete with a certain young man for her affections."

"It's just as well." His lips twitched. "My own affections are engaged elsewhere."

Heavens, the air was getting quite close in here. Or perhaps

Cassie had laced my bodice too tightly. I tried to draw an even breath. "Susannah's concerned about the rumors surrounding her stepfather. I want to speak to Louisa about it. Have you seen her?"

Kendall put a hand protectively at my back as one of the wait staff brushed behind me rather closely. "She greeted me when I arrived half an hour ago, but I haven't seen her since. It's hard to find anyone in this crush."

"It's about to become more crowded still." I nodded towards the vestibule. I wasn't the only one who was late. "The school choir and their parents have arrived."

He snorted. "A children's choir is to accompany the famed Miss Stephens? That's like hitching an expressman's wagon to a thoroughbred."

I chuckled. "Where's your Christmas spirit? They may surprise you." I stepped toward a passing waiter. "Excuse me— have you seen Mrs. Lockwood?"

"She was in the dining room with Mrs. Cartwright a few minutes ago. Down the hall, around the corner to the left."

The murmur of two voices—neither sounded like Louisa— drifted through the closed doors of the dining room as I drew closer. After checking the corridor to be sure I was unobserved, I put my ear to the crevice.

"How could the foolish girl have misplaced it?" It was Judge Rowe's voice. "She's always losing jewelry. This carelessness has to stop."

"I know, Lucius," Clara Rowe's voice was contrite. "But Allison and I made an extensive search for the necklace. We cannot find it anywhere."

I bit my lip. Were they discussing the Margharita necklace? If so, maybe Morris hadn't put it back as promised. But he'd be a long way from Chicago with his lady friend by now if that was the case. There'd been no talk of Rowe's secretary abruptly leaving.

I moved away quietly before I could be noticed. Where was Aunt Lou? Perhaps the library?

I was heading down the hall in that direction when I heard sniffling sounds. I'd know that sniff anywhere. Susannah. I followed the sound to an alcove behind the marble balustrade. She had her face to the wall, shoulders quivering.

"Susannah? What's wrong?"

She stiffened, then turned a tear-streaked face toward me. "Willie's father has forbidden him to-to see me again. Willie came here only to tell me, and then he left."

"I suppose his father heard about the unaccompanied ride in the family carriage?"

She nodded. "Here I was, worried about *my* family finding out."

I suppressed a sigh. Young love was so exasperating.

Faintly, on the other side of the wall, I heard something. I tipped my head to listen. "Is that...*barking*?"

She gestured to a plain door tucked into the corner, likely opening onto the servants' stairs. "Plato's been shut in the cellar for the evening. He's not good with strangers."

No surprise there. But back to the business at hand... "Susannah, I'm trying to find your mother. One of the staff thought she was in the dining room, but I've had no luck."

"Mama and Edgar went to the study a while ago to confer on something—I don't know what." She gave a wan smile. "I didn't hear any shouting. A good sign?"

"Let us hope so." I realized then that I hadn't seen either of our hosts. "Is your father going to make an appearance tonight?"

"He'll come out when Miss Stephens is ready to sing. He'd already greeted some of the early arrivals—the Rowes, the Cartwrights, and Mr. Crofton. Mama and I were helping him. Mama says I need practice in hostess duties. Oh—I met Mr.

Kendall, too. Mama says he's a good friend of yours." Her eyes took on a mischievous glint. "He's quite handsome, don't you think?"

I waved a dismissive hand. "Yes, yes, we're all aware of that, including the gentleman in question. So—your mother and stepfather went to the study?"

"That's right. They left me to welcome the guests by myself." She blew out a breath. "It was an exhausting task, let me tell you."

"I'm sure you comported yourself admirably."

She snorted. "Better than Edgar. The way he greeted people was…awkward. Even Mama noticed."

"Awkward? How so?"

"He was telling everyone we should dedicate the evening to old friends lost and how it was important to cherish any effects of theirs one might run across. What do you think he meant?" she asked.

Old friends lost. Eileen Crofton, most likely. But cherishing a memento… Had Eileen given Edgar some token during one of their trysts? It seemed in particularly bad taste to be so overt about it.

No, wait—he must have meant Eileen's appointment book. Louisa had said she planned to show it to him. I wanted a look at it even more badly now.

"Miss Hamilton?" she prompted.

"Difficult to say, dear. The more important question is— what did the others think he meant?"

She shrugged. "People seemed a bit confused, but nothing more."

I didn't like it. I'd better find Louisa. I pressed the girl's hand. "See you later."

I decided to try Lockwood's study next, only to discover Judge Rowe, alone, going through the drawers of the mahogany desk. He froze.

"Looking for something?" I asked.

"It is no matter," he said gruffly. "What are *you* doing here, young lady?" His heavy jowls deepened as he gave me an icy stare.

That sort of authoritarian deflection was not going to work with me. "I asked you first," I said mildly.

"*Hmph.* School-yard semantics."

"Perhaps I should fetch the butler, then." I turned toward the door. "You can describe whatever it is you're looking for."

"Cigars," Rowe said tersely. He tapped the bulge of a hard case in his pocket. "I discovered I'm out."

I gave him an appraising look but knew I wasn't going to get anywhere with this one. "I'll leave you to your...search."

I left the door ajar on my way out.

Strains from the piano reached me as I headed toward the library. If the performance was starting, perhaps I'd missed Louisa in the process of circling the main floor and she'd returned to the salon. Mercy, how absurd to not be able to find one's hostess. Edgar was likely on his way there, too.

I decided to stop briefly at the library on my way to the music salon, just in case. Oddly, the lamps were off. The only light was the moon, streaming through the skylight.

The room wasn't empty, however. On the far end, in silhouette, stood the buxom form of the young Miss Rowe, being kissed ardently by a long, lean man. He stood deeper in the shadow of a pillar, so I couldn't see whether he was dark or fair. My heart lurched. *Please, not Phillip.* His avowal of feeling had seemed so genuine. Had I been deceived?

Suddenly I felt a hand grab my arm just as the other hand covered my mouth. "*Shh,* Pen," Kendall's voice breathed softly in my ear. "We don't want to interrupt the love-birds."

We retreated deeper into the shadows. My mind spun with a dozen questions even as I relaxed. He dropped his hands. We stayed there in the recess of the library door, waiting.

Though it seemed an eternity, it was actually a minute or two. In the distance, the piano music grew more boisterous, and finally Allison stepped back. "We should join the others before we're missed."

"I'll go first," the man murmured. As he stepped into the light on his way out, I could see it was John Crofton.

Once Allison had disappeared down the hallway after him, Kendall closed the door and turned up the lights. "That was close."

"How did you happen to be here without them noticing you?"

He ducked his head sheepishly. "I was already in here, looking for something."

What was going on with everyone tonight? I folded my arms. "Don't tell me you were looking for cigars, too? I know you don't smoke them."

Kendall's eyes narrowed. "Who was looking for cigars?"

"The judge—supposedly. I discovered him rummaging through Lockwood's desk."

"Interesting."

"So? What were *you* looking for?" I asked.

Kendall hesitated as we heard Miss Stephens's rich tones. "Tell you later. We'd better head to the salon. Did you find Mrs. Lockwood?"

"No. But she must be there by now."

As might be expected, the music salon was exceedingly crowded, and the footmen were setting out extra chairs against the back wall. Even so, many remained standing, spilling out and blocking the doorways. Kendall and I stood in the hall. I didn't mind. We could still hear clearly, and the strains of "Hark the Herald Angels Sing," "Adeste Fideles," and my favorite, "Silent Night," were thrilling to experience. Miss Stephens's voice blended seamlessly with the children's—who were surprisingly good—and her solo rendition of "O Holy Night" made me sniff. Was I growing sentimental with age? Surely not.

Without looking in my direction, Kendall passed me his handkerchief. It was large, clean, and smelled like him.

When the music was over, the performers were met with rousing applause and led out to the ballroom for refreshments. Kendall and I watched people stream through the doors, waiting for the Lockwoods to emerge. Susannah came out, radiant with contentment. She spied me and hurried over.

"Oh, Miss Hamilton, wasn't it wonderful? How I wish I could sing like that." Then she noticed Kendall and stopped. "I beg your pardon. Hello, Mr. Kendall."

"Miss Adair." He bowed gallantly.

To give Susannah credit, she rose to the occasion, without a hint of a blush or a stammer. "Thank you for attending our little musicale."

"My pleasure."

I glanced at the doorway as the last of the patrons filed out. "Where are your parents?"

"Mama is still in there, gathering the donation baskets. I haven't seen Edgar, though. He might have been in a seat farther back. In this crowd, it was impossible to see everyone."

I stuck my head inside the room. Sure enough, there was Louisa, stacking be-ribboned wicker baskets in a footman's arms. No sign of Edgar.

"He must be in the ballroom already," Susannah said, peering over my shoulder. "Shall we go on, too? Mama will join us shortly. I helped her with the menu, you know." Her face brightened in animation, her smile crinkling the corners of her doe-brown eyes. "We have all sorts of Christmas delectables planned for the guests."

"That sounds lovely, dear," I said, "but I'd like a word alone with your mother. You two go ahead."

Kendall smiled at Susannah as he gently threaded the girl's arm through his. "Lead the way, Miss Adair."

When they left, I stepped into the salon. "Aunt Lou."

She whipped around, still holding one of the baskets. I could see the dark hollows of sleepless nights beneath her eyes. "Oh. Hello, Penelope. I wasn't expecting you." She handed off the last basket to the footman. "Take these to my sitting room for now."

He bowed and left.

"I arrived rather late," I said. "I hope you don't mind me coming."

"Of course not. It's good to have you," she said dutifully, her voice toneless. Her eyes were equally lacking in animation.

I glanced around. We had the room to ourselves now. "Susannah told me some of what happened at the banquet. You mustn't heed the gossip-mongers. As I said before, I don't believe Edgar killed Eileen."

She stiffened. "I don't know what to believe. Of course he denies it all—including the affair—but he refuses to tell me what he's really up to. I want to-to believe him." Her voice broke.

Edgar's close-mouthed approach to the operations of the board was hardly surprising. I remembered the man's dismissiveness when Louisa asked him before about possible malfeasance at the Benevolent Society. And if he was culling through suspects…the instinct to protect his wife was frustratingly understandable. "Did Susannah tell you what she overheard between Edgar and Cartwright Sunday evening?" I asked.

"No, but if it was similar to the awful things I'd heard, I can hardly blame her for failing to mention it."

"Edgar threatened Cartwright with an audit. Once he takes over as chairman, he can make good on that."

Her expression brightened with interest. "An audit…that could implicate a number of men on the board, not just Cartwright. So that's what Edgar's been up to? Why not tell me?"

I shrugged. "You know him better than I."

"He *is* quite protective," she admitted.

"There's something else—Eileen's book. I assume you showed it to him?"

"Yes. He couldn't make sense of the writing any more than I could. Today he sent off a letter to a friend of his who may be able to translate it for us." She flashed me a rueful look. "He agreed with me that we shouldn't entrust it to anyone official, such as your Mr. Pinkerton. No offense, my dear."

"Where is it now?"

"The library safe. Edgar's idea."

"When do you expect to hear back from his friend?"

"I don't know."

I made a face. We needed answers quickly. "Aunt Lou, it's past time we have a frank discussion with your husband. We must know his plan."

She shook her head. "If it has to do with board business, it's best we stay out of it."

"What if he's engaged in a broader investigation that goes beyond an audit? Susannah said he made some pointed declarations tonight, while greeting the guests."

She frowned. "He mentioned lost friends and…mementoes, I think."

"Mementoes—such as Eileen's appointment book?"

Her mouth formed a silent *o*.

"If he's also trying to solve her murder," I went on, "he may corner someone desperate."

"Good point." Her jaw set in a grim line. "I haven't seen him this past hour. He must be at the buffet. Let's go."

The attendees were taking advantage of the ballroom's more comfortable size and the sprawl of the generous buffet to circulate more freely. Despite my unease over our anticipated conversation with Edgar, I must admit my heart was warmed by the congenial mingling of workaday folks in their best clothing— still rather rough by wealthy society's standards—and the silk-gowned, stiff-collared attire of the Prairie Avenue elites. Perhaps, too, the heady scents of clove and ginger, mingling with the cut evergreen branches that ornamented the tables, helped boost my mood.

Kendall approached us almost immediately and gave Louisa a little bow. "My congratulations, Mrs. Lockwood, on a successful event." He nodded toward me as he handed me a plate laden with turkey croquettes, poached pears, and a slice of mince pie. "Miss Hamilton, I took the liberty of preparing you a plate. I'm afraid the coconut drops are gone." He crooked his head toward the choir boys. "They must have inhaled them. There's no other explanation."

Aunt Lou touched my arm. "I'll find Edgar and be right back."

Kendall frowned at her departing back. "Is she all right?"

"She will be—as soon as we get some answers from her husband. Have you seen him?"

"Can't say that I have."

Appetite gone, I set down my plate and surveyed the room. I didn't see him, either. I followed Louisa's progress as she circulated among the guests. Mrs. Rowe and Allison were conversing in animated fashion with Miss Stephens, whose light laugh was nearly as charming as her singing voice.

After stopping among them, Aunt Lou stepped out to the balcony, where Judge Rowe and Richard Cartwright were smoking. The judge had found the cigars at last, it seemed. She spoke to them, and they shook their heads.

She walked briskly back inside now, heading toward Mrs. Cartwright, who was chatting with Susannah. She stopped there only briefly before turning hasty steps in our direction. The first ripple of fear ran up my spine at the sight of her pale face.

Kendall followed my glance. "A problem?"

"I fear so."

Aunt Lou, Kendall, and I began a search in earnest. While she inquired of the butler, Kendall and I explored the first floor rooms, beginning with Lockwood's study.

It looked much as I'd left it when the judge was here—

curtains drawn, desk lamp dimmed, chair pushed against the desk, writing blotter neatly aligned on top.

"The judge is a tidy searcher, at least," I said, opening drawers as Kendall combed through the waste bin, searching for a clue as to where the man could be.

"Rowe told you he was looking for cigars when you surprised him here?" Kendall asked.

"That's right. An obvious fabrication. Why not send a footman to fetch them?" I straightened and arched an eyebrow. "There's been quite a lot of searching going on tonight."

Kendall met my eye. "You have a question?"

"Have you and the judge been looking for the same thing?" I was fairly sure it was Eileen's book, but how would Kendall know of it?

"Most likely."

I put my hands on my hips. "Well? Are you going to tell me what it is?"

"Let's find Lockwood first." He sighed. "Shall we move on to the library?"

Aunt Lou walked in. "Never mind the library. Someone saw Edgar putting on his coat about forty-five minutes ago."

"He left in the middle of his own party? Did he have the carriage brought 'round?" Kendall asked.

She shook her head. "He must be somewhere on the grounds, though Heaven knows why."

"He was meeting someone." Anxiety prickled along my spine. To be gone for nearly an hour… "Where should we start —the coach house?"

Kendall frowned. "Not private enough, if indeed he was meeting someone. Too many drivers and groomsmen loitering there on a night like this."

"And the gazebo's too open," I mused. "What does that leave—an equipment shed, perhaps?"

"What about Susannah's pottery studio?" Aunt Lou suggested.

Kendall let out a low whistle. "She has her own studio?"

Aunt Lou looked down modestly. "A *small* one, with just the basic necessities— a potter's wheel, kiln, sink…that sort of thing. She's quite keen on pottery these days."

Kendall nodded. "All right, then, let's go."

"Should we have the staff help us look?" I asked.

Aunt Lou shifted uneasily. "I'd prefer to do this discreetly."

In that vein, we opted not to fetch our coats. Aunt Lou already had her shawl, Kendall lent me his jacket, and we liberated a lantern from the back porch. Thus equipped, we crossed the grounds behind the house, passing the topiary garden where Susannah had found the sack of jewels, stopping briefly to check the gazebo at the center of the grounds—no one there—until we reached the studio, tucked away on a side path near the fence line.

"Look!" I pointed at a stout bar, jammed through the curved hasps of the double doors. I glanced at Aunt Lou. "Is it typically secured this way?"

"No, never." She frowned. "I'll go around and look in the window." Heedless of her gown, she waded through the brambles that grew between the fence and the side of the structure. "Edgar!" she called.

Kendall's expression was grim as he reached for the heavy piece of iron.

As Aunt Lou had taken the lantern and I couldn't see much besides Kendall tugging at the bar, I decided to follow her. I held up my skirts as prickly vegetation snagged my stockings and hampered my steps.

She was holding the lantern up to the double-hung window. "See anything?" I asked.

"Nothing untoward, but my view is limited." She blew out an exasperated breath and tapped on the window. "Edgar? Edgar?"

I went back to check on Kendall's progress. "How's it going?"

"It's...stuck." Kendall's voice was gritty with frustration.

"Should we get some help?" I went over to assess what he was dealing with.

"I can get it. Just a few more inches." He clenched his teeth and tugged again.

"Here, let me help." I leaned close to push from the other end. I sniffed. "Do you smell something?"

"Not really," he muttered. He yanked roughly at the last few inches of scraping metal to clear the handles.

"But something's not—"

I felt a whoosh of hot air and a roar in my ears as the doors flew at us, knocking us to the ground.

CHAPTER 18

I don't know how long I lay insensible. I remember feeling sturdy hands grasping my shoulders and dragging me away from the structure—now on fire—and over to the lawn.

I sat up. "Phillip! Louisa!" I yelled, surveying the scene. Through the smoke and flickering glow, I saw the outlines of people running out with water buckets. Flames arched up to the smoky sky. I scrambled to get to my feet.

"Easy, miss," a woman's voice said. It was the parlor maid. "You have a nasty cut on your head."

Automatically I touched my temple and felt the wetness.

She wrapped an afghan around my shivering frame. "We should get you inside or you'll catch your death of cold. Can you walk?"

"In a minute. Where are Mrs. Lockwood and Mr. Kendall?"

The maid pointed to the butler and one of the guests— Richard Cartwright—carrying Aunt Lou as quickly as they could from the side of the burning studio. They laid her down at my feet. The housekeeper came along, armed with towels and a blanket.

"Oh, Louisa," I murmured in dismay, taking in the sight of

the cuts upon her face and the blood matting her hair. But she was breathing, thank heaven.

She groaned, and her eyelids fluttered, but nothing more. It was probably a kindness that she was unconscious from the pain. I didn't try to rouse her.

"She should be brought inside," I said to the housekeeper, who crooned over her mistress and covered her with a blanket.

"Someone's rigging a stretcher now," she said briskly.

I looked around. "Where's Mr. Kendall?"

"Who? Oh, the gentleman." She gestured to the far side of the lawn. My chest clenched at the sight of the prone figure under one of the shed doors. Several men were pulling him free. In wobbly, lurching steps, I made my way over to him.

"Phillip!" I reached for his hand. "Are you all right?"

"I will be," he grunted. He brushed at his sleeves and torso, a futile exercise, as it left more streaks of dirt and rust upon what was once a pleated evening shirt of pristine white. I didn't look any better. I gazed ruefully over my ash-smeared, aquamarine satin. Apparently I was down to one evening gown.

"What happened?" he asked.

In the distance, I heard a siren from the nearby fire station on Eighteenth. We Chicagoans take fire very seriously. "An explosion. I caught a whiff of something but didn't put it together before we inadvertently sparked it."

"Gas? In the studio?"

I nodded. "Susannah's gas-fired kiln. It shouldn't have been a hazard, unless someone left the valve open."

"Where's Louisa?" he asked.

I nodded toward the lawn. "She's alive, but her condition looks serious."

We heard a cry behind us. "Mama!" Susannah rushed though the kitchen door, pushing past a steady line of servants carrying water buckets. I couldn't see her expression in the dark, but a world of anguish was embedded in that one word. She ran over to her mother, who was being lifted onto a makeshift stretcher.

"Please, miss," came a pleading voice at my elbow. The maid had followed me. "You should come inside, before…" Her voice trailed off as she turned her head toward the smoking structure, nearly doused now.

I knew what she meant. Lockwood. He must have been in there. He could not have survived.

But Kendall wasn't paying attention to the maid. He squinted at the studio. "Thank heaven the fire didn't spread to the surrounding—" His breath caught at the sight of a blanket-draped form being lifted by two footmen onto another stretcher.

The maid turned away with a sob.

All of the guests save for Phillip and myself took their leave amid murmured sympathies to no one in particular, as Susannah was upstairs by her mother's side. I didn't witness much of the leave-taking myself, as the parlor maid led me to a guest room to help me clean up and change into a borrowed shirtwaist and brown serge walking skirt that was a bit short. At least it didn't smell like smoke and blood. I assumed Phillip was also being tended to.

There was a knock on the door when I was done, and a gentleman in a smart, black suit carrying a medical bag entered.

"Miss Hamilton? I'm Mrs. Lockwood's physician." His gaze lingered at my temple. "Let me have a look at that. Any other injuries?"

I lifted my right elbow. "A bit scraped up and singed, but nothing serious."

As he led me to a seat closer to the lamp, I asked, "How is Mrs. Lockwood?"

"Resting comfortably. She suffered cuts to her face and neck, but it's her head injury that worries me most. What a terrible accident."

I didn't bother to disabuse him of the notion. "How bad is her injury? Does she know about her husband?" I winced as he applied something stinging to my forehead.

"She roused only briefly. She's sleeping now. No one has said anything to her as far as I know. I've left strict instructions that she not be disturbed tonight. Or her daughter, for that matter, who was in near hysterics and needed a sedative."

Once he was finished with me, I headed to the parlor to find Kendall waiting there already. No one had explicitly told us to remain, but we each had a sense that someone in authority would have a good many questions for us.

I handed back his now-filthy evening jacket. "I'm sorry it's in such sad shape."

He lifted an indifferent shoulder. "No matter."

At least he looked in better condition than his coat. Only a few scrapes were visible at his face and neck, and there was a bandage on his chin.

I sat down across from him. "Phillip, we need to deal honestly with each other. What were you searching for tonight?"

His eyes flickered briefly at my use of his Christian name.

I shrugged—as we'd nearly been blown up together, I was not about to worry about decorum.

"I had the sense," he began, "that Edgar was in possession of something of Mrs. Crofton's. It seemed important. I was curious."

Ah. I breathed a small sigh of relief. Even though I'd been *nearly* sure that's what it was, a small bit of doubt about the former thief's honesty had lingered. Pre-conceived ideas are the hardest to relinquish. "So you heard Edgar hinting at finding something of hers?" At his lifted eyebrow I added, "Susannah told me."

"That's right, but he seemed to direct the comment at the rest of the group rather than me. So there *is* something?"

I explained about the book Louisa had found. "I suppose it isn't so surprising that something of the sort exists. Eileen seemed the kind of woman who liked to document everything, especially if it gave her a hold over someone."

"Have you seen it?" he asked.

I sighed. "Not yet. Louisa says it's written in some sort of shorthand that no one can read. I proposed we have Mr. Pinkerton try to decipher it. Louisa might have been amenable to that before she found out about her husband's affair with Eileen, but afterward...she didn't want it out of her keeping, fearing it could compromise his reputation. She showed it to Edgar only. He was making arrangements to have it examined privately."

Kendall nodded. "And the judge searched Lockwood's study tonight—sounds like something he would very much like to have."

"Far better than the cigars he claimed to be hunting for," I agreed.

"Why hint at the book at all? Was Lockwood trying to gauge their reactions?"

"If I had to guess, I'd say he was growing impatient. He didn't want to wait for his translator friend to work on the book. He'd already been biding his time for a look at the board's financial records."

"And that interval gave Cartwright time to falsify or destroy important evidence," Kendall said.

I nodded. "No doubt Edgar was aware of that possibility. So it was all the more frustrating for him to have to wait on both pieces of evidence and risk something important slipping through his fingers."

"Then Lockwood was trying to use the existence of the dead woman's book to get the answers he needed about Cartwright more quickly," Kendall mused, "because Rowe or Crofton might know the sort of secrets she would record in there."

"Exactly. Then he retired to his study before the performance started. Except for the short conversation he'd had with his wife, he wanted to be alone to encourage one of them to come forward."

Kendall winced as he shifted to get more comfortable. "But Cartwright was there when Lockwood dropped his hints, too. He certainly wasn't going to cooperate. On the contrary, he would have regarded it as a threat rather than an opportunity."

"True." Which was Edgar's goal—carrot or stick?

"Why didn't Lockwood remain in the study and instead head to the pottery studio?" Kendall asked.

"I can't explain that, I'm afraid."

There was a short knock, and two uniformed policemen entered, their hats tucked politely under their arms. A barrel-chested man with stripes upon the shoulder of his tunic stepped forward. "Miss Hamilton? Mr. Kendall? I'm Sergeant Ganley." He jerked a thumb behind him, toward the tall man who maintained a watchful stance by the door. "Patrolman Tatum. We're investigating the death of Mr. Lockwood." He gestured to a wood chair. "May I sit?"

I wearily waved him into it.

Ganley sat, carefully keeping clear of the delicate arms of what was likely an antique.

"Now then." He looked at us over his spectacles. "Why are you the only two people to have remained after the incident?"

Kendall lifted an eyebrow. "Ironically, the others aren't here to answer you."

"The staff should have kept the guests here," he grumbled. "Now I'll have to search hither and yon to interview everyone."

"How unfortunate for you," I retorted. "Meanwhile, a young lady has lost her stepfather and very nearly her mother. What have you learned about the explosion? You've questioned the staff, I assume?"

He nodded. "Everyone swears the gas valve to the kiln was properly shut off earlier that day, when the young lady was finished with it. And yet, we have an explosion to account for." He pulled out a notepad from his tunic pocket. "And what's this I hear about the doors being barred from the outside?"

"It's true," Kendall said. "A heavy iron bar had been wedged through the handles, preventing anyone who might be inside from escaping."

The sergeant tested the pencil on his cuff and made a note. "So Lockwood was still alive when his attacker turned on the gas and left."

"We didn't hear any pounding or cries for help coming from inside the structure, though," I pointed out. "Was he already unconscious from the gas?"

Ganley shrugged. "The doctor hasn't finished examining the body, though he tells me there aren't any wounds that can't be attributed to the explosion. Now then—I was informed this was an indoor musical function. How did you two and Mrs. Lockwood come to be outside, near the pottery studio?"

"We were searching for Edgar Lockwood," I said. "The butler told Louisa that he'd been seen putting on his coat."

The policeman nodded. "I was informed of that as well. Go on."

"Since no conveyance had been called on his behalf, we judged it likely he was out on the grounds somewhere. For what purpose, we didn't know," I added, anticipating his next question.

"I see. So, Miss Hamilton, what is your relationship to the victim?"

"Which one?" I asked impatiently.

"I meant the one who is no longer with us. Edgar Lockwood." He waved a hand. "But take your pick."

"I didn't know Mr. Lockwood all that well. His wife, however, is acquainted with my mother. We had a chance meeting a couple of weeks ago." I was reluctant to reveal the case I was working on, but the events of this evening were very much connected to it.

He raised an eyebrow at my silence. "And?" he prompted.

I was too fatigued for further evasions. "When she discovered I was a private detective," I said bluntly, "she engaged my services to investigate the death of a close friend of hers."

He expelled a gratified breath and sat back. "At last, we are making progress."

"If you already knew I was a Pinkerton," I asked peevishly, "why not get to the point?"

"I like to know the mettle of those I'm dealing with," he said, unruffled. He gave me a severe look. "I cannot brook evasion and half-truths, you understand? I must be privy to everything you know." He grimaced. "Private detectives are not always forthcoming with police." He turned to Kendall. "And you, sir? What is your connection to the family?"

Kendall waved a careless hand. "I'm a private detective, too."

I blinked at the answer at first, but he was right—Kendall was a detective now, not simply some rogue for hire, as I'd long considered him. I flashed him a grateful look, which he returned with warmth in his eyes. If there was anyone I'd pick to help me navigate this morass, he'd be at the top of the list. Along with Frank, of course.

"Indeed?" The sergeant tapped his pencil. "How is it we have two detectives attending a social event in which one host is killed and the other gravely injured? Doesn't sound to me as if you're earning your pay."

I clenched my hands in my lap. "We weren't here as protection for the family."

"Apparently not."

I ignored the jibe. "The invitation to tonight's event was purely social—at least, originally. But I don't deny I'd hoped to find answers to Louisa's concerns."

The sergeant straightened. "And those concerns, Miss Hamilton? I cannot ask the woman at the moment."

"I just told you—Mrs. Lockwood wanted to catch her friend's—Mrs. Crofton's—killer."

"Crofton…that was the woman who lived in the mansion behind this one?" Ganley asked. "She died in a robbery last year."

"Mrs. Lockwood didn't believe it to be a robbery, and after looking into it further, we've speculated that the jewels were taken as a ruse. Susannah Adair found them shortly after the woman's death, concealed in the Lockwoods' topiary garden."

"Mrs. Lockwood's daughter?" Ganley was writing notes at a furious pace. "And why didn't Miss Adair report the finding of these items?" He didn't bother to look up.

"She didn't know they were connected to a murder. She's quite young—her parents had shielded her from the unsavory details at the time. I cannot speak as to what conclusion she drew when she found them, but she decided to employ them for her own purposes. I only found out myself this week."

"And what purposes were those?"

"You'll have to ask the young lady that, when she wakes. If you wish to examine the sack and its contents, Mr. Pinkerton has them in his office safe."

"I will do that, believe me," he said. "Why didn't you turn them over to us immediately? You must have known we'd want to question Lockwood about a murdered woman's jewels being found in his own garden. He can't answer such questions anymore."

"I only learned of it myself a few days ago."

He waved off my excuse. "You people make our jobs twice as difficult as need be. Did you at least ask Lockwood about the jewels?"

I shook my head in regret. "Louisa suspended the case and wouldn't allow me to question him."

"Why?"

"She feared a scandal. She was devastated to learn her husband had had an affair with Mrs. Crofton."

Ganley nodded grimly. "I'd heard from the staff about the

couple's rather loud argument on the subject. Mrs. Lockwood got more than she bargained for in launching the inquiry."

I looked down at my hands. She certainly had.

"When she hired you," Ganley went on, "she must have had a specific person for you to investigate, correct?"

"Yes—Judge Rowe." Had William Pinkerton heard those words, he would have aged ten years. Here we thought the danger of Rowe learning of our inquiry had passed.

At least I had the small satisfaction of having turned the sneering sergeant speechless.

When he didn't ask the obvious question, I went on. "Mrs. Lockwood knew that her friend and the judge had had an affair years ago."

His eyes widened. "She'd had an affair with him, too? The lady got around."

I ignored that. "In the process of her, *um*, liaison with Rowe, Eileen learned a secret detrimental to the judge's reputation. She blackmailed him with it on at least one occasion of which I'm aware. But there's more."

"Of course there is." He licked his thumb and turned over a fresh page.

I explained the content of Eileen's letters to the judge, where she expressed her concerns about the financial dealings of the Widows' Benevolent Society at the hands of Richard Cartwright and her request to install Lockwood on the board.

Ganley looked up from his notepad. "So the focus of your inquiry shifted from Rowe to Cartwright?"

"That's right. Mr. Pinkerton is still looking into Cartwright's finances to see if there is anything amiss. I was obliged to consider Edgar Lockwood as well—not only because of the jewels found in his garden, but because he had no alibi for the night Mrs. Crofton died. He *seemed* to be working on her behalf, but I wanted to be sure. I hadn't gotten any further, however, when Louisa suspended my investigation."

"And now the poor fellow's dead," Kendall pointed out, "so we know he's not guilty."

Ganley shook his head at me. "Lord save me from capricious females who cannot make up their minds. So—which fellow killed Mrs. Crofton? Cartwright or Rowe?" He sneered. "Why not add her husband to the list?"

"John Crofton was out of town at the time," I said sharply. "He couldn't have killed her."

"Fair enough, but he was here *tonight*," Ganley said. "The two deaths, a year apart, don't have to be connected."

"Lockwood's death doesn't make much sense otherwise. Susannah told me her stepfather threatened Cartwright with an audit a couple of days ago."

Kendall leaned forward. "And Lockwood dropped a hint about the book when he was greeting guests tonight."

Ganley frowned. "What book?"

I explained the appointment book Louisa had found in Mrs. Crofton's hat box a few days ago. "I haven't seen it, but Louisa said it's written in some sort of code and is unintelligible. She showed it to Edgar, who was arranging for it to be translated."

"Rowe was after it," Kendall chimed in.

Ganley's eyes brightened in interest. "Is that so?"

I nodded. "I caught him going through Lockwood's desk earlier this evening. He claimed to be looking for cigars."

"Where's this appointment book now?"

"In the library safe, according to Louisa. At least, I *hope* it's still there."

"We'll have to get in and see," he murmured to himself. "Any idea how Lockwood came to be out at the pottery studio? He didn't say anything to the staff."

"I hadn't seen him all evening," I said. "And he didn't share his plans with his wife. Were you able to determine who saw him last? Besides the murderer, that is."

Ganley shrugged. "Obviously, I haven't had a chance to question everyone, but one of the maids saw him putting on his coat"—he flipped back a few pages in his notepad—"shortly after nine o'clock, just before the choir children arrived."

"And we headed for the studio around ten-fifteen," Kendall said. "More than an hour after."

"If he'd been overpowered as soon as he got there," Ganley mused, "and locked in the building with the gas turned on, he could have been dead before the explosion." He stood. "I have no further need of you tonight. You can go." He waggled a finger at me. "But no more investigating, you hear? This is a police matter now."

Kendall insisted upon accompanying me on the ride home.

"You're rather quiet," he said. "How are you feeling?"

"I'm all right. At least *I* didn't awaken with a door perched upon my chest." My glance lingered at the bandage on his chin.

He touched it ruefully. "Not an experience I care to repeat. What do you think the sergeant is going to do next?"

"His first order of business should be getting into the safe," I said. "Interviewing the other guests, particularly Cartwright and Rowe, would be a close second."

"If I were the judge, I'd be destroying Eileen's letters."

"I'm not so sure. Even though she made reference to the affair and a secret she had over him, he'd kept them for a reason."

"What reason?"

"To prove he was working with her and Lockwood, rather than against them. With Lockwood's death, proof of that is even more important."

"You believe Cartwright is our man."

"He had the most to lose. Lockwood was already trying to impose his authority as the new chairman with the threat of an audit. In a few weeks, he would have had access to all of the ledgers, invoices, and receipts he'd care to have examined.

Combine that threat with Lockwood's hint about Eileen's appointment book, and Cartwright might have been tempted to revisit the desperate measures he'd used before."

And yet, something about the theory bothered me. Just as with Lockwood, the circumstances behind Cartwright's guilt looked a bit too damning. It felt as though we were being shown carefully constructed shadows of the moving parts.

CHAPTER 19

*T*he next morning, I took a hansom back to the Lockwood mansion. My profligate use of cabs was definitely eating into our budget.

The maid let me in and took my coat. "Miss Susannah is talking to the policeman right now. Do you want to wait in the master's—I mean, in the study?"

"How's Mrs. Lockwood?"

The girl bit her lip. "She had a rough night, miss. She woke for a little while but didn't seem aware of anyone. She's sleeping again."

Dread settled like a stone in my chest as I followed the maid to the study. What if Aunt Lou didn't recover?

After what seemed an eternity of waiting, the door opened, and Susannah came in. The little white dog, Plato, trotted at her heels.

I braced myself for his usual expression of outrage, but instead, he wagged his tail and came right up to me. I dangled a hand for him to sniff.

"He's getting used to you, I expect," Susannah said.

I gave a thin smile. "I'm here often enough these days." Up close, I got a good look at her. Her face, usually glowing with the

215

K.B. OWEN

vitality of youth, was pallid and hollowed, her eyes red-rimmed. "Are you all right?"

"I suppose." She looked around the room and shuddered. "I'd rather not be here. Come up to my sitting room."

Susannah's sitting room was a welcoming space, with walls papered in a delicate vine pattern and comfortable upholstered chairs covered in slate-blue crushed velvet.

Atop her writing desk, I noticed a shallow, open box with a necklace of dark stones inside. "What's this?" I lifted it out, and the stones—rubies—brightened to reveal their red sparkle. *The Margharita necklace.* "Susannah? How did you come by this?"

She plopped herself into an overstuffed wingback chair. "Allison left it for me last night. I never noticed in all the confusion. I found it this morning. I haven't spoken to her yet today. I'm guessing she felt guilty and gave it back."

"Hardly surprising," I said dryly. "You see why your mother didn't want her to know?"

Her jaw clenched defensively. "It's hard not to confide in Allison. She's my best friend."

I set the necklace aside. "She's in a difficult position now. Her parents are upset over its disappearance. I overheard them arguing last night. She's allowing them to assume it's been lost or stolen." At least Morris had kept his end of the bargain.

Susannah blew out a breath. "Please don't scold me. I have enough to worry about."

True enough. I changed the subject. "What did the policeman have to say?"

"He wanted the appointment book you told him about. But Mama obviously can't tell us the combination, and Edgar is dead…"

"No one else in the household knows it?"

She shook her head.

"Where's Ganley now?"

"He's gone to interview more of last night's guests."

That should keep him out from underfoot for a while, I

mused, recklessly ignoring his warning about interference. "I have a friend who might be able to open the safe. Do I have your permission to try?"

Susannah and I hovered as Kendall pulled tools out of his kit. He looked back at us in annoyance. "I'm not accustomed to an audience," he said peevishly. "Would you wait outside, please?"

We paced the hall until he waved us back in and placed a leather volume in my hands. "This is the only item matching the description. Mrs. Crofton's name is inside the cover, but nothing else except for the date notations is intelligible."

I riffled through several of the thick, fine-quality pages, gilt-edged and neatly lined. He was right—nothing I recognized as names in the entries, only odd squiggles mixed in with roman letters, none of it comprehensible.

"What now?" Kendall asked. "Do we take it to the sergeant?"

I turned to Susannah. "Did Ganley say when he would return with someone to open the safe?"

"After dinner."

I exchanged a look with Kendall. "Are you thinking what I'm thinking?"

He grinned. "Let's get this to the office and see what Mr. Pinkerton can do."

∾

Though Pinkerton was out, it was his secretary, Mary, who proved the most helpful.

"I've learned several varieties of shorthand during my years here," she said, turning the pages. "Mm-hmm, yes—that would be—I see…" She reached for the pencil in her topknot and then glanced up at us, startled. "Why are you still here? I can't work with you standing over me."

Kendall flashed me a meaningful look. "I know exactly what you mean, Mary. We'll leave you to it."

"Come back in two or three hours," she murmured, adjusting her spectacles.

"So, what shall we do with our time?" he asked, as we stepped back out to the sidewalk on a blustery December day. And by blustery, I mean more than our usual stiff breezes. "Shopping, perhaps?" he suggested. "Do you have any Christmas gifts left to buy?"

I smiled and shook my head. "Already taken care of. My gift list is typically short."

He leaned toward the curb to hail a cab. "It seems to me you're in need of a gown to replace your ruined one." He shook his head. "Such a pity—blue is definitely your color."

A hansom drew up to the curb for us.

Kendall leaned close as he helped me in. "Yes, especially that shade of pale blue—it matches your eyes perfectly."

I snorted as I settled my skirts. "And your morning coat matches yours, but you don't hear me going on about it."

He laughed. "Fair enough." His eyes lingered at my collar, where I wore the silver key pin. He didn't say anything but squeezed my hand before letting go.

I changed the subject. "Now that I think on it, Saint Nicholas *should* bring young Henry a couple of toys." I smiled to myself. Our parlor would be overrun with even more detritus, but it *was* Christmas, after all.

His eyes lit up. "Of course! How old is the little fellow? I have yet to meet him."

"Nearly three."

"Perfect." He tapped on the roof, and the driver slid open the hatch.

"Where to, sir?"

"Your closest toy shop, my good man."

I felt the lurch of the cab, and we were off.

I have to admit, Kendall's lively mood was infectious. I've

never enjoyed myself so much in a toy store before. Of course, part of it might be that I didn't have to keep my eye out for hoisters. Being a mere customer felt like a veritable luxury.

Kendall looped my arm through his as we entered, and I let him, only because I still felt chilled by the outdoors.

"I know all about what boys like," he boasted. "Aren't you glad you brought me along?"

I smiled up at him. "If we're going by your tastes, I'd say boys like shiny objects."

"My dear Miss Hamilton, how little you know about me. Shiny objects came much later."

We passed by the section devoted to hobby horses—rejected on account of how much space such a one would occupy in our modest-sized dwelling—and turned to the displays of wooden blocks, trains, and large spinning tops.

I picked up the smooth blocks of a set painted in bright, appealing colors. "Look—they have alphabet letters and animals on them. He can learn as he plays."

The young lady staffing the counter smiled. "As you can see, the blocks are varied in size. They correspond to the animal painted upon them—the ant and the turtle are on smaller blocks than the elephant and the whale." She stacked them enticingly upon the counter.

Kendall beamed. "Perfect. We'll take them."

He also insisted upon buying Henry a stuffed bear and an india-rubber ball before we finally extricated ourselves.

"That was fun," he said. "I like shopping for other people's children. All of the enjoyment and none of the work."

I had to agree. "Thank you for paying for the gifts. You didn't have to do that."

"My pleasure. I was wondering—might I see the lad open them on Christmas morning? If I wouldn't be in the way, that is."

I smiled. "I'd like that. You wouldn't be in the way."

"You're sure? I wouldn't want to intrude in case you and Frank—I mean, I thought you two spend the holidays together."

"Not for quite some time."

He gave me a searching look. When it was obvious I wasn't going to provide anything further on the subject, he said, "Well then—let's see what Mary has come up with."

Mary turned from the filing cabinet when we walked in. "Ah, there you are. I've finished transcribing it for you." She nodded toward a stack of notepaper beside the leather-bound journal. "No one's using the conference room, if you want to read in there."

Kendall and I divided up the pages and settled at the large oak table, scarred by cigarette burns and ink stains. I had the more recent half of the appointment book, though that was a bit of a misnomer. Yes, Eileen's social and professional appointments were noted, but in between were lengthy writings about the people in question—what she'd observed of their behavior, what gossip she had gathered, what she'd been told in confidence.

I turned over the first few pages with a sigh. "So far, I'm reading about the women of her acquaintance and their various indiscretions and spending habits. Nothing yet about Lockwood, the Society, Cartwright, or Rowe."

Kendall gave a grunt as he set aside a sheet and kept reading.

Finally, I found mention of all four on the second to last page.

2 pm Wednesday, 30 September, 1886

Lucius was reluctant to accede to my request, but I left him no alternative. As his last act before turning over the chairmanship to Cartwright, he will appoint Edgar Lockwood to the board of the Widows' Benevolent Society. Edgar has agreed to quietly investigate the malfeasance I suspect is going on in the organization but could not prove.

I was tempted to go to my husband about the matter as he also serves on the board, but he's an ambitious man to whom expediency is all. Sadly, I trust Edgar over my own husband to find proof that Cartwright and others are lining their pockets at the charity's expense. I hope he will be successful. I cannot abide the idea that funds meant for destitute widows are being diverted to such a man.

One problem, of course, is that John will see Edgar's promotion as preferential treatment, since Edgar has not been a member as long as would be expected for such an appointment. But John will be promoted to Treasurer in my place, so he may not mind it so much. At least I won't be overshadowing him anymore—a frequent complaint of his.

However, I fear John will suspect that I've exerted some sort of influence upon the judge to effect Edgar's appointment. He knows of my past affair with Lucius. Will he believe I've taken on a new lover in Edgar? That is Lucius's opinion, certainly. I find it a notion too ridiculous to refute. Louisa is my best friend.

Cartwright may cultivate the rumor, if only to ensure my suspicions aren't taken seriously. I dare not confide to my husband the real reason for Edgar's appointment. John is too close to Cartwright. I must count upon Lucius addressing the rumors on my behalf.

"Phillip, look at this." I passed him the page and waited while he read.

He let out a low whistle. "That confirms your theory."

"Another important detail," I said, "is that Edgar and Eileen were *not* lovers." If only Edgar had confided the entire scheme to his wife. Louisa had dearly wanted to believe he was telling her the truth in denying the affair.

"I wish we knew more about Cartwright's finances," Kendall said.

"We're still working on that." William Pinkerton stood in the doorway. I wondered how long he'd been there.

He pulled over a chair. "That employment agency you told me of seems to be the key. We're narrowing our efforts there."

"Employment agency?" Kendall asked.

"The Osage Ladies' Employment Agency," I clarified. "When I searched Cartwright's study the night of the auction, I found a number of canceled checks from the Benevolent Society made out to them."

"The agency exists," Pinkerton said, "but as to whether it does what it purports to is another matter. And we have yet to locate the designee, the elusive S. Parker." He eyed the sheets in front of us. "Mary says you have some interesting reading."

Kendall passed over the page in question. "Your secretary has impressive skills."

"That she does." Pinkerton smiled and skimmed it. "Any other entries of value?"

"Notations that confirm Mrs. Crofton and Judge Rowe had had an affair," Kendall said, "and some extraneous tidbits regarding certain ladies of her acquaintance. Nothing worth killing her for." He put a self-deprecating hand to his chest. "At least, in my humble opinion of the fairer sex."

"The book ends December of 1886," I said. "Eileen was killed just a few weeks later."

"Lockwood had begun his term on the board by then," Kendall said. "Had he learned something so soon that proved dangerous to Cartwright?"

"If he had, he would have been the one killed," Pinkerton said, "rather than Mrs. Crofton. And his death was nearly a year after hers."

"Just when he was about to assume the chairmanship," I mused.

Kendall straightened the stack of pages in front of him. "We could be looking at different motives for each death. And possibly two different killers."

If Cartwright hadn't killed Eileen… I thought over the other possibilities. Lucius Rowe? Except for the fact that she held a secret over him—not lightly dismissed, of course—they seemed on good terms. He'd helped with her scheme and had kept quiet about it all this time, even after her death. John Crofton? Eileen had worried he would resent Lockwood's rise and suspect her of having an affair. Had that been the case?

"Could Crofton have killed his wife?" Kendall asked. "Or does he have an alibi?"

"Mrs. Wynch here has already asked that question," Pinkerton said.

Kendall raised an eyebrow in my direction, but whether it was over the question or Pinkerton's use of my married name, I didn't know.

"His account has been confirmed by his mother," Pinkerton explained, "and the servants of her household. He arrived at her home in Cincinnati the afternoon before his wife's death and stayed overnight. He didn't leave until after receiving the butler's urgent telegram the next day."

"So everything circles back to Cartwright," Kendall said.

Pinkerton blew out a sigh. "It's best left to the police now. I'll turn over Mrs. Crofton's journal and jewelry to them. Where was the book found?"

"The Lockwoods' library safe." I exchanged a glance with Kendall.

Pinkerton narrowed his eyes at Kendall. "You broke into another safe? Why didn't the police take charge of it at the time?"

"No one knew the combination," Kendall began, "and then—"

"Susannah found it written down, but not until after they'd gone," I interposed. I disliked lying to my employer, but better than Kendall earning a reputation as a safe-cracker. He'd only worked for the agency these past two weeks.

Pinkerton flicked a look in my direction. "*Hmph.* Who's the man in charge of the case?"

"Sergeant Ganley," Kendall said. "Irascible fellow."

"Not all that fond of private detectives, either," I chimed in.

Pinkerton shrugged. "A common sentiment."

"I wish we could capture the killer ourselves," I said irritably. "He's caused a lot of heartache."

Pinkerton shook his head. "Remember what I said about tender-heartedness, my dear."

I stiffened. "You know quite well that reason guides my decisions. However, sentiment does have a role to play, as it is the substance of *why* we investigate." I paused to collect my thoughts. The issue had been on my mind a great deal lately.

"The wrongdoers we pursue," I went on, "whether poor or wealthy, rough or educated, are thieves of the worst kind. They steal not only valuables, but virtue, peace of mind, and yes, lives." I met Pinkerton's eye. "If you're accusing me of being tender-hearted because I cannot help but want swift justice for Susannah and her mother, I am not ashamed of it."

He flicked a glance over at Kendall. "You see why I hired her."

I felt a flush creep up my cheeks. For William Pinkerton, it was the equivalent of glowing praise.

"How are the two women faring?" he asked.

"Mrs. Lockwood slips in and out of consciousness and cannot be questioned yet," I answered. "Susannah is distraught, naturally, but is trying to remain calm and helpful. I wish she had more than one friend and confidant to turn to in such a difficult time."

I blinked. *One friend and confidant.*

Allison, who knows all the gossip. Allison, whom Susannah could not resist telling her secrets to. Allison, who visits frequently—and, if I remembered correctly, stayed with the Lockwoods *one night in particular*. Why didn't I realize it before?

The idea settled into my abdomen with a cold certainty I've learned to pay attention to. I glanced down at the transcribed notes in my hands. If I was right, it meant that none of this—the coded notes, Lockwood's covert investigation, whatever evidence of financial malfeasance existed—made a difference, at least in Eileen's death. That motive was as old as time itself. And then Lockwood's death had become entangled in hers.

"There's an important piece of information we didn't share with the sergeant," I said to Kendall.

He raised an eyebrow. "What was that?"

"The amorous scene we witnessed between Allison Rowe and John Crofton. And it wasn't the first time I'd seen them together. Last week, at the riding stables, they were—well, not quite so *en flagrante* as what you and I had seen—but there was a familiarity that bespoke more than a recent acquaintance."

Kendall shrugged. "Sordid, but irrelevant. Think about it from a practical standpoint—if Crofton was occupied in romancing Miss Rowe in the library, he couldn't be out at the studio killing Lockwood."

"I'm not so sure," I said slowly. "We saw the couple just as the music was starting at nine-thirty. Ganley said Lockwood had put on his coat and headed out a little after nine. Who's to say Crofton didn't take care of Lockwood first and then turned his attentions to Allison?"

He grimaced. "What a horrible notion. But what about a motive?"

"Cartwright may have told Crofton of Lockwood's threat to bring in an auditor. He's the treasurer, after all."

Pinkerton leaned forward. "Lockwood threatened to bring in an auditor? When was this?"

I explained again what Susannah had overheard. "If Cartwright was scheming with Crofton, he'd want to warn him," I finished.

Pinkerton shook his head. "The treasurer of the Benevolent Society killing the new chairman would invite the very inquiry he'd wish to avoid."

"Not if it was made to look like a suicide. Edgar would have died of the gas, if we hadn't inadvertently triggered the explosion."

"The doors to the pottery studio were barred from the outside," Kendall pointed out.

"Indeed they were," I conceded. "However, it wouldn't have

been difficult for Crofton to go back later and remove the bar once Lockwood had succumbed. He wouldn't have expected anyone to be prowling the grounds on a cold night. We got in his way."

"How did he get Lockwood there and overcome him?" Kendall asked. "The sergeant told us the doctor found no suspicious wounds on him."

"I can only guess at how he lured him. We know Lockwood wanted the ledger. Perhaps Crofton pretended to cooperate, promising to hand it over in that out-of-the-way location. As to how Crofton overcame him without a sign of struggle..." I shrugged and looked at Pinkerton.

"Chloroform would do it," he said. "But why would anyone believe Lockwood did away with himself?"

"Rumors were circulating about Eileen and Edgar," I said. "In addition, word had gotten around about Eileen's jewels having been found in the Lockwoods' garden. It was the topic of whispered conversation at the banquet Sunday night. Edgar had no one to corroborate that he was at home in the early morning hours of her death. So, in the face of his apparent suicide, people would believe he couldn't face his guilt becoming known. Which brings me to the second part of Crofton's motive. He wanted to shift the blame for Eileen's death so as to protect the real murderer—Allison Rowe."

CHAPTER 20

*B*oth men gaped at me.

"B-but," Kendall sputtered, "Miss Rowe? She's just a girl."

"She's seventeen. Well—sixteen, when Eileen was killed." I looked across at Pinkerton. "I believe her relationship with Crofton precedes his wife's death, and she killed her at his bidding."

Pinkerton got up to pace the room, hooking his thumbs in the armholes of his pinstripe waistcoat.

It was a lot to absorb. I waited for him to work through the possibilities.

Finally, he turned and faced us. "It would explain why Crofton had such a solid alibi for his wife's death. He knew he'd be suspected, so he made sure his whereabouts could be verified."

I nodded. "He also would've been sure to instruct Allison ahead of time—leave a key where she could find it, tell her which door to go in through, and apprise her of the servants' night-time routine. She arranged to stay the night at the Lockwoods' as Susannah's guest after the ladies had returned from a late concert."

"But to actually kill someone," Kendall protested, "requires steely nerves and a great deal of strength."

I could see he was struggling to accept the notion. Oddly, I was not. I'd seen what my sex was capable of. "I haven't known her long, so I cannot speak to nerves. However, in terms of strength, she had only to smother Eileen with a pillow as she slept—the lady customarily took a sleeping draught, according to the police report. Crofton would have known that, too. Allison wouldn't even need to turn on a light. After that, she'd dump the contents of the jewelry box in a sack, hide the sack in Lockwood's garden, and slip back inside to bed."

"Why Lockwood's garden?" Pinkerton asked.

"It was easier, as she had to cross both backyards to return. But there may have been more to it than that. If the burglary was suspected to be false, suspicion would shift to Lockwood once the bag was discovered. Crofton devised the plan, remember. If he thought Eileen and Lockwood were having an affair, then exacting a bit of revenge had appeal." I turned to Pinkerton. "Speaking of the sack, I should like another look at the contents. There's a gold chain bracelet that looked familiar."

Pinkerton called for Mary, who produced the bag. I rummaged inside. "Here it is." I held up a delicate, braided gold chain bracelet. "I noticed Allison wearing a necklace of this design at the Cartwrights' auction. She wore no matching bracelet. On another occasion, I overheard her father complaining that the girl was always losing jewelry." I passed it to Kendall. "And look—the clasp is loose. It could have slipped off without her noticing as she plunged her hand in the sack."

"The clasp *is* loose," Kendall said, turning it over in his hands.

"And there's something else—Lockwood's account to the police has been bothering me, but I couldn't figure out why until now. It has to do with the Lockwoods' dog, Plato."

Kendall blinked. "I beg your pardon—did you say *dog*?"

"The police asked all the neighbors and servants the same

basic question—did you see or hear anything unusual that night? Everyone answered in the negative, except for Edgar Lockwood. He said the only unusual thing was their dog had been whining to be let out."

"Not much of a detail." Pinkerton frowned. "How is it significant? Dogs frequently whine to go out."

I smiled. "Yes, and they typically bark at people they don't know very well. Plato barked at me the first few times I visited the Lockwoods, but not today. He's gotten used to me. Lockwood's account only noted Plato whining—*not* barking."

Kendall's brow cleared in understanding. "You're saying the dog would have barked if Cartwright, Rowe, or a stranger hired by one of them had been the person creeping into the Lockwoods' garden to leave the sack?"

"Exactly. But Allison's a regular visitor. Plato's used to her."

Pinkerton frowned at Kendall. "I've never met Miss Rowe. Is it possible she did it?"

"Perhaps." Kendall cleared his throat. "She's a…well-nourished young lady."

"And Eileen was a generation older," I said.

Kendall sat back and folded his arms. "All right—let's assume Miss Rowe killed Eileen at Crofton's behest. Although I have difficulty with a young lady being so blindly in love with a man that she would agree to something so horrible, I'll set that aside for now. What of Crofton's motive for having his wife killed? It didn't have anything to do with the graft scheme, did it?"

"No, though it was something just as craven. He wanted to be free of his wife and marry Allison."

Pinkerton shot me a look. "Sounds like pure conjecture."

"Is it? Eileen was a good fifteen years older than her husband and came into the marriage as the wealthier of the two. Although John had had some success in his career and possessed a comfortable income, it was his wife's money that supplied their lavish lifestyle. She was connected to powerful men—some more intimately than others—and navigated their sphere with a self-assurance not many women of her generation possess. She'd become the first woman on the board of a male-only organization. She was rather ruthless, if the book is anything to go by." I inclined my head toward where it rested on the table. "She viewed those in her circle—including her husband—with a cynical eye and meticulously documented their faults."

"You believe Crofton resented it?" Kendall asked. "That he killed her because he felt intimidated by her?"

"It's quite a shadow to live under," I said. "She even wrote of it that way in her journal—'At least I won't be overshadowing him anymore.' And the contrast between Eileen and Allison likely aggravated the feeling. Allison is everything Eileen was not —young, pretty, naïve, and unquestionably enamored of him. Crofton inherited Eileen's wealth at her death, and marrying Allison at the appropriate time would gain him even more money and connections."

"Was Allison really at risk of being discovered?" Pinkerton nodded toward the gold chain on the table. "That's not proof at all. And over the past year, there hasn't been the slightest hint that she's to blame."

"If she perceived it as a risk, it was real enough. Susannah told her a detective was looking into the pouch's discovery. Coupled with the realization that her bracelet had been lost and might be in the bag, Allison could have panicked." I looked over at Kendall. "You asked if Allison had steely nerves. To do the deed, perhaps—a few minutes, and it's over—but what about the aftermath? Could these latest developments have rattled her enough to turn to Crofton? Would he not act to assure her—and himself?"

Kendall pursed his lips. "So now what? We've already pointed the sergeant toward Rowe and Cartwright and subjected those fellows to untold scrutiny. Going back to him with a new theory about a murderous young girl—the judge's daughter, no less—will not be well received."

"True," I answered. "However, if we set a trap for Allison, using the book as bait, I'm confident she'll go straight to Crofton with it. She's his weakness—his tender-hearted spot, if you will," I added, resisting a smirk in Pinkerton's direction.

∽

After a bit more persuasion, Pinkerton agreed to the plan. Kendall dropped me off at the Lockwood mansion so I could talk to Susannah in private and make my arrangements. I kept the gold chain in my pocket.

I didn't look forward to telling the girl. Her stepfather had been murdered, her mother gravely injured, and now to inform her that her best friend had been using her—it felt as if I was ripping the poor girl's heart out a piece at a time.

Susannah was sent for as soon as I stepped into the hall, and she came down quickly. "Any news, Miss Hamilton?" Hope animated her features and smoothed the furrows in her brow.

"We've made a few discoveries and have a working theory. How's your mother?"

Her shoulders slumped. "No change yet."

I glanced over my shoulder at the maid, hovering nearby as she hung up my coat. "Can we talk somewhere in private? I need your help with something." Here would be the real test of the girl's resilience.

We settled into Susannah's sitting room once again.

"What do you need me to do?" she asked eagerly. "Is it related to something you found in the book?"

"Partly. First, there's something you should know about." I explained the scheme Mrs. Crofton and Judge Rowe had devised to have her stepfather covertly investigate possible graft on the board of the Widows' Benevolent Society.

Her eyes went wide. "The organization that just held the

awards banquet? Where everyone was acting so strangely toward Edgar and whispering behind his back?"

"Exactly. Mrs. Crofton asked your stepfather for his help, in confidence. That was the source of the secrecy between them. They never had an affair. We were wrong about that. Such a rumor was being circulated to discredit them both. When your mother wakes"—*if* she awoke, but I firmly pushed the thought out of my mind—"we shall have to make sure she understands that."

"That's why he mentioned an audit," Susannah murmured. She met my eye. "This scheme—is it why my stepfather was killed?"

"It's…complicated. There were several motives behind it."

"Who did it?" Her voice rasped.

I explained my theory about Crofton. "Did you notice anything strange in his behavior toward Edgar at the musicale?"

"He seemed much the way he usually does—charming and attentive, even when Edgar made that odd statement about old friends lost." She pursed her lips thoughtfully. "I remember Mr. Crofton was quite cordial to me, asking me how I was enjoying my pottery studio. He mentioned he'd like to get a tour of it sometime. Nothing remarkable."

"Did he? Interesting." That was the only cue Edgar needed, I was sure. Had Crofton agreed to give him something or to discuss Cartwright? And once he'd lured Lockwood to that spot…

But it wasn't proof. None of this was.

Susannah slouched against the cushions with a sigh. "I don't know him well, but he seems like a nice man. It's hard to believe. Did he kill his wife, too?"

"Actually, he couldn't have—he was out of town, which has been verified by several trustworthy sources. But I'm convinced he got someone to do it for him. Someone very close to him." I waited for her to make the connection. I was sure she knew something of Allison's relationship with Crofton.

She searched my face, expecting more. When I stayed quiet, her expression turned thoughtful…then grew horrified.

"Allison?" she whispered through whitened lips.

"You know she's been seeing him—without her parents' knowledge."

"Of course I know," she said impatiently. "But that has only been since his wife's death."

"Are you sure?" I pressed. "What if their relationship began before Eileen was killed? Then it's awfully convenient that she died, is it not? His mourning period is nearly up. He's quite wealthy now, and not so old that her parents would object to the match."

Susannah got up and paced the room. "You're accusing my best friend of adultery and murder. That's not possible."

I persisted, even as I hated doing so. "Consider the night Eileen Crofton was killed. You and your mother and Allison returned here from a concert, correct? Didn't Allison remain as an overnight guest? The police report said as much."

"It was too late for her to go home. She said she was very tired and what fun it would be to stay—oh!" She put a hand to her mouth. "It seemed spontaneous at the time."

"I'm afraid it was part of the plan—Crofton's plan. Along with stealing the jewelry to make it look like a burglary—"

"But when her parents gave her the Margharita necklace as a gift, wouldn't she have recognized it as the one she took?" Susannah interrupted. "If what you say is true, then she would have been the one to put it in the sack with the other things."

"Good point." I looked over at the necklace, carelessly jumbled in its box. Without the light to catch the fire of the rubies, it looked like a dark cluster of unremarkable stones. "She would have been working in dim light and rattled by what she'd just done. It's possible she tipped the trays of Eileen's jewel case into the sack without examining anything. Then she concealed the bag in your garden as quickly as she could." I fished in my pocket for the gold chain bracelet and held it up. "Have you

233

seen Allison wear this? It was inside the pouch with Eileen's pieces."

Susannah narrowed her eyes for a good look. "I'm not sure. She has a lot of jewelry."

"She was wearing a braided chain necklace very like this at the auction. I only noticed because she mentioned offering to lend it to you instead of her pearl bracelet."

"This is horrible." Susannah buried her face in her arms.

I passed her a handkerchief. "I'm sorry."

She wiped her eyes and blew her nose. "What do we do?"

"We must *know*, once and for all, what the truth is. Right now, all we have is conjecture. But I have a plan. I'll need your help."

While detective work can be exhilarating, much of it can be tedious. This was one of the latter occasions, as I sat in Lockwood's study with all the lights out, attired in the dark worsted dress I liked to wear for reconnoitering. My double-barrel derringer rested in my lap. I didn't expect to have to fire it at Allison, of course, but if the young lady decided to recruit help in securing the book, I was ready.

Susannah had played her part admirably. She'd called her friend—perhaps one of these days a telephone will no longer be a luxury only for businessmen and the wealthy—and asked for the consolation of her company that night. The two were now sequestered in Susannah's bedroom. This was where Susannah would have to implement the second part of the plan and confide to her best friend that she'd gone through her stepfather's desk and found a book from the late Mrs. Crofton that implicated her husband in a scheme of wrongdoing at the Widows' Benevolent Society. Knowing how close Allison was to John Crofton, what should she do?

I'd tutored Susannah on how to convincingly feign sleep so

that Allison would feel emboldened to make her search. The book was currently sitting in Lockwood's bottom desk drawer.

As I waited, the wind picked up outside, rattling the windows and rasping branches against the roof. A storm was coming. I prayed it wouldn't interfere with the plan, for Allison taking the book was merely the first step.

I couldn't tell the exact time in the dark, but I estimated it was close to three in the morning when I heard a sound that didn't come from outside—the creaking of floorboards overhead. Someone was on the move. I crouched in the shadow of the tall wingback chair.

The door soon opened, and I caught a glint of her blonde hair in the light of the corridor before she stepped in. My eyes had adjusted to the gloom, but hers had not, evidenced by the sound of a thump and a stifled gasp as she banged into the desk. She hesitated, then proceeded to open and close drawers until she found the book.

She took it over to the French doors to examine it by what moonlight showed between the scudding cloud cover. I could see her better now. She was fully dressed, though her hair was down and spread across her shoulders. Her frown deepened as she paged through the book. And no wonder. We couldn't have figured it out without Mary's help.

She bit her lip. I knew what she was trying to figure out. The book was unreadable—how could her friend know about Crofton's guilt? Susannah's lie was becoming clear.

Allison stood there a few minutes more, clearly unsure about what to do.

I was sure, however, and I was prepared. If only she would do it soon. My knees were protesting this extended crouch, but I daren't move.

Finally, she tucked the book under her arm, opened the door to the garden patio, and slipped out.

I hurried upstairs, where Susannah anxiously paced the dark room.

"Miss Hamilton! Did you see her? She left the room a while ago."

I nodded. "She's on her way to Crofton's now. Here, I'll show you. Leave the light off."

She followed me to the window, where I carefully shifted the curtain an inch or so. Allison was already through the back gate of the Crofton property, hugging the protection of a stand of fir trees as she made her way to the side of his house.

"You were right," Susannah breathed. "She's heading to tell him."

"You can't see from here, but she has the book with her. She couldn't understand why you'd lie to her about what it revealed, as it's obviously illegible to the untrained eye. She needs advice as to what to do next. And look." I nodded toward the man dressed all in black, who slipped behind Crofton's arbor, tracking her movements while staying out of sight. "Mr. Kendall."

Susannah squinted. "I don't…ah, yes, I see him now. So you knew she'd go to Crofton?"

"I considered it likely. Crofton was the mastermind of the original scheme—ah, you see?" I watched in satisfaction as Allison stooped over an object on the ground—a pot, perhaps—straightened, and leaned close to the side door. "She knows where he keeps the spare key."

Susannah shivered. "But for Allison to do something so monstrous as to kill a woman who had never done her any harm…"

I blew out a breath. "I know. Some women are so desperate for love they will do terrible things in the name of it." I watched Allison go in and saw Kendall glance behind him, up toward our window.

I turned to Susannah. "It's time to call the station number on the card the sergeant gave you. Do you remember what to say?"

She nodded. "That I looked out my window and saw what appeared to be a burglar, sneaking into the Crofton mansion."

"Good. I have to get over there." I clasped her hand in a quick goodbye and hurried out.

Kendall was still keeping watch within the cold, dancing shadows of Crofton's arbor when I caught up to him. I shivered as the wind plucked at the coat I'd hastily pulled on and mis-buttoned. No time to fix it now. "The police should be on their way." I had to lean close to his ear to be heard over the wind that lashed the vines beside us. "She's still inside?"

"Up there." He nodded toward a second-floor window, where light glowed at the edges of the curtains.

"Good," I said. "You should go before they arrive. We don't want you getting caught and accused of being the intruder Susannah called about." Large, cold raindrops began to spatter us. *Wonderful.*

"I don't like leaving you alone, Pen." His breath warmed my ear. "These are desperate people."

"I'm only here to intercept Allison. She'll try to escape out the back when the police arrive. I can handle her." I tipped my ear to listen. Even over the sounds of the storm, I could hear two coaches clattering down the avenue at a rapid pace. "Better go."

He breathed a sigh and slipped away.

At the sound of brisk knocking upon Crofton's front door, I sidled closer to the service porch's side door. That's where Allison had entered the house, and it was shielded from view of the street by thick shrubbery.

I didn't have long to wait. Within moments, the door eased open. A tall, lean form wearing a man's hat and overcoat stepped out briskly.

My breath caught. It wasn't Allison. It was John Crofton, satchel in hand.

And I'd sent Phillip on his way, *drat it.*

Heart pounding in my chest, I pulled out my derringer. "Stop right there, Mr. Crofton," I said in a loud, stern voice.

He halted and cautiously swiveled his head toward me, his eyes wide in disbelief. "Miss Hamilton! What are you doing?" His glance fell upon the gun. "Why on earth are you pointing a weapon at me?" He took a step closer.

I leveled the derringer at his heart. "I said, *stop.*"

The ferocity of my tone made him hesitate. I raised my voice to try to counter the sound of the wind howling between the buildings. "We're back here!" I called, but it felt as if my words were being forced back down my throat. I wasn't sure anyone at the street could have heard me.

Crofton gave a grim smile and advanced another step.

I backed up. "Where's Allison?" I shouted.

He shrugged. "Does it matter? She's no longer part of the plan."

I had a bad feeling about that. Kendall had said she was still inside. "What did you do to her?"

"You thwarted me once before, Miss Hamilton. I won't let it happen again." He took another step.

I put a bit more space between us, still holding the gun steady. "Thwarted you? How? Lockwood's dead. We couldn't rescue him."

He scowled. "You got to the studio too soon. I couldn't arrange the scene to make it look—" He shook his head. "*Enough.* I'm leaving." He took a purposeful step closer, to get past me and reach the back gate.

"I will shoot you if I must." The wind tore at my hair, and set my eyes watering. I backed up and felt my heel hit something solid. I risked a quick glance over my shoulder. I was up against the hatch of the root cellar.

In that moment he swung the satchel, hard, toward the gun. I pivoted my opposite forearm into the blow, pointed the gun low and across my torso, and fired. Less-than-ideal aiming— Frank would have clucked his tongue at me holding the gun stock sideways like that—but even so, I managed to clip Crofton in the thigh. He gave a yowl and dropped.

There's one thing to be said for shooting a gun in a windstorm—the sound is sure to carry, even when a voice cannot. Lights came on, doors opened, and a number of people—policemen, Crofton's staff, and neighbors clad in their night attire—headed towards the source.

First on the scene was Sergeant Ganley, his billy club raised high. He lowered it with a grunting exhalation—part relief, part exasperation, I have no doubt—at the sight of me holding the derringer and standing over Crofton as the man clutched his leg.

"Miss Hamilton," Ganley said, holding out his hand for my weapon—which I relinquished—"if you would simply allow us to do our jobs from time to time, I would be most grateful." He glanced down at Crofton and turned to the man I recognized as Patrolman Tatum. "Fetch the doctor and send back a couple of men to get this one inside while we wait."

The man nodded and hurried off.

"Where's Miss Rowe?" I clasped my coat closer to my chest.

Ganley pocketed my gun and gave the groaning Crofton a steely-eyed look as two uniformed men emerged. "Carry him to the front parlor and watch him," he instructed.

"Sergeant?" I asked, as they tramped off, Crofton hefted between them.

He shook his head. "She's dead, miss. Strangled." His eyes narrowed as I shuddered. "Let's get out of this wind."

hristmas Day, 1887

"Henry," his mother prompted, "you have another present. Here, give Mama the tissue paper, there's a good boy."

Cassie laughed. "It's always the way, isn't it? The box and the paper are as fun as the toy."

We were tucked comfortably in the parlor—Cassie, me, Tilly, Henry, Phillip, and our lodgers. Even the reclusive Mr. Grissom had deigned to keep us company this Christmas morning. Miss Walterson was playing with the new stacking rings she'd given the boy, Mrs. Hodges was trying to get Mr. Grissom to admire the stuffed bear, and I was frantically finishing the last handkerchief for Frank before he stopped by. There'd been little time this past week.

Cassie glanced at the mantel clock and jumped up. "I should peel the potatoes and check on the turkey."

Sadie was spending the holiday with her brother's family and wouldn't return until next week. Fortunately, Cassie didn't mind cooking. I was happy to leave her to it. My cooking abilities don't extend much further than tea and toast.

"It smells wonderful already," Miss Walterson said, sniffing appreciatively. "Will the meal be ready early enough for us to attend the Sunday school's Christmas performance afterward?"

"We'll have plenty of time," I said. "It doesn't start until six."

"Do you need any help, Miss Leigh?" Phillip asked, from his cross-legged position on the parlor rug next to the child.

"There isn't much to do," Cassie said. "I'll be back."

I lifted an eyebrow in his direction as she left. "You know how to cook?"

He chuckled. "I know how to stir things." He turned back to Henry, who was fumbling with the ribbon. "Now then, my good fellow—let me help you with the knot." Phillip's long fingers brushed the boy's short, chubby ones, and the bow was swiftly untied. "There."

Both mama and child cooed over the bright stack of blocks, which were promptly knocked down and scattered about the floor.

"I'd say the morning has been a success." Kendall stood and dusted off his trousers. "I should be going."

Tilly scooped Henry into her lap and flashed Kendall a warm look. "So many lovely gifts. Thank you."

I set aside my needlework. "I'll see you out."

"So what are your plans next?" I asked, as he shrugged on his overcoat. "Will you continue working for Mr. Pinkerton?"

"For now." He lifted a shoulder noncommittally. "We're taking it case by case. He's sending me to San Francisco next week, in fact."

"Oh?" Disappointment plucked at the back of my throat, but I affected a nonchalant tone. "For how long?"

"A couple of weeks, at least."

"You must be looking forward to the change of scene."

"I always enjoy a challenge." He gently touched the key pin

on my blouse before clasping my hand. "But I'll miss you, Pen. Promise you'll stay out of trouble while I'm away?"

I raised an eyebrow. "You asked me that the last time."

"Good point." He chuckled and turned toward the door. "I should know better."

~

By the time Frank stopped by that afternoon, people had begun to disperse—Tilly to put the child down for a nap, our lodgers to visit friends in town, Cassie in the kitchen tending to supper. We had the parlor to ourselves.

Frank sank into a cushioned chair, stretched out his long legs toward the fire, and gratefully accepted some of the holiday punch we were keeping warm on the stove all day.

"I haven't had a chance to catch up on the resolution of your case," I said, sitting across from him with my own cup of punch. I took an appreciative sip. *Mmm*, nice. Cassie liked to add more nutmeg than Sadie.

"I'm sure you've seen mention of it in the papers," he said.

"Indeed, I read about Dutch Dan and the Mosers being charged in Brinkerhoff's death. Nice work. They found the body, I take it?"

He nodded. "Olivia told us where to look. Once she was cornered, she gave up the others quicker than you can say 'Jack Robinson.'"

"Finally, an occasion where she couldn't brazen it out," I mused.

"She's playing the victim now, saying it was all Moser's idea —that he made her go along with it, and so on. Even if a jury believes it, she'll be in prison for a while."

"That will be a relief to Tilly. By the way, did you ever learn what Bert O'Neill was up to when you saw him talking to her?"

"Pinkerton got to the bottom of it. Turns out the fellow's been anxious to impress and get promoted quickly. Decided to do a little investigating on his own and keep it secret." Frank rolled his eyes. "Thought he could get information from Tilly if he started seeing her romantically, but she wasn't having any of that."

I gave a snort. "Not surprising."

"It's a wonder our surveillance wasn't blown right then. Luckily, she was on our side—in a fashion. How is she?" He gestured to the pile of toys beside the sofa. "Looks like they're settling in."

I smiled. "I'd say so. Both are doing fine."

"What are her plans?"

"I haven't been home long enough to talk with her about that, but she's welcome to stay until she figures it out."

"That's kind."

I chuckled. "I'm a tender-hearted woman, or hasn't Mr. Pinkerton told you that? Never mind." I waved a hand at his confused expression. "Long story. But in that vein"—I reached for a flat box beside the hearth—"I have something for you."

His eyes lit up at the set of white cambric handkerchiefs I'd hemmed and monogrammed. "They're perfect, Pen. Thanks."

"An improvement on those rags you've been using. Don't look too closely at the stitching, though. Definitely not department store quality."

"I actually have something for you, too." He groped in his jacket pocket and pulled out a tissue-wrapped bundle.

I pulled it apart with all the abandon of young Henry Sohren. "Frank, how marvelous! These are the specialty lockpicks I wished I'd had last year. And a jointed key, too! How did you know?"

He shrugged. "Just a guess. Pinkerton has been using you a lot lately."

"How considerate." I gave him a warm smile. "Thank you."

He flushed. "Of course."

We were quiet for a while, sipping punch and gazing at the play of light upon the andirons.

"Pinkerton told me about Crofton's capture and Miss Rowe's death," he said finally.

My throat tightened. I set aside my cup. Despite what she'd done, I wished Allison had been spared.

"How could he possibly believe he could get away with it?" Frank asked.

I shrugged. "Crofton had a lot of cash in the satchel he was carrying. His plan was to book passage to Antwerp once he reached the Port of New York. From there, he had enough money to settle comfortably somewhere in Europe."

"Why kill the girl? Why not simply send her back to the house, destroy the book, and brazen out the speculation?"

I made a face. "Crofton suspected the trap I'd set. He didn't want any…hindrances."

Sergeant Ganley had shared only an abbreviated version of Crofton's confession when he'd paid me a visit yesterday, but it confirmed a great deal. "Even before that night," I went on, "Crofton had been making plans to flee. He'd grown uneasy when Lockwood's murder didn't go as expected."

"What do you mean, *as expected*?"

"As I'd surmised, he wanted to kill Lockwood for two reasons—to shift the blame for his wife's death firmly away from Allison, and to eliminate the threat of an audit of the Widows' Benevolent Society. In order to make that happen, Lockwood's death had to look like a suicide, ostensibly as remorse for killing Eileen Crofton."

"It didn't look like a suicide, then? I'm not familiar with the details."

I explained that our search for Lockwood had interrupted Crofton's plan to return and unbar the door. "And Pinkerton was right," I added. "He'd overcome Lockwood with chloroform, so that no wound would arouse suspicion."

"How did Crofton lure him there in the first place?"

"With the promise of the ledger. He pretended that Cartwright had pressured him to go along with the scheme, when in reality he was an eager partner and was profiting from it." I wondered what role Crofton had had in maintaining the spurious employment agency that received much of the money, but the sergeant hadn't had the time to go into specifics.

Frank shook his head. "The man has a lot to answer for."

I flashed him a grim look. "Judge Rowe is using his influence to make sure of it."

I'd no sooner seen Frank out the door when a familiar carriage pulled up, and out stepped one of the Lockwoods' footmen, juggling an enormous basket and a large, flat box. The driver jumped down to help him.

"*Mercy*, what's all this?" I opened the door wide as they approached.

The footman, recognizing me, grinned. "Merry Christmas, miss. Compliments of Mrs. Lockwood and Miss Susannah. There's a note in the box."

I stepped out of the way to let them in. "You can put them on the credenza. How's Mrs. Lockwood doing?" I'd received word from Susannah two days ago that her mother was finally awake and cognizant of her surroundings. She didn't share what would have followed Louisa's awakening—the difficult task of breaking the news about Edgar's death.

"Gettin' stronger each day, miss," the footman said. "She was able to come downstairs and share some of the holiday with Miss Susannah this morning."

A subdued holiday, no doubt, though there was still much for them to be grateful for. They had each other. "Please ask them to send word when she is well enough for a visit."

He gave a bow and followed the driver out.

"Who was that?" Cassie asked, peering around my shoulder as I opened the box.

"The Lockwoods' staff, dropping off gifts from Louisa and

Susannah," I murmured, taking in the sight of my aquamarine satin gown, cleaned and mended.

Cassie's eyes widened. "Look—a matching pair of opera gloves, a shawl, and a fan, too. How wonderful! It's a shame you have no elegant affair to attend in the near future."

I laughed. "I've had quite enough of those for the time being. But I can wear the shawl to the children's Christmas party tonight." I lifted out the soft cashmere, worked in a paisley pattern of black, cream, and pale blue. An envelope tumbled out. *Penelope* was written across the front in a shaking hand.

As Cassie explored the basket, exclaiming over the bounty of edible treats within, I sat on the hall bench to read the note.

Dear Penelope,

I am grateful for your efforts—along with Mr. Kendall's— in trying to rescue Edgar. I grieve at my husband's death, but I'm determined to recover my strength for the sake of Susannah.

I am also grateful to you for catching the man responsible. Seeing him brought to justice will make this time of mourning a little easier for us.

Should I ever have occasion to see your mother again, I will be sure to tell her all about the brave, clever, and capable daughter I had the privilege of meeting.

Yours,

Aunt Lou

"Miss Hamilton! Miss Leigh!" a voice called from the dining room.

I roused myself as Tilly came down the hall, wiping her hands on her apron. "The table's laid and supper's ready."

Cassie flashed me a smile and hefted the basket. "Perfect! Let's feast."

∿

THE END

AFTERWORD

I hope you enjoyed the book. Please consider leaving a quick review at your favorite online venue. A single sentence as to whether or not you liked it, along with clicking on the star rating you see fit, can go a long way.

Ratings create a digital "word of mouth" that help readers find books they will love, particularly those written by independently published authors. Thank you!

KB Owen Mysteries

A note on research:

The plot of *The Twelve Thieves of Christmas* called for in-depth research into various aspects of 1880s life, particularly as they pertained to Chicago—its department stores, city streets, neighborhoods, and crime. Much of my research focused upon Chicago's wealthy class of the time period, which provided the backdrop and fictitious character renderings of the story.

The following list (with commentary) contains the databases, sites, and indexes I used, should any of my readers wish to learn more.

Thanks for reading!

~K.B. Owen, September 2021

Books:

75 Years of Gas Service in Chicago. Wallace Rice. The Peoples Gas Light and Coke Company, 1925.

~~Useful information about the development of Chicago's gas and electrical infrastructure during this time period.

The Bon-Ton Register, 1879. HathiTrust.org.

~~In addition to providing names and addresses of the wealthiest and most socially connected residents of Chicago at the time, the Register is replete with etiquette tips and advice.

Chicago's Mansions. John Graf. Images of America, Arcadia Publishing, 2004.

~~A valuable source of information about the mansions owned by Chicago's wealthiest families—Pullman, Marshall Field, McCormick, Kimball, and more. The book is rich in photographs, descriptions, and locations of the houses, and even at times provides detail about how the owner's priorities influenced the room features and architectural choices.

The Elite Directory and Club List of Chicago. The Elite Directory Company, 1888-89.

~~A compendium of names, addresses, and social clubs.

The Lakeside Annual Directory of the City of Chicago. Chicago Directory Company, 1887.

~~A treasure trove of business entries, addresses, advertisements, etc. Gave me a good sense of where business districts/types of businesses were located in the city so I could create credible fictitious versions.

Remembering Marshall Field's. Leslie Goddard. Images of America, Arcadia Publishing, 2011.

~~Although most of the book focuses upon later years than the time period I was looking for, several sections provided helpful information as to Field's business philosophy and general store operations of the time.

Maps:

Rand McNally & Co. Map of Chicago, 1886. From Encyclopedia of Chicago database. http://encyclopedia.chicagohistory.org/pages/10605.html

~~This was so useful I actually enlarged and printed a trifold, poster-sized version for reference.

Chicago in Maps.

https://www.chicagoinmaps.com/historicmaps.html

~~An index to all sorts of historical maps of Chicago, from 1834 to 1940.

Websites and Webpages:

Chicagoancestors.org

~~This site covers a lot of ground. I found it especially helpful for directories that provided the locations of fire stations and call boxes.

Chicagodetours.com
~~Useful information about Chicago's mansions.

Chicalogy.com/transportation/northchicagostreetrailroad   and
/westchicagostreetrailroad
~~A basic overview of the streetcar lines, locations, and
means of propulsion, via both horse and cable-pulled.

ChroniclingAmerica.loc.gov
~~A digitized database of historic American newspapers

GlessnerHouse.org
~~Lots of photos and descriptions to help conceptualize
mansion interiors. I learned a lot about wallpapers on this site as
well.

HathiTrust.org
~~A wonderful resource for primary documents. I used it
primarily to access city directories from the 1880s, several of
which are cited above.

LOC.gov
~~The Library of Congress's digitized archives

Women in the American Art Pottery Movement, Wisconsin101's
site.   https://wi101.wisc.edu/2020/04/20/women-in-the-
american-art-pottery-movement/
~~This provided useful context for one of my plot points.
Cool to learn there were successful women potters back then!

Special thanks to:
Jan Whitaker, author, researcher, and blogger of historical
restaurants and department stores, for her help with a research
question. Her books and blog can be found at: https://
restaurant-ingthroughhistory.com/

EXPLORE MY OTHER HISTORICAL SERIES...SET IN A 19TH CENTURY WOMEN'S COLLEGE!

THE CONCORDIA WELLS MYSTERIES

Set in a fictitious 1890s women's college, this cozy-style series features Miss Concordia Wells, a young lady professor who cannot resist a little unseemly sleuthing when those she cares about are at risk. Who knew higher education could be...murder?

Start with:

*Dangerous and Unseemly, book 1. Winner of **Library Journal's** "Best Mystery of 2015: SELF-e"!*

"A fun historical whodunit with a delightful background of the early days of women's collegiate education."
~*Library Journal*

ALSO BY K.B. OWEN

ABOUT THE AUTHOR

K.B. Owen taught college English at universities in Connecticut and Washington, DC and holds a doctorate in 19th century British literature. A long-time mystery lover, she drew upon her teaching experiences in creating her amateur sleuth, Professor Concordia Wells and from there, lady Pinkerton Penelope Hamilton was born.

kbowenmysteries.com
contact@kbowenmysteries.com

www.ingramcontent.com/pod-product-compliance
Lightning Source LLC
Chambersburg PA
CBHW071252250626
47159CB00004B/1152